Shadow in the Rain

Harriett Ford

Shadow in the Rain

Helm Publishing

For information address:
Helm Publishing
3923 Seward Ave.
Rockford, IL 61108
815-398-4660

www.publishersdrive.com

ISBN 0-9778205-2-1
LCCN Applied for
Printed in the United States of America

"No evidence is more compelling than a suspect's confession. For why would anyone confess to a crime he did not commit? Yet false confessions have become legion in the criminal justice system. Blatant flaws in the system from faulty DNA and fingerprint matching, prosecutorial misconduct, incompetent counsel, eyewitness error and plain old-fashioned perjury have repeatedly sent the innocent to death row. "—**Stanley Cohen,** author of *The Wrong Men,* a must read for anyone who doubts that the innocent are wrongfully convicted. Cohen, an award-winning journalist, documents one hundred such cases across the country. All these hapless victims would have been executed had not journalists, family, pro-bono lawyers and others labored tirelessly to correct the demon of injustice.

"One witness shall not be enough to convict a man accused of any crime or offense he may have committed. A matter must be established by the testimony of two or three witness."
Deuteronomy 19:15-20 NIV. Also **Numbers** 35:30.

"Veteran investigative reporter for the Rockford Labor News, a weekly newspaper in Rockford, Illinois, the intrepid Harriett Ford encountered a murder case which left her strongly believing the wrong man had been convicted. After she zealously pursued the case, interviewed witnesses and worked with private investigators, she wrote an eye-opening fictionalized story based on the case. Can this good read convince you, too?" —**Ruth Westphal, Ph.D.**, former senior editor for Harcourt, Brace & Javonovich and editor in chief for Cook Publishing in Milwaukee, Wisconsin.

"As editor of the Rockford Labor News, I have watched the Ted Kuhl murder investigation unfold chapter by chapter in the weekly editions of our paper. Harriett Ford's book is a riveting fictionalized account of a similar crime based largely on the Kuhl case. And as always, the basis of truth for the story is stranger than fiction."—**Don Brady**, editor

"My dad, the late private investigator Joe Lamb, intended to write a book on the injustices in Ted Kuhl's case before his untimely death. He would be so proud of Harriett."— Rockford native, USA Today editor and award-winning novelist, **Joyce Lamb** whose books include *Caught In The Act*, *Relative Strangers*, and *Found Wanting*.

Publisher's Note

For many years, I have seen injustice in the judicial system committed by those sworn to abiding by the law, upholding truth, and forsaking all means of bribery. For too long this naïve viewpoint was held in my mind believing that the innocent would be vilified. No more. Crimes against the affluent, and influential are condoned and pardoned every day, from corporations accused of embezzlement, and fraud, to political cronies seeking favors for votes. It is time to speak out warning those we voted in and make them accountable to right the wrongs committed by themselves or their predecessors. We need laws to protect and serve the working class people of the United States of America. These laws are the only things keeping our rights from becoming no rights at all. When we see or hear of forensic evidence mishandled, judges being bribed, state, or defense attorneys becoming corrupt in pursuit of their selfish ambitions, and blinded to falsifying or omitting crucial facts in a case, especially one involving the prosecution of a man who has not been proven guilty beyond reasonable doubt, what recourses do we possess?

The court has become likened to a TV series only to be mocked and ridiculed by the people themselves, but still no action is taken. I urge the general public to believe the time is come to stand up for moral beliefs and never, ever give up.*

Read the last pages of this book very carefully. Ted's incarceration is a farce, according to professional investigators. It was based on not a whit of evidence, but possibly upon political cowardice hiding behind the overwhelming need for reelection.

If you have any ideas and would like to help Ted in his cause to be set free, please contact Helm Publishing on the copyright page.

*These are Helm's opinions based upon media coverage of cases seen on TV, heard on radio, read in the news, personal experience and in no way do they reflect the author's views.

FOREWORD

The Unrightable Wrong?

Once in every journalist's life comes a story that must be told. This is mine.

I first began looking into a cold case, fully believing that police have better things to do than to arrest an innocent man. What I found was a series of errors, theory without proof, no forensic evidence, and unsound conclusions. It was a startling experience.

Rather than to write another documentary on the miscarriage of criminal justice, I have chosen to write a fictional story based on this real life case. The story unfolds through the eyes of a fictional reporter, for the purpose of drama and because she can do things I cannot do (and look better too). After all, Angela Lansbury has already played the grandmotherly investigative writer in the "Murder She Wrote" television series.

Most scenes are entirely fictional. However details of the actual investigation, witness statements—and a second murder possibly linked to the first—are as accurate as possible, based on police reports and interviews.

Names, dates and places have been altered for the protection of the innocent. The characters of Tia Burgess, Cap Nemon and Mr. Phillips—and all scenes involving them—are entirely fictional.

In order to separate fact from fiction, a fascinating analysis of the real life case is included in the addendum, written by a nationally known forensics scientist.

Readers may find themselves asking—does the court really want to send a message to police investigators just to bring prosecutors a signed confession and forget the forensic and scientific evidence?

Has the criminal justice system made a serious mistake? And if so, are wrongful murder convictions—those without any DNA evidence—becoming the unrightable wrong?

ACKNOWLEDGMENTS

I wish to express my sincere gratitude to the Rockford Police Department for their assistance, and also for their professionalism and high level of skill in gathering evidence and solving crimes.

My thanks also to my publisher, Dianne Helm, Ray Null, assistant editor, and to Don Brady, editor of the Rockford Labor NEWS, without whose encouragement, this book would not have been possible.

I offer my gratitude posthumously to investigator Joe Lamb, for his exhaustive investigation of the case.

My fabulous husband and two beautiful daughters also deserve medals for outstanding service on the home fronts while I was busily clicking away on my computer keyboard.

ARE THE TWO MURDERS LINKED?
THE TRUTH IS AS PLAIN AS A...

SHADOW IN THE RAIN

INTRODUCTION

The following account is based on a description furnished by police reports, video surveillance tapes, and the theory of a nationally known criminologist/forensic scientist on which this story is based. Added details are from witnesses who came forth after the original investigation.

December, 1999
Woodsville, Wisconsin, located on the state line between Illinois and Wisconsin approximately 20 miles from Rockford, Illinois

Like a vampire wrapped in the black velvet cloak of night, he waited for the moment.

A sickle moon cut holes through the bellies of the clouds, momentarily silvering objects on the street below. Trees and vehicles vanished into shadows as the clouds merged once more, blotting out the icy moonlight. He welcomed the darkness.

The house sat at an angle on a circle drive. Curtains had been tied back and yellow light streamed through windows on the side of the frame home, allowing the watcher a partial view of the living room.

He could see the woman as she passed back and forth. She was alone, occupied with placing ornaments on a Christmas tree. He felt a momentary shiver of anticipation. This was it.

He'd had a close call earlier in the week. That snoop-nosed neighbor woman kept staring at his car, finally writing down his license plate number. Since then he'd traded in the car for a plumber's used commercial van and only approached the street after most of the residents on the block had returned home from work and were having supper. Still he was careful to avoid parking under the lonely streetlight.

Reaching for the door handle, he rolled his eyes and hit the steering wheel with a clenched fist as a car pulled into the driveway. He froze, watching a dark-haired woman exiting, walking up the steps and knocking at the front door.

The watcher cursed under his breath. His hand smarted from the angry blow. He could wait, but not past another dawn. She had escaped too many times already in past two weeks. The boss was tired of waiting. Inside the cheerily lit bungalow, he caught momentary glimpses of the two women chatting together as they finished decorating the tree.

What the hell were they doing now? Minutes crawled by. He was cold and hungry. Frost began to form on the inside of the windshield. He wanted the visitor gone. The deal done. Now.

His target, the blue-eyed blonde, was out of his line of vision. But an hour later he could see her answering the telephone beside the window. With the receiver pressed to her ear, she smiled and nodded her golden head, eagerly turning to the other woman, an apparent question on her lips.

In moments the two women had put on their coats, locked the front door and climbed into their separate cars. He waited until both vehicles pulled out of the drive, down the street and around the corner. Then he started the plumber's van and followed as closely as he dared, not wanting to lose them. Only a few blocks away, at a busy strip mall where holiday shoppers were still out in droves, the two women parked nine stalls apart and walked toward the Green Onion Bar & Grill.

The watcher pulled his van into the parking lot, left the engine running, and opened a pack of Camels. It was 9:40 p.m. The heater warmed him. He inhaled the cigarette, thinking he'd have to quit one of these days. Okay, he thought. This is going to take awhile. Let her enjoy her last supper. The boss would approve.

He decided to visit the game arcade next door to the restaurant. Stepping out of the van, he slipped on an icy patch of pavement, fell to one knee and cursed the cold. The wrench to his lower back was jarring. Anger at the blonde welled up, as if she were somehow to blame. With oath he vowed she would pay.

At 10 p.m. he left the game place and headed back to the van, where he smoked another cigarette. An hour later he moved the van, parking on a side street. It was better not to risk someone jotting down his plate numbers. Then he walked back to the parking area, and kept moving in a slow circle around its perimeters, wanting to be in the right place when she walked out.

Just after midnight she had not yet left the restaurant. The game arcade soon would be closing. He would no longer have a place to get out of the cold. The temperature had fallen to 28 degrees, so he walked briskly on his aching knee, pulling his bomber jacket tightly around him.

One of the mall's security guards approached him. "What are you doing?"

"None of your f----n business!" he snarled.

"I said what are you doing?" the guard repeated in a more authoritative tone.

Realizing he had answered foolishly, he used a less offensive manner. "I'm just waiting for someone in the bar." This time he headed straight for the three outdoor pay phones installed at the north end of the lot, quickly dropped in some coins, dialed and listened to the mechanical connection. No answer. Instead the cell phone in his coat pocket started ringing. Holding it to his ear, he muttered something, nodded and ended the call.

At 1:15 a.m. the mall's parking lot lights blinked off and the security guards went home. Darkness settled like a black shroud over the area, lit from inside by the faint glow of storefront business signs in bright neon splashes. These lights cast a multi-colored, murky glow for a few yards, but nearer the car where the watcher stood, he blended into the night, almost invisible.

Dark enough, he thought, pleased with the location of the car. It wasn't the place he would have chosen, but it would have to do. People were leaving the game arcade, starting vehicles, scraping frost off windshields. Good. The parking lot soon would be empty. Nervous and edgy, he lit another cigarette.

Then he saw three people walking out of the Green Onion Bar & Grill. There she was, still with the same woman and a man.

Too many people. Should he wait? Another couple walked together in a path that would intersect the three friends, who were laughing companionably as they stopped at the brunette's vehicle. Miss Brunette started her car, turned on her radio and reached for an ice scraper.

Now it was just the woman and her man walking toward him. Good. He could take her out easily enough and then go for the other one if he had to. The watcher quickly dropped to one knee on the far side of a nearby car and bit his tongue to keep from crying out. He had unwittingly landed on the newly-injured knee and a spasm of pain shot through it.

Completely unaware of his presence, the man and woman were standing at the driver's door, talking about a Christmas party tomorrow night and saying their I-love-yous. After they shared a goodnight kiss, he heard the sound of footsteps walking away.

It was their last kiss.

Leaping up, he aimed the .357 Magnum at her head. He could see sudden terror in her eyes in the brief flash of gunfire. Her startled scream cut short as her knees buckled and blood exploded from her head.

Immediately turning his gun toward the stupefied man, who was whirling around, the gunman took aim and fired, squeezing off another three or four rounds. He didn't know if the bullets struck the man or the brunette, because neither was standing. After a quick glance at the body on the tarmac, he ran for the van.

Shocked silence. People running. Shouts of rage and grief. Cars screeching out of the lot. It was done before dawn, just as he had planned.

Twenty-nine-year-old Nancy Jurowksi lay crumpled in a pool of blood on the icy pavement with a bullet blasted into her brain.

Woodsville, Wisconsin Fall of 2002

Chapter 1 - Danger

"Will you have dinner with me tonight?"

Tia Burgess was already shaking her head no into the receiver, when Rip Tyson added, "I have something to talk to you about that I think you're going to find very interesting."

"What?" She asked, already certain she didn't have time for this. There were three more stories on her desk at the news office in need of proofreading before she could even think about leaving.

"Murder." He spoke the word calmly into the phone, almost seductively.

Had she heard him right? Without a second thought she heard herself saying, "Where and what time?"

What am I doing? She asked herself as she wrote down the name of the restaurant. She had planned to go straight home tonight as usual. But working for a small, weekly paper, she knew only too well that the chance for scooping the daily didn't come along very often. However, she'd known Rip Tyson for a couple of years. As a scuba diving instructor, he knew people from every strata of society, judges, lawyers and doctors to bikers and even parolees who frequented the biker bar near his scuba shop. Rip probably had a story worth listening to.

Not that she expected a scoop. Just maybe a different angle on a story that probably had already seen major coverage in Woodsville's daily paper.

Murder. If Rip had answered with any other word in the English language, she would have stuck with her original plan. He had known how to pique her interest all right. Maybe he knew someone involved in the—never mind. She wasn't going to think about it now. Not with unedited copy still lying on her desk.

Two hours later, running a comb through her hair and straightening her skirt, Tia left the News office. She had called from the office and arranged to pick up her friend Carmen Morelli, who surprised her by wearing a blonde wig.

"What are you doing with that thing on your head?" Tia almost laughed while Carmen buckled her seat belt.

"You're going to be talking about a murder, and I don't want anyone knowing what I look like if the killer is still loose!" Carmen exclaimed. "I've had my share of being threatened by a murderer after I had to testify in a homicide trial. Once is enough. I won't be getting involved with another murder case until I kiss a frog that turns into a handsome prince. And how likely do you think that is?"

"Well, I haven't seen you kissing any frogs lately, but I have to say a couple of your ex-boyfriends almost fall into the toad category," Tia noted.

Carmen rolled her eyes. "That slimy Murphy. What a jerk! And to think I almost married him." The two women agreed Carmen had avoided the mistake of her life as they drove out to the Green Onion Bar and Grill in a business district just north of Woodsville. This was the very parking lot where Nancy Jurowski had been murdered two years earlier. Tia chose not to mention that to Carmen.

Excited to be included in Tia's plans, Carmen was adamant about her disguise. "You can say my name is, um—Karen! I don't want anyone to know my real name, or how gorgeous I am without this platinum wig, dahling!" She dramatized in her Eva Gabor voice.

Tia suppressed a laugh. This was hardly cloak-and-dagger stuff. But the story could involve a real killer, so maybe Carmen wasn't too far off the wall for wanting to remain unknown. Even if the killer were already in prison, he probably still had friends on the outside.

"And what about this Riptide guy anyway? How do you know he's not some shady character?" Carmen was asking.

"His name is Rip Tyson. He was our scuba-diving instructor."

Carmen raised her eyebrows. "I should have known it, with a name like Riptide. Sounds like some comic-book character."

"Rip's probably not his real name. He's a good guy," Tia answered.

"You know lots of guys. And they're all good guys. Why don't you give one of them a second look?" Carmen pushed the subject.

"Because, dahling, I just adore a penthouse view, and I'm staying put in mine," Tia announced, picking up Carmen's Gabor accent. "Besides, as you've often told me, men can be dangerous."

"I'll help you weed out the dangerous ones. You know so many, you can take your pick."

"I know lots of guys because I'm a reporter. Good guys and dangerous guys. I stay away from them all."

Carmen knew full well that she was treading on taboo territory but couldn't resist saying, "One of these days you've got to give one of them a chance."

Tia didn't respond. This was a subject she avoided like she would avoid talking about cockroaches at the dinner table. She parked the Bronco and they entered the restaurant, winding through crowded tables toward the back of the place where Rip Tyson waved from a group of people seated at a large round table. He introduced the group, all longtime friends or relatives of Ben

Krahl, the man who had been sentenced over two years ago for the murder of his girlfriend, Nancy Jurowski.

Tia introduced Carmen as "Karen, my associate and friend." Only when they were ordering did Tia slip, saying, "Carmen, would you share a pasta dinner with me?" Dark eyes flashed Italian fire at Tia, but Carmen kept her lips pressed together.

Both women assessed the group one by one as they spoke in concerned and sincere voices. At the table were Ben's two brothers, Jim and Jerry Krahl, his sister Mary and her husband Joe, and Eddie Manelli, a former longtime next-door neighbor. They didn't look like people who would be involved with a murderer, Tia thought. Nobody resembled Jack Nicholson dragging an ax around inside a snowy maize. No Anthony Hopkins smiling evilly at Clarice from behind prison bars. The group looked more like the cast members from "Everybody Loves Raymond." But she supposed even the most normal looking families can spawn killers.

Ben didn't do it. We've known the man his whole life, they each insisted solemnly. He absolutely is not capable of murder. Rip looked directly at Tia and said in a voice firm with conviction, "I was there that night. Ben didn't kill Nancy."

Tia could plainly see that Rip believed what he was saying, however she was immediately skeptical. She had read enough police reports to know police have more important things to do than to go around arresting innocent suspects.

She listened first, then started asking questions.

First off she wanted to know, "Why have you waited until now to get hold of me with this story? It's been almost two years since the trial."

Tia had covered the story of the Jurowski homicide at the time. She'd also reported on Ben Krahl's conviction. Although she had not attended the actual trial, she didn't question the jury's verdict. She figured the police had done their job. The evidence was there to convince the jury.

Rip answered, "Because Ben's post conviction appeal is finally on the docket, and truthfully, I just thought of you when I saw a copy of your newspaper the other day. I hope you won't think I'm presuming on our friendship, but the daily paper has no interest in this case. And besides that, the state's attorney sits on their board."

"So why did Ben sign a confession if he was innocent?" She asked the obvious question, thinking nobody signs a confession unless he's guilty.

Rip had a ready explanation. "It wasn't a confession to murder. It was a description of an *accidental* shooting—a hypothetical scenario made up by the police. That's no confession at all. But you're right, of course. He should never have signed it."

A waitress arrived at the table and took drink orders. Rip paused to order coffee, then continued his story. "The detectives interrogated Ben for 14 hours after he had put in a full day at his job. They were shouting at him. Calling him a liar. Telling him he was going to get the death penalty."

Tia listened. She had never been aware of this kind of police interrogation in Woodsville. It sounded to her like the stuff of bad TV-cop dramas.

After ordering a steak sandwich and fries, Rip waited until the rest of the orders had been given. Then he continued, "They filled him up with coffee and wouldn't let him go to the bathroom. He was exhausted. Finally, they told him to just sign their friggin' statement and he could go home. By that time, he'd been without sleep for over 23 hours. He was ready to agree to anything just to get out of there."

Clearing his throat and wrinkling his brow, Rip explained, "I know it sounds stupid, but Ben really believed that they would do their jobs and he would be cleared. Besides they had invented a scenario that didn't fit the facts of the case. He thought it was so ludicrous nobody would believe it. He would have had to be left handed to shoot Nancy from the position they had him in their hypothetical story."

The question in Tia's mind was why the investigators didn't arrest him on the spot after they got their confession. She knew that veteran cops feel certain of their suspect if they can make an arrest within 24 hours of the crime. They're fairly comfortable making an arrest within 48 hours. After that, they wonder if they will ever solve it. But several days went by before they arrested Ben Krahl. That bothered her. She remembered thinking they must have had some questions about his guilt before they finally charged him.

"I still can't imagine anyone signing any kind of confession if he wasn't guilty," she stated her doubts. She didn't know it then, but people serving on a jury feel exactly the same way. Anything smacking of a confession carries a lot of weight for a conviction.

Rip spoke slowly and distinctly, "Tia, he agreed to sign a statement saying he tried to take the gun away from Nancy, and it accidentally went off—that's a big difference from confessing to premeditated murder."

"So why didn't he ask for a lawyer during this long interrogation?" She could already guess the answer. Had detectives purposely not arrested him so they could question him without reading his Miranda rights?

"Of course that would have been the smart thing to do," Rip agreed. "But Ben didn't think he needed a lawyer. He was innocent, so why hire an attorney?"

It was a simple argument. Just simple enough to be believable. After all, in his shoes she would have reasoned the same way. The more questions she asked, the more answers she got that held a ring of plausibility. Still, she remained unconvinced.

She wanted to know, "What evidence did they have besides the statement he signed?

The group answered almost in unison. "Rocky Miller."

They explained that Rocky, Ben's longtime best friend, was the eyewitness who testified he saw Ben aiming the gun. Significantly, the only eyewitness to make this claim.

"But Rocky also changed his story sixteen times," Rip continued. "Most police don't usually give a flip-flopping witness that much credibility unless they have forensic evidence to back up the claim. In Ben's case, there was no forensic evidence. None at all."

That didn't sink in right away. Tia thought it highly unlikely that a man had been convicted without forensic evidence of some kind, something more than a questionable witness with an ever-changing story.

"So what do you want me to do?" She asked the group. They each looked so desperately hopeful. Their unwavering faith in Ben Krahl tugged at her heart rather than her logic.

Rip explained that while Ben's post-conviction relief appeal was actually in the courtroom, they were planning to carry picket signs on the sidewalks in front of the Black Woods County Courthouse. He was asking her to give Ben's case some coverage in the Woodsville Weekly News.

She didn't promise anything. But this picketing event seemed deserving of a little attention.

The waitress had served their table, and she nibbled at her half of the pasta. Blonde-wigged Carmen had already finished hers, and incredibly had remained silent throughout the conversation, as quiet as a rabbit in a den of foxes. Tia smiled inwardly, knowing what a difficult feat that was for Carm, who loved to talk.

"I know this is a lot to digest at one time," Rip acknowledged. "We'll talk again. You need to know more about the group of people who were with Ben and Nancy on the night she died."

Tia silently agreed, but made no promises.

Later, when the two women were in the Bronco driving back across town, they discussed the story.

"I just don't know about this one," said Carmen, still laughing over being introduced as Karen and then called by her real name the rest of the evening. "I should have known you'd do that! Now everybody at that table must think my name is Karen-Carmen!"

The two women laughed at their failed deception, and Carmen thought it was good to hear Tia laugh. She knew Tia's sense of humor was not completely dormant. It was just difficult to trigger.

"Well at least they don't know how gorgeous you are even without your blonde wig, dahling," Tia said as she stopped the Bronco in front of Carmen's condo. She thanked her friend for going with her on this unusual venture out after hours.

7

"No one will ever recognize you. I don't think you're in any danger," she assured Karen-Carmen.

Danger. Now that was a word Tia seldom used even though she wrote about crime every week and was well aware that Black Woods County had its share of drug dealers, street gangs and violence. This was simply a fact to be lived with, like deer ticks and Rocky Mountain spotted fever. You know the problem exists. You just try to avoid the places where you could become a victim.

Fear was not part of her daily life. Not yet.

She decided to write a letter to Ben Krahl before she committed to writing his story. She wanted to hear from the man himself why he had signed that police statement.

She also wanted his take on why Rocky Miller, his longtime best friend, had fingered him as the shooter.

Chapter 2 - Men

After mailing her letter to Mr. Krahl at the end of her next workday, eyes tired from proof reading, Tia called Carmen to see if she wanted to get a bite to eat. The two women sometimes shared a meal during the week, because both lived alone and neither liked to eat alone.

They decided to make the short drive across the state line to Rockford, Illinois where they could enjoy the free taco bar at the Irish Rose restaurant downtown. Carmen was all chatter as they pulled into the parking lot on East State Street. "I know I'm Italian, but I still love tacos!" Her enthusiasm never waned. "So how's it going with handsome Rip?" Carmen asked as she directed Tia to a parking space.

"What are you talking about? Oh, you mean Rip Tyson. Forget that right now Carmen. He's got an eye for blondes."

"Yeah, but I heard he's in blonde-ruptcy right now, and he sure didn't mind looking at you last night." Carmen had that gleam in her eye again. The one that said, let's get you out into the dating scene. You've been alone three years and that's long enough.

Tia turned the tables. "You were the one wearing the blonde wig, dahling, so he must have been looking at you. Shall I tell him you're available?"

Carmen sighed. She was getting nowhere. Besides, she could hardly wait to break the news. "I'm not available! I've met this really cool guy. He plays lead guitar in a fifties band, and he's a lot more exciting than the chess player."

Tia wasn't surprised. Watching a chess tournament is about as exciting as watching a sapling grow into a tree.

They locked the car and entered the Irish Rose, Tia listening with amusement to Carmen's glowing description of her latest romantic interest. He won't last either, she thought to herself.

She was convinced her fiery Italian friend with the flashing black eyes and strong opinions was more of a challenge than most men were up to. Carmen was independent, a threat to the traditional breadwinner. A successful physical therapist, she had purchased a condominium, drove a classy car and had made some lucrative investments.

Her string of ex-boyfriends, and a few broken hearts along the way, just continued to grow. Now at age 29, she was unlikely to meet many professional men who were not already married. And in her words, the divorced guys usually carried too much emotional baggage, not to mention kids and child support payments.

Both women agreed the good guys were already taken. For Tia however, it was a different story. Carmen knew the tragic details. With her insatiable curiosity and genuine concern, Carmen had pried it out of Tia a little at a time, usually while they were seated in a booth at the Irish Rose.

Carmen thought it romantic that Tia had married her college sweetheart, adventurous, athletic and rugged Jeff Burgess. When Jeff's computer company transferred him from Missouri to a branch business in Woodsville, Wisconsin Tia had come along enthusiastically, expecting to raise a family and settle in as a freelance writer, working from home.

Woodsville could easily have been a slightly smaller twin city to its southern neighbor, Rockford, Illinois which was billing itself as the state's "Second City" in the mid 1990s—second in size only to Chicago. Tia later learned the two cities also shared a high incidence of crime as well. Winnebago County was racking up the highest violent crime rate per capita of any county in the entire state of Illinois. However, crime was the last thing on her mind at the time.

Tia had decided she would enjoy the best of both states. She liked Woodsville's easy traffic flow and neighborly attitude. She also had access to all that Rockford had to offer just a few minutes down the road, and for big city attractions, Milwaukee and Chicago were not far away.

Jeff's career had taken off in the fast lane. Promoted to management in just two years, he had purchased a second vehicle and saved the down payment for their first home in the posh Whispering Winds Estates.

Tia had not sold many stories, but she was undaunted, fully expecting to break into a writer's market eventually. Jeff's encouragement bolstered her confidence.

The couple had a bright future. A future filled with promising dreams and hopes—wiped out in a shattering instant when a drunk driver crossed a centerline on Illinois Route 173 during a rain-soaked night.

Mercifully, Tia could not remember the accident, or much about the weeks that followed except a parade of white coats, stethoscopes and the antiseptic smell in the Intensive Care Unit at St. Anthony Medical Center in Rockford. She was in and out of consciousness for days, suffering from a severe concussion.

When at last she did wake up, she wanted to go back to sleep again rather than face a life without Jeff. . . and their precious unborn child.

She had been shocked to learn that Jeff's sadly lacking insurance policy left her with just enough to pay off her astronomical medical bills and one vehicle after burial expenses. The drunk driver didn't have insurance.

She'd been forced to sell their dream home and move into a small upper apartment on Wood Hills Road. With bills staring her in the face, Tia applied for a reporter's position at the Woodsville Weekly News, just as their senior reporter, Sara Blake, known around town as the Hat Lady because she was never seen without one, had retired. Tia liked her editor and the office staff. It was more than a job if she stopped to analyze it. They had become a substitute family, her lifeline for survival.

Whenever her mother insisted that she move back to Missouri, she used the excuse that she wanted to finish writing her book. In truth, she felt her husband's nearness in the area where they had lived and planned a life together. She knew it wasn't rational, but she feared distance would dim his presence, which she clung to with a kind of desperate fierceness.

Still, the words wouldn't flow to the computer keyboard when she wrote at home. It seemed all her inspiration had died with the man she loved and the baby her empty arms still ached to hold. However at the news office, the words came easily, a way to focus her mind on making the words fill the empty pages . . . and the pages to fill the gaping hole in her life.

As long as she concentrated on developing snappy leads and stories with sizzle, she managed to exist inside a cocoon spun tightly enough to numb the ache in her heart and all other emotions as well.

Therapy. Writing had always been a form of therapy for Tia. Better than any pill or counselor could be. Now her very survival depended on it.

It wasn't long before her editor sent her downtown to cover the police beat. Of course this had intrigued Carmen, curious about possible romantic interests, but the city officers kept a respectful distance after noticing Tia's wedding band. Most were unaware that she was a widow. She'd managed to sustain this slight deception, primarily because she maintained her reserve.

However, she took an instant liking a retiring Woodsville Detective with the unlikely name, James Bond, who preferred to be called Jimmy, although with his portly middle and balding head, he was not easily mistaken for the devastatingly handsome Double-0-Seven. After she wrote a clever feature on the span of Mr. Bond's police career, he informed her that he was taking her to lunch to fill her in on a few things she had missed in her crime beat column.

Since she knew him to be a happily married man and a member of her church, she decided it couldn't hurt to go. After all, who wouldn't want to have lunch with a detective named James Bond? Besides he might be able to help with crime stories from time to time. Aside from Carmen and her editor, James Bond was her only friend since the accident.

And that was the way it went. Work at the paper all day. Home to an empty apartment at night. Sometimes church on Sunday. More often not.

If it weren't for her faith, Tia knew she would be as helpless as a feather sucked into a whirlpool drain. Still, she asked all the tormented and typical questions: Why, God? If I had prayed harder and had been a better person, would my husband still be here? The answers were as elusive as a smoke ring hidden inside a cloud.

It was during physical therapy for her injuries that she first met Carmen and was immediately warmed by her outgoing personality. Of course Carmen had determined to write some happier chapters into her friend's life. Maybe the Irish Rose was just the place to begin. Because it was located in the heart of Rockford's River District where law offices abound, many professional men gathered there in the evenings. Carmen knew some of them from her years working as a law clerk before she earned her Physical Therapy degree. Perhaps she could introduce Tia to one when the time was right.

"I'm so glad you called me tonight," Carmen chattered, "Come on, my stomach's growling."

Rising from her chair, Carmen accidentally collided with a tall stranger who grinned down at her. "Any chance you could do that again, honey?" he asked as he looked her up and down with approving eyes. "You can brush up against me anytime."

"Excuse me," she answered. Returning his impudent boldness, she looked him up and down with a critical eye. Pointing at his chest she demanded, "What are you doing wearing a tie like that with your blue shirt? It makes you look like a dweeb. You really need a nice stripe or a pale yellow."

Taken aback, he glanced down at his tie as Carmen brushed past him on her way to the taco bar. Tia followed, amused at the way Carmen handled the flirtatious comment.

A dangerously handsome man took a seat at a nearby table, and Carmen's eyes widened. "Ooooh! He makes my liver quiver!" she whispered as she nudged Tia to look in Mr. Handsome's direction.

Tia appraised him. Then she said quietly, "Carmen, he's gay. Look, he's holding hands under the table with the man beside him."

"Oh no!" Carmen moaned, "You're right! All the good ones are taken."

The frown on her pretty face passed, and her eyes brightened. "But wait till I introduce you to Brett Hanson. He plays rhythm guitar in the band with Joe, and he's dying to meet you!"

"I don't think so," Tia announced firmly.

Carmen rolled her eyes with momentary exasperation, then looked at the taco on her plate. "*Mangia, mangia!*" she urged, following her own directive and digging in with enthusiasm.

She had tried before.

She would try again, certain that eventually, she could get things moving in the romance department for Tia somehow.

Chapter 3 - Ben's letter

Ben Krahl tossed on a bunk in the Green Bay Correctional Center in Green Bay, Wisconsin.

He moaned in helpless protest as his dreams wrapped him in tumultuous darkness. Again, he relived the echoes of gunfire. The wailing sirens from approaching squad cars. Nancy's lifeless form lying in a pool of blood on the freezing tarmac.

Rage at his helplessness in the presence of Nancy's violent death burned white hot, leaving him exhausted and troubled in the morning.

He was not a young man at age 42 when the Judge handed down the 40-year sentence. For Ben it was, in effect, a life sentence. A living nightmare. The sound of those heavy doors clanging shut on his life, his hopes and dreams.

Every prisoner knows the surreal quality of those first few weeks. The profound alarm and the logic-defying belief that someone will have the good sense to rectify this impossible mistake and all will be put right again. As weeks turn into months and years, a mind-numbing routine slowly leeches vitality out of the soul.

At night Ben longed for daybreak. At dawn he wished for the night. Neither brought relief from the painful loss, the endless monotony or the terrible reality that his life was irrevocably altered. Nancy's death had been, in a very real sense, his own death as well. Without her, he felt as much enthusiasm for life as he might for eating a road kill rabbit. But there was his son Jarrod. A reason to go on. There were appeals. His lawyers were working on the case.

Something had to break.

Hope of release is a survival rope an inmate clings to as fiercely as a drowning man clings to a life preserver in the middle of a raging flood. Ben wound his hope-rope a little tighter in order to keep despair from drowning him. Long before morning, he had pen and paper in hand, ready to answer the Woodsville Weekly News reporter's questions in a letter he had received only a day ago.

Mrs. Tia M. Burgess wanted to know why he'd signed the so-called "confession" prepared by the police. Naturally she would want to know that. He had asked himself the same question over and over so many times.

Why, why, why? The answer was just plain stupidity.

Stupid, stupid, stupid. He wrote down the words and looked at them. How was he going to explain such stupidity to a reporter who had never even met him, but who was asking honest questions that deserved honest answers.

He had to try. Maybe at last someone would hear his side of the story and not some ludicrous and damning theory. Prosecutors were expert at speaking dramatically with absolute certainty in their voices. They knew how to use sarcasm. They were very good at making jury members feel totally dumb for daring to disagree with an erudite counselor's scholarly opinion. Truth was tangled until it got lost in a preponderance of speculation. And Ben's freedom got lost in the tangle.

After opening his letter with an expression of appreciation for Mrs. Tia Burgess's interest, Ben wrote the following:

"Thank you for your letter. As you can imagine, mail in this place is something we all look forward to. It's our only link to our family and friends. Now let me try to answer your questions. Why did I sign such a statement?

"Stupid. Broken. Defeated.

"Stupid for talking with the police for as long as I did without an attorney. But not wanting to appear guilty by asking for one, or by walking out.

"Broken by hours and hours of being yelled at, cursed at. Called a liar, threatened with life in prison, physical violence, and even lethal injection.

"Finally, my will and fight were gone. Seeing this, the police told me that if I signed a statement I could go home and everything would be over. I read the statement which was not written by me. It made absolutely no sense or logic. I would have had to be left handed to shoot Nancy from the position they said I was in. The facts didn't match their theory. I believed police would soon discover that and find the real killer. Knowing that I had done nothing wrong, I signed and was allowed to leave.

"I was defeated. On the way home, I was shaking so badly from the cold, (they kept my coat) from lack of food, lack of sleep, and the shock of what had just happened. I could not drive in a straight line. I had to park my truck and compose myself before I could continue on my way home. Unless you have experienced an interrogation of this magnitude, I cannot expect you to understand why I signed that statement. I can only attempt to explain it.

"Well, there you have it. You have no idea how many times I've kicked myself for signing that paper. But I truly believed the system would protect me.

"I thought the police would do their job and find out who the real killer was. And even now, I still believe it was not the system which failed me, but some people who failed the system.

"Why would my long-time best friend Rocky Miller name me? Self preservation.

"I believe the police threatened him and treated him as badly as they treated me. Rocky said in the police report that his biggest fear was not being able to spend the rest of his life with his family. We both folded under the pressure. But in different ways.

"I signed a statement. He named me as the shooter. The police asked me if I thought Rocky did it. I told them no. They tried to convince me, telling me how suspicious he was acting, leaving the crime scene. Making inconsistent statements. Calling to check if I was hurt, etc.

"I told them Rocky did not do it.

"I feel no anger toward Rocky, knowing the grueling interrogation he went through, being shouted at and called a liar. I would have told them most anything just to get them off my back. And after awhile I did change my story to agree with whatever fit their theory of the crime.

"You said you pray for the entire truth to be revealed. As much as I love—and miss—my freedom, I love and miss Nancy more. The entire truth will reveal the name of her murderer. And I believe she deserves at least that much."

Ben once again thanked Tia for her interest and signed the letter. He desperately hoped that she would be able to stir up enough questions that the real killer would be found.

He had to believe that sooner or later, the scumbag would make a mistake. Slip up. Get a girlfriend or a buddy angry enough at him to spill the story or turn him in for the reward. Someone out there knew Nancy's killer. Someone, someday was going to talk.

*The above is an actual letter written by the man on whose story this book is based.

Chapter 4 – Cass Peters

The rain fell hard. The old man was lonely. The voluptuous young waitress was naïve or simply stupid.

"I was wondering what you would look like all wet," he uttered, hungry eyes turning from the rain-washed windows to the teenage girl waiting to take his order.

Tia couldn't help overhearing their conversation at the cozy restaurant where she had stopped for dinner on her way home from the news office. She glanced his way, thinking he looked old enough to be the girl's great-great grandfather. Instead of a clever comeback, the young waitress giggled and patted his shoulder, apparently enjoying his leering attention. Either that or she was hoping for a big tip.

Tia turned around and gave her attention to a bowl of soup. She told herself she'd stopped here because she especially liked the Old English House soup. In truth, she dreaded entering her dark and empty apartment on this rainy fall night. The light and warmth of the restaurant was a good place to have supper and read over Ben Krahl's letter, and she was eager to see what he had to say.

"May I join you?"

Caught off guard, Tia looked up to see a tall man with chiseled features smiling pleasantly down at her. "Unless you're waiting for someone?"

The stranger seated himself before she could answer. His eyes admired her, not lasciviously but with sincere appreciation.

"I'm sorry, but I am waiting for someone," Tia lied.

"Then I'll just sit here until he arrives. Anyone foolish enough to keep you waiting deserves to lose his place at your table."

"He'll be here at any moment, and he really won't appreciate finding you beside me."

"What's your name?" the stranger asked, ignoring her remark.

"That's none of your business."

"Mine is Cole Nemon, and I think you're absolutely gorgeous."

"Mine is Totally Unavailable, and I think you're treeing up the wrong bark—barking up the wrong tree," she stumbled over her words.

His grin broadened. "Not at all." He leaned back and adopted a thoughtful pose. "I can tell by your accent that you're not a Georgia-peach tree, but you are a peach from the south."

"Missouri," she said, immediately angry with herself for giving him even that much personal information. "Now you really must be going."

"I'll be going as soon as you let me buy you a cup of coffee. Oh, Miss?" he called to a nearby waitress. "Can I please have six cups of coffee when you get time?"

"You'll be going now, or as soon as I call the police." Tia demanded. The guy was too determined and she didn't like it at all. He looked crestfallen. "Hey, can't blame a guy for trying." But he still didn't move. "Look, I know I'm a total stranger, but how is a guy supposed to meet a lovely lady like you if he doesn't move while he has the opportunity?"

The persistent stranger stopped a second waitress passing by their table, "Pardon me, Miss. Could you do me a favor? Introduce me to this beautiful lady here. Tell her my name is Cole Nemon, and I'm a professor at the college."

The waitress played along, formally introducing Mr. Cole Nemon and then asked, "And your name, Ma'am?"

"Sorry, I don't give my name to strangers in restaurants," she answered.

"I'm not a stranger now. We've been properly introduced." He reached across the table and took her hand, shaking it formally. "I know this sounds really cliché, but I've seen you someplace before."

"You're right. It sounds totally cliché."

Nemon released her hand. "Were you ever in a scuba diving class?"

"Yes. With my husband." Tia announced pointedly.

Instantly the charming grin turned serious, the smiling eyes darted to the previously unnoticed wedding band on Tia's finger. "I see. Then I must apologize, Ma'am. I was out of line. Please accept my apology," He got up to leave. "And tell your husband he's a fortunate man."

Tia breathed a sigh of relief as she watched him walking away. Looking up at the waitress she asked, "What is it with men? Some of them just need to be locked up until their hormones shut down completely. It would do them good."

"That would be a crying shame in his case if you asked me," the waitress sighed, watching the stranger as he walked away. Then she refilled Tia's coffee cup.

Briefly toying with the idea of writing a feature on corny pick-up lines for the next edition of the news, Tia turned her attention back to the letter she had received from the prisoner. She read it carefully, thinking Ben's words held a ring of truth. Here was an ordinary guy who happened to be in the wrong place at the wrong time and made some really dumb mistakes.

Or else he was an incredibly clever, manipulative, cold-blooded killer who had planned to murder his girlfriend in a

21

parking lot full of witnesses. Did that make sense? How clever was that?

Okay, she thought, I need to talk to the people who were there other than Rip Tyson. She checked her list of names, acquaintances and friends involved with Ben and Nancy.

The next morning, Tia cleared her assignments to a manageable pile, then decided to dial the 'motive' that had been sold to the jurors, Cass Peters, Nancy's best friend who had been dubbed "the other woman" at the trial.

She found the number, hesitated to call Cass at work, but decided it was as good a time as any. After introducing herself and explaining the reason for the call in a friendly and non-threatening manner, Tia was pleased to find Cass willing to talk.

"I think about that night all the time," Cass murmured in a quiet voice, "It's hard to sleep."

"How close were you and Nancy?" Tia posed her question gently, listening for any telltale signs of jealousy.

"Nancy and I were friends from the seventh grade on when we started attending a private Christian school together. She was like family to me." Cass paused to blow her nose, then continued describing the relationship.

"I was the one she called in the middle of the night if she was ever upset. She was there during my teen years, my marriage, my kids' births, and my divorce. She even used her key to my house to sneak presents under the tree for me, so my kids wouldn't be the only ones to open presents on Christmas day."

Well acquainted with grief, Tia recognized the painful emotion in Cass's voice. This was obviously a tender subject. Three years had passed since Nancy's death, but for Cass Peters, the pain had not dulled. She mentioned other examples of Nancy's generosity and special times they had shared over the years. Each time Cass brought up a cherished memory, her voice choked a little more.

Tia listened, waited a moment then asked, "Why did Nancy move out of Ben's house after they had lived together for nearly a year?"

Regaining some composure, Cass explained in a tired voice, "Nancy was 29 years old and not getting any younger. She wanted to get married and have a baby. Ben was older. He was divorced and already had a son. He didn't want any more kids."

Tia nodded, taking notes as she listened. "But they still saw each other?"

"All the time. She was over at his place practically every weekend."

"How did anyone ever get the idea of an affair between you and Ben anyway?"

Cass's voice took on a slightly defensive tone. "That was a total lie," she insisted. "Yeah, there were jokes about Ben and other women, but they were never taken seriously by anyone. Just the kind of jokes that friends make to boost a guy's ego. After all, Nancy had already moved out of their house. He was open game supposedly. But everyone knew they still loved each other.

"And even if it were true—I mean—let's say Ben's got these two women, and we're still good friends. We're planning a trip to California together after the New Year for my mom's graduation from tech school. Ben even buys Nancy a plane ticket. We all three get along great, so why does he need to kill one of us?"

Why indeed? Tia echoed the question in her mind.

Perplexed, she asked, "So the prosecutors just made up the story of the affair for no reason at all?"

Cass sighed, "For the first two nights after the murder, I spent the night on the couch at Ben's place. I was scared. I'd just seen my best friend get killed and I didn't want to be alone. It was my ex's weekend to have the kids. Besides, the killer knew that I saw him. How did I know he wasn't coming after me too?"

"You SAW him?"

"I saw a figure, but I couldn't see a face."

Tia could understand why Cass had feared being alone those first couple of nights. She could also understand how the sleepover would arouse police suspicion.

Cass continued, "And because I asked Ben to go with me to buy a dress for Nancy's funeral. The prosecutor told the jury that Ben bought the dress for me. But I paid for it myself and I have the VISA receipt to prove it." There was both regret and anger in Cass's voice.

It was time to end the conversation. Tia thanked Cass for her willingness to answer questions. After she hung up the phone, she didn't need a lie detector for what she intuitively knew. Cass Peters was telling the truth.

Who but another woman can understand the bond that develops between females such as existed between Cass and Nancy? Women reveal themselves to one another in ways they cannot to the men in their lives. Tia strongly doubted that Nancy had ever feared losing Ben to her best friend.

So what did she have in her notebook so far? A woman who loved the victim like a sister. A woman still deeply and profoundly shaken by the murder. A convicted boyfriend with no obvious motive. And a crime with no murder weapon.

Tia decided she would be at the Black Woods County Courthouse to cover Krahl's appeal.

* * *

Under a colorless October sky with high clouds racing on a stiff breeze, picketers walked outside the Black Woods County Courthouse. Shivering but determined, Rip Tyson and several others carried homemade signs as they paced the sidewalk. The signs proclaimed Ben Krahl's innocence.

Tia pulled her jacket hood up over her head and snapped a few photos, her fingers numbed by the chill. Then she hurried inside and took the elevator up to the third floor.

In Chief Judge Mitchell Moroz's courtroom, Ben's new defense attorney, Bill Crane, moved back and forth between his notes and the witness stand. He was short, slender and wiry built with black hair and piercing eyes under darker brows, knitted together in concentration.

Tia watched the proceedings with great interest. This was, after all, the legendary Bill Crane. She didn't often have the time to see him in action. Word around town was that Crane could get Hannibal Lechter acquitted if he took the case. Still, she was well aware a jury of twelve men and women had already found Ben Krahl guilty of first-degree murder.

Even though he was experienced as a criminal defense lawyer, unlike Ben's trial attorney who mostly handled DUI cases, Crane was fighting an uphill battle.

The state's star witness, Rocky Miller, was seated on the witness stand.

"So Mr. Miller, do you remember Ben saying to you at the bar that night that he was going to kill Nancy?" Crane asked.

"No."

"Didn't you testify earlier that you had heard him make that threat to harm Nancy?"

"I don't remember."

"You don't remember making a statement to police that Ben told you at the bar that he was going to kill Nancy?"

"No, sir." Rocky remained motionless in the witness chair, eyes downcast. He never looked up one time during the questioning.

"Well if he had said those words to you at the bar or anywhere else, and then Nancy was killed that very night, don't you think you would remember it?" Crane thundered.

Miller said nothing.

Tia almost applauded. Here it was. Miller was not a credible witness. And he was the state's only witness.

"No further questions, your honor," said Crane.

Then in a surprising twist, Crane called the prosecutor to the stand. Tia's interest grew. She had never seen an assistant state's attorney on the witness stand. This was highly unusual.

After establishing that the Assistant State's Attorney had prosecuted the Jurowski case, Crane asked, " Mr. Clark, isn't it a fact that you knew Mr. Miller changed his story 16 times before you put him on the stand?"

"Yes."

"And isn't it a fact that you knew he changed his story about hearing Ben threaten to kill Nancy?"

"Yes."

"And you did not reveal this information to Mr. Krahl's defense attorney?"

"Yes."

"And don't you think this would have made a huge difference in the way the defense handled the case?" Crane emphasized forcefully and dramatically.

Before the prosecutor could answer, Crane exploded, "Of course this would have affected the outcome—the defense could have had a heyday with this one!"

Anyone in the courtroom could see that a good defense lawyer would have chewed up Miller's story and tossed it on the rubbish heap. The jury would have had plenty of reasonable doubt, because Miller was the strongest part of the case, since there was no gun, no motive or forensic evidence. There was nothing at all to point to Ben Krahl as the murderer except Miller's testimony.

Chief Judge Moroz was unmoved. It was apparent to Tia that Moroz already had his mind made up. In the end, while he did acknowledge that the state had made an error, he said it was not strong enough to change the outcome of the trial.

What were they thinking?

Tia was dumbfounded. The whole case smelled stronger than a garlic milkshake. Ben Krahl lost the appeal. However, he had won a reporter who was willing to become a tyrant for the truth.

Whatever the truth might be.

Chapter 5 – Cecelia Jurowski

"What's the scariest thing you can think of?" Tia asked Carmen as they spoke on the telephone that night.

"Let's see. When I was five, it was the monster under my bed. When I was eight, it was Stinky Pete Wilson. But since I'm an old maid at age 29, it could be finding out that the last guy who asked me to marry him would be the last. Why?"

Tia paused for a moment, listening to the clock ticking on the nightstand beside her bed. The sound emphasized the stillness of the night. A small reading lamp cast familiar shadows on the wall.

It was a rather stark room, devoid of decoration. She didn't think of it as lonely. However she welcomed Carmen's frequent telephone intrusions into her refuge perhaps more than she realized. Carmen usually called a couple of times a week full of questions about current news, but her real motive was to check on her friend's welfare. "So what scares you?" she asked.

"What if you had said yes to the last guy's proposal?"

"Come to think of it, that would have been pretty scary." Carmen faked a horrified voice. "What things scare you?"

Tia put down the book she had been reading. "King Kong used to scare me half to death when I was a little girl. Then when I grew older it was mammograms. But there are scarier things. One of them is being locked up for something you didn't do."

"Have you been charged with a crime?" Carmen pretended to be astonished.

"Not yet. But I could be if I decide to hire a couple of thugs to work this character over until he tells the truth!"

"What character?"

"The man who lied and pointed the finger at his best friend."

"Oh, that Rocky Miller! Do you think he killed Nancy?"

"No, but I'm starting to think Krahl didn't do it either. I'm really stumped. I can't find any rational reason for the man to murder his girlfriend," Tia puzzled.

"What did the prosecutors say was his motive?" Carmen asked, her curiosity sensors on full alert now.

"They argued it was a crime of sudden passion, a lover's spat. Ben supposedly flew into a rage because they were quarreling over his supposed affair with Cass."

"But they charged him with first-degree murder! That means premeditation—not sudden rage or a crime of passion," Carmen fumed. "So he kisses her goodnight, turns and walks fours steps away, and the next instant he shoots her? I don't think so."

"Neither do I. Three witnesses at the scene all saw him kiss Nancy. The next instant she's dead. That gives him about two seconds to go from tender touch to torrid rage."

"So what are you going to write about next?"

The public's response to her first story on the Krahl case had surprised Tia. "Carm, I've got people from all over the community calling me to say Ben Krahl is innocent. There are a few key people I want to talk to."

Out of habit, Carmen began warning her, "You just be careful. There might be a killer out there who won't like it if he knows you're poking around."

"I thought you believed in guardian angels," Tia pretended surprise.

"I do, but you don't want to give them more work than they can handle."

"I'm not in any danger, Miss Karen-Carmen. But if it makes you feel any better, I'll borrow your blonde wig."

After their phone chat, Tia poured a cup of hot chocolate.

She flipped the television to the American Movie Classics channel and watched John Wayne getting beaten up by an Oriental dwarf for a few minutes. A Karate dwarf beating up the legendary movie hero? Did she need eyeglasses? No. Just sleep.

She punched the off button and climbed into bed. Sleep was a late arriving guest. Still awake after midnight and feeling like howling a duet with the groaning wind, Tia rolled out of bed to get the bottle of anti-depressant capsules and sleeping pills sitting in her bathroom cabinet.

She had visited the psychiatrist for grief counseling only once at Carmen's insistence. She'd had the prescriptions filled. Both plastic bottles sat in the bathroom cabinet, unopened.

Nightmarish scenes sometimes rose up from beneath the layers of sleeping consciousness, offering her bite-size glimpses of things she did not want to remember. Tempted now to take the pill, which might offer some respite, she picked up the small white plastic bottle. This was the medical community's most popular answer for plagues of the mind. Just pop a pill and be normal again. Somewhat normal. Artificially normal.

Does normalcy really come in a capsule? It was tempting. But no matter how many pills she swallowed, she couldn't bring back the life she had known before the accident, the husband, or the child she had loved and lost before it came to be.

Tia placed the bottles back on the shelf, crawled back into bed and pulled the comforter up around her chin. The mournful wind finally ushered in a few hours of mercifully dreamless sleep.

When sunlight filtered through the apartment blinds, striping her quilt with alternate bands of light and shadows, Tia sat up yawning, unrefreshed. Would she ever sleep well again? Glad that she had a workplace and friendly greetings to go to, she dressed in gray slacks, a pale pink sweater, swallowed a sip of juice and headed for downtown Woodsville.

At the news office, Pat greeted her warmly, as always, the bright spot in her day. "Elvis Presley called you already this morning," he said after taking her jacket.

"Already? What did Elvis want this time?"

"He's doing a show for the senior citizens at the Jubilee Center and says he wants some advance publicity."

"No Elvis sightings? No Elvis-is-alive story?"

"Not today, but he said he would have a serious scoop about Elvis's faked death for you very soon."

The desk was waiting with notes from her Cass-Peters interview. The last words she had jotted down were, "No affair." Sorry Elvis. I'll get back to you, she muttered. Tia was eager to talk to the murdered woman's family members and discover what they thought of the man.

Dialing the number of Nancy's grieving mother, Tia spoke with Cecelia Jurowski, who was anything but gentle. "There's no way in Hell you can convince me that Ben Krahl didn't shoot my daughter!" Cecilia exploded, hostile and angry at the world. "He's an evil, cold-blooded man. Ben and that Cass Peters woman are both pathological liars."

Tia steered the conversation as gently as possible, trying to find out how much Cecelia knew about Nancy's relationship with Ben. "Was your daughter serious about Ben?"

"Nancy loved Ben with all her heart. She moved out because she wanted to have a baby, and he didn't want more kids. The no-good sonuvabitch!"

Once more, Tia waited for the woman's string of expletives to subside. Then she asked, "When did you first suspect Ben was the killer?"

Cecelia answered somewhat calmer, "I first suspected Ben the day before the visitation when he stopped by and said he was taking Cass to buy a dress for the funeral."

Tia remembered that a very frightened Cass had asked Ben to accompany her on that outing and had in fact purchased the dress with her own Visa card.

Cecelia was adding in a voice dripping with sarcasm, "Of course Cass wouldn't come inside my house. She had already told me that she was having an affair with Ben. She even confessed it to Nancy!"

The affair story again. Why ever would Cass want to confess this kind of thing to Nancy's mother, of all people? Oh by the way, I'm having an affair with your daughter's boyfriend. Just thought you'd like to know.

Even more doubtful was the California trip. Why would any two women be planning a trip together if they were both sharing the same man? It defied logic and everything Tia knew about human nature.

Then Cecelia brought up the lie, "I told you Ben is a pathological liar. He sat on my step with his head down in his hands that morning, until I finally asked him what he was thinking about. He said he was thinking about all the guys he had saved in Vietnam, but he couldn't save Nancy. The lying bastard never even went to Vietnam!"

Cecelia added a few more bitter words about the man her daughter had "loved with all her heart."

Okay, Tia acknowledged to herself. She knew Ben had lied about serving in Vietnam. And like so many stupid people in all the cop stories, he had dug a deep well for himself with that lie. A well he might never be able to climb out of.

The prosecutors had used the Vietnam lie to stress to the jury that Krahl was deceitful from the onset of the investigation, and that "innocent men do not lie like that." The judge later referred to the Vietnam lie as one of the main reasons he chose not to grant Ben's appeal for a new trial. What did that lie have to do with the murder anyway? Tia puzzled.

A lie is never without consequences, no matter how benign, she mused. Still it did seem that 40 years in the pen was a steep price to pay for that small, ego-inflating deception.

31

Changing the subject, she asked, "Did Nancy keep a diary?" Rip had mentioned the diary and hoped it could be found, possibly as a source of refuting the affair theory.

Cecelia spewed out a very firm no. "My daughter always told me everything. I would have known it if she kept a diary. We were very close."

It was obviously painful for the grieving mother to read any story questioning Ben's guilt. Tia could understand raw grief and outrage. How well she could understand it. But why wouldn't Cecelia want to know it if the wrong man was in prison?

What if the man who killed her daughter was still walking the streets of Woodsville? And if Ben Krahl really was the one who pulled the trigger, what difference would it make if Tia asked a few questions? The truth is the truth and has nothing to hide. Any new information she might dig up would not change it.

When she tried to suggest this, Cecelia only became angrier. She wanted Ben to remain in prison.

So did Tia. *If* he was the one who pulled the trigger.

Her doubts were growing with every interview.

Chapter 6 – Riptide and Captain Nemo

Lightning kicked out of the sky and set its silver toe down somewhere near the Wood Hills Apartments where Tia was curled up under a blanket. She was reading her notes for part three of her Krahl series when the phone rang.

"Hello."

Nothing but heavy breathing on the line. Oh boy, I've got a pervert here, she thought. Starting to hang up the receiver, she heard a male voice ordering, "Back off the Krahl story."

The voice was deep and the tone almost casual. The sound of it had a quality that set off alarm signals in Tia's head. Instantly alert, she asked, "Who is this?"

"I said back off the Krahl story, reporter girl." There was a hint of authority as if he were accustomed to instant obedience. There was also a hint of chilling malevolence.

The line went dead before she could respond. Icy chills tiptoed up her spine and hair prickled on the back of her neck. She had never in her wildest dreams expected this. Was it a real threat?

Was it the killer? Someone who knew him? Was she in danger? For the first time, she considered that possibility. She dialed her detective friend James Bond's number at once.

"Could be a prankster," he suggested after Tia described the call. "Or it could be a member of Nancy's family. Didn't you tell me they wanted you to back off the story?"

"You're right," she answered, calming herself. "It could be one of them. They aren't happy with me." Bond advised her to be cautious, to be very aware of her surroundings, and not to be out alone at night.

"He knows my phone number, *Mr. Bond.* That means he could easily find out where I live."

He smiled when she said his name with the same inflection as the movie characters used. It was something he'd heard from coworkers over the years, but when Tia said it with her southern Missouri accent, she always made him chuckle. This time he restrained his amusement.

"Okay, Miss Lois Lane," he played along, "Get a deadbolt lock, and I'll ask a friend of mine in patrol to pass by your place at night for awhile."

After hanging up, she wrapped the blanket tighter around her and turned out the lights. Lightning silvered the room in brilliant strobe-like flashes, but the late autumn storm was already moving east. Thunder grumbled, less and less angry. It was a long time before she was able to drift off to sleep, only to dream fitfully of Jeff holding out his hand to her.

No matter how she struggled, longingly stretching out her arms toward his, she could not reach him.

* * *

Ben Krahl is an innocent man callers declared to Tia at the office each time the Weekly News hit the streets with her series. Tia began receiving letters from people all over the community, people who knew the convicted man and were hoping to see him set free. The clerk at the gas station where he stopped for morning coffee. Boy Scouts who had been members of his troop. People who had worked with him over the years.

She was amazed at how well liked he had been and curious as to why his trial attorney had never called a single character witness. It appeared he had so many decent, hard working people in his favor. If only the jury could have seen him through their eyes.

Tia decided not to mention the threatening phone call to Pat, because she knew her editor worried over her like a protective father. His concern was welcome. With no one to come home to at night, no one wondering where she had been if she arrived late, or if she'd had a good day, Pat's concern was like a warm ray of sunshine in the middle of a frozen winter. It felt good to know that somebody cared.

He often praised her columns and that felt good too, a satisfying end to the workday. After picking up a to-go sandwich and settling in at her second level apartment, Tia decided to call Rip Tyson. She was looking for a motive, anyone with a reason to kill Nancy, and she wanted to ask Rip a few more questions.

"Sure, let's meet at the Green Onion in Mackenzie Park. I know it's probably not your favorite place, but I'm always hoping that something there will trigger a forgotten detail."

Tia started to decline. She didn't really want to go out again, but she was at a place in her series where she needed more information. "I'll be there in half an hour," she agreed. Since Carmen was out with Guitar Man, Tia drove to the Grill alone and parked the Bronco Close to the entrance, keenly aware that this was the very parking lot where Nancy had been shot to death on a bitterly cold December night.

Dead leaves skittered across the pavement, rattling like dry bones tap-dancing on cemetery crypts. Multi-colored neon lights from business storefronts cast a muted glow in the L-shaped strip mall. Tia did not notice a driver watching her from a parked van as she entered the restaurant.

Rip Tyson was sitting at a table with his date, a blonde named Sharon. He also introduced Tia to "Captain Nemo," otherwise known as Cole Nemon, a scuba instructor who sometimes helped out at Rip's diving school. She recognized him instantly as the tall stranger who had tried to so determinedly to pick her up at the Old English House restaurant.

Nemon did a double take. He'd come along with Rip for the meal only, expecting to meet a widowed reporter and probably be totally bored since he'd already heard Rip's take on the murder many times. Instead he was pleasantly surprised to see the woman who had spurred his uncharacteristically bold behavior at the Old English House.

So this was the *widow* Rip had told him about. He realized he was staring at Tia, and extended his hand with a pleased grin. "Just call me Cap. Captain Nemo is a name Rip uses to keep our scuba students in the mood for the thrills of deep-water diving."

"Well, Mr. Nemon, we meet again." Tia said formally, raising a cool eyebrow. For a fleeting instant, it crossed her mind that scuba diving with this man would be thrill enough for most students, the girls anyway. He wasn't handsome in the ordinary sense, but something about him was certainly arresting. She ignored the surprised recognition and genuine gladness in his startlingly blue eyes, but noticed the way a single lock of dark hair brushed over his broad brow. If she thought about it, she would have to admit she liked his well-defined mouth curved in that appealing, lop-sided grin.

She deliberately chose not to think about Cap Nemon. Instead she turned her attention completely to the matter at hand.

Cap, on the opposite side of the table, couldn't keep from watching Tia who seemed completely unaware of his presence. He remembered the jolt of disappointment when she'd informed him she was married. The reaction had surprised him at the time, but he'd left the Old English House thinking that he would just have to find her twin somewhere in the world.

Now here she was again. He was even more dazzled than before. Pretending to focus on the conversation, he was captivated by the way she tilted her head while listening, her tapered, elegant fingers as she took notes, the fringe of sooty lashes that swept up when she lifted her dark eyes.

She seemed very intent on what Rip was saying, all business and completely focused, a reporter zeroed in on her story. Not once did she glance his way. He hoped he had not offended her completely during their first chance meeting at the restaurant.

The group's pleasantries immediately turned to talk of Ben Krahl. It was apparent that Ben's imprisonment was eating away at Rip. Keenly disappointed that Judge Moroz had thrown out Ben's appeal for post conviction relief, Rip nevertheless thanked Tia for getting the story out in the open at last.

"Rip, is there anyone you can think of who might have a reason to kill Nancy Jurowski?" she asked.

Rip shook his head no.

The waitress interrupted to take their orders. Once again it was hamburgers and fries, except for Tia who stuck with a bowl of soup.

"Do you think something was going on between Ben and Cass Peters?" Tia asked after the waitress gathered their menus.

"I'm very aware of body language and glances between men and women," Rip paused briefly while the waitress filled their coffee cups. "There was nothing going on between Ben and Cass. I would have known. I was around them a lot," he emphasized.

Then he changed his tone. "Now there's Rocky. Cass told me she thought he was acting weird that night, flirting with her and pouting."

"Was there something going on between Rocky and Cass that might have put Rocky in a bad mood that night?"

"Rocky was married, and Cass wouldn't encourage him. He was moody later on that evening, but I figure that was because he wanted Ben to leave and go someplace with him instead of with Nancy. He'd hoped Ben would be spending more time with him after she moved out."

"How were Ben and Nancy getting along?" Tia asked.

"They were having a good time. We all were. Just kicking back, having a few drinks and laughing. Nobody wanted to leave.

The bar owner kept the place open later than usual just for us. I was sitting right there beside Ben and Nancy. If there had been even the slightest disagreement between them, I would have known it."

"Who left first?"

"Rocky walked out first. Then Ben, Nancy and Cass all walked out together. The next thing I know, Ben and Cass come running back inside, Ben is as white as a sheet and shouting, 'They shot my girl!' I jumped up and ran outside with him. Rocky had already split in his van."

Tia jotted down on her notebook, Rocky fled the scene. "So where did Rocky go?" she asked.

"He called 9-1-1 from several blocks away—said he floor boarded it out of there as soon as the gunfire started."

"Then Ben was never alone in the parking lot with Nancy?" Tia asked.

"Never," Rip shook his head. "Cass was there the whole time. There were two or three other couples walking out at the same time. And Rocky Miller also was there when the gunman fired."

Tia wrote, Ben never alone in lot.

"Mackenzie Park Police cars pulled up in minutes. They handcuffed Ben and put him inside the back of a squad car."

"Why the handcuffs?"

"Ben was fighting mad. He wanted to hurt whoever had shot Nancy. He thought the shooter was some druggie or gang banger because they sometimes hang out at the game place in the strip mall."

Tia jotted, fighting mad at the gunman. Angry.

Rip continued, "Ben's anger worked against him. The Mackenzie Park Police Chief did not think anger was the appropriate behavior for a grieving boyfriend. He told one of his detectives to check Ben's pickup for a gun."

The gun. The significantly never-found gun.

"Did Ben ever carry a gun?"

Rip shook his head. "Never. I would have known it if he had. Now Rocky Miller had guns in his van. He liked to go trap shooting. He took Ben with him sometimes. But Nancy hated guns. She never wanted to be around them. Kinda eerie don't you think? Like she had a premonition."

Where did the gun go? Tia underlined the words twice.

"Police and firefighters scoured that parking lot with toothbrushes. They even checked the roof of the mall. They never found it."

"Do you think he could have tossed it in Cass's car?"

"No way. He first ran to Nancy's body and then grabbed Cass and they ran straight back to the Green Onion. Then I went back out with him to check Nancy's condition. He didn't have time to hide a gun. Somebody would have seen him."

"You said the police put him in the squad car, so they surely patted him down. Obviously they didn't find a gun. Wouldn't that have been in the report?"

Rip shook his head. "It should have been there, but it wasn't." he stressed. "Whether Mackenzie Park investigators checked Ben's pickup and Cass's car for the weapon was left out of police reports that night. This affected the outcome of the trial. If police could have testified the gun was not in either vehicle, the defense could have used it to point to Ben's innocence. But because it wasn't noted in reports, it couldn't be argued. That left the gun issue open for the prosecutors to imply that the gun had to be there."

"You're telling me that even though police checked for the gun, they left it out of their reports so the defense couldn't use this in court? An officer couldn't testify that he didn't find the weapon in either vehicle?"

Rip just nodded his head affirmatively, a look of frustration in his eyes.

Attorneys played by the rules. Some of them good rules, some of them stupid. The rules had backfired in Ben's case, Tia thought.

"Tell me about Rocky," she requested.

Rip's words rolled out like water from a faucet turned on full force. "Rocky Miller was the state's star witness. He was 105 feet away when he saw the gunman and the flash. Yet, the manager of the bar said it was so dark that he could only see about 40 feet because the parking lot lights had been turned off after midnight."

Pausing to allow his words to sink in, Rip continued, "A Mackenzie Park Police Officer at the crime scene wrote in his report that he needed to keep the headlights of his squad car switched on in order to see the body . . . from only five feet away. How come Rocky could see so well in the dark?" Rip emphasized this question with skepticism in his voice.

"When he called 9-1-1, he said he didn't know who the shooter was. That was the moment of truth."

Tia asked, "So what did Rocky say in that call?"

"Rocky first described a tall thin suspect, maybe six-foot, weighing around 130-140 lbs. He was wearing a baseball cap and a biker jacket. If Rocky really saw Ben shoot Nancy, why didn't he tell the police immediately?"

Tia silently agreed, thinking Rocky would not have had time to invent a cover story for his friend. She wondered aloud, "Why didn't the police investigate Rocky more thoroughly? He had guns in his van. He walked out ahead of the others. He was moody that night. And I find it very interesting that he was the only one who left the crime scene."

"But he didn't have a motive," said Rip.

Neither did Ben, Tia thought. Aloud she asked, "So why did Rocky point the finger at Ben?"

"One reason. He thought they were gonna pin it on him."

Tia didn't want to believe that any police officer could make such a huge mistake and charge an innocent man with murder. She trusted the Woodsville police she had come to know. They were hard working, honest crime fighters. They wouldn't do such sloppy work.

However, the Mackenzie Park police force was a different law agency altogether. She knew those officers seldom had murder investigations on their hands in the much smaller suburb. They weren't nearly as experienced. Honest errors?

The missing pieces of the Krahl puzzle bothered her even more as she listened to Rip. The waiter brought their orders.

40

Sharon and Cap Nemon were already digging into burgers and fries.

Conversation turned to other things, but she wasn't listening. She was thinking about the letter she had received from Ben Krahl, and merely toyed with her soup. After Rip picked up the check, Tia glanced at her watch. "It's getting late and I have to go, but thanks for the dinner."

Cap stood up to help her with her coat. "Let me see you to your car," he offered.

Promising to talk again with Rip if she had further questions and making her farewells to Sharon, Tia headed out with Cap. Suddenly mindful of the mystery caller a few nights ago, she was grateful for his company.

"Say, we're taking a scuba class up to Lake Geneva for an open water dive tomorrow. Why don't you come along for the boat ride?" Cap suggested.

He was thinking she had better say yes, or he would simply have to throw himself under the wheels of the next car that passed by.

Tia started to make an excuse, but Carmen's repeated urging to get out and go—it's been three years—echoed in her mind. A brisk breeze on the water might also blow some color into what her boss said were her "too-pale cheeks." Maybe I'll go, she thought. After all, the guy had backed off respectfully enough when he learned she was married. He would likely keep his distance.

Cap was even more pleased when she agreed to meet them at the dock the next morning. He saw her safely buckled inside the Bronco and closed the door, then walked to his own car whistling a tune that sounded a little like *Pretty Woman.*

* * *

The driver of the van watched Tia's Bronco as it pulled out of the parking lot. Then he started the engine and pulled out after her. In his haste to stay on her tail, he ran a red light.

Of all the rotten luck! A Mackenzie Park squad car was right behind him, red and blue lights flashing. He pulled over to stop and pounded the steering wheel with a clenched fist.

What the--! Now he'd have to get rid of the van.

As he pulled out his driver's license, pain shot through his hand and up his arm. He swore again. He must have struck the wheel harder than he realized. With an oath, he vowed the reporter woman was going to suffer for it.

Autumn 2002

Chapter 7 – Lake Geneva

Saturday was one of those bright fall days in southern Wisconsin when the orange, gold and scarlet leaves paint a colorful contrast against a brilliant azure sky. The sun-drenched day was warm, in spite of the breeze playing through the blue spruce trees and giant oaks common to the Woodsville area.

Tia dressed warmly in blue jeans, a bulky sky-blue sweater and brown boots. She brushed her short chestnut hair back and pulled on a stocking cap. She could almost hear Carmen urging her to do the Bambi-eye thing with mascara. Not today. A little lotion on her face to keep from getting a sun or wind burn would suffice.

She drove her Bronco to Lake Geneva, a lakeside community in southern Wisconsin that could be reached on pleasantly winding, tree-lined lanes. It was a trip that Tia and Jeff had loved to take, especially on glorious autumn days. They had once spent an anniversary at a quaint little bed and breakfast on the outskirts of Lake Geneva, a village filled with sprawling Victorian homes, blocks of antique malls, and curio shops lining the shores. Feeling his absence keenly by the scenic reminders of happier days, she struggled to put on a cheerful face as she pulled up to the dock.

Rip and his helper, Captain Nemo, waved to her from the dive boat, where their students, already dressed in full wet suits, were boarding. It would be a chilly dip, but a necessary one for divers seeking their scuba certification.

Cap extended a hand to help her aboard and she was instantly aware of the strength and warmth of his grip. They buckled life jackets and sat down on the floor of the dive boat, somewhat sheltered from the breeze. Water shimmered and began to form a frothy wake as they chugged out from the shore.

"So, Miss Reporter, what do you do when you're not out chasing down information for cold murder cases?" Cap asked Tia, flashing his boyish grin. He was thinking she looked absolutely charming, even in the bulky sweater that made her shapeless and the cap that covered her chestnut locks. Most women can't wear a cap and look that lovely, he thought as he watched that fringe of sooty lashes sweeping up at him. She wasn't really seeing him though. That disappointed him.

Tia didn't register that he had used the word "Miss" instead of "Mrs." Instead she was vaguely aware that he had sea-blue eyes filled with a refreshing enthusiasm. "Oh, you know, the usual" she answered without thinking, "Read. Walk the neighbor's dog. Wash the car."

Cap laughed, "I'm not buying that. You've got to have a social calendar that's all booked up." He was thinking he would like to put his name on that calendar.

Outside the news beat her life must seem very empty to a casual observer. But even so, she wasn't ready for socializing. Deciding to ignore his comment, she pushed a strand of hair back under her stocking cap and asked, "So, Captain Nemon, what do you do when you aren't teaching scuba-diving?"

"I'm an instructor at Woodsville College. I teach criminology and criminal law classes."

A fringe of dark lashes swept up as she turned her eyes to his. Now he had her full attention.

"Oh that's right. You told me when you introduced yourself at the Old English House. Are you familiar with the Nancy Jurowski murder?" she asked him, immediately interested in his opinion, her reporter's radar locked in on the subject.

"That case is one that stinks as far as I'm concerned. I've never seen a more bungled case in my life."

Her curiosity kicked into high gear. "Bungled? How?"

Pleased that he had her attention Cap began, "First off, no person should have been allowed to leave the crime scene that night. The cops should have separated all the witnesses and taken their statements individually. They should have checked everyone and every car for a gun. And that is one thing they probably did. Even the greenest cop knows to do that. Unfortunately, they left out that part in their reports."

Both Detective James Bond and his former fellow officers had often said the same thing. It was a significant omission. Tragically so for Ben Krahl.

Cap continued his list of should-haves. "Police should have gone door to door in the immediate neighborhood to ask if anyone had seen or heard anything suspicious. They should have taken the license plate numbers of every car in the lot. More importantly, Three separate law agencies got in on the act. Wisconsin State Police, Black Woods County Sheriff's police and Woodsville officers. Then of course, they didn't communicate well with each other."

Tia was well aware that different law agencies compete with each other, sometimes fiercely. She thought they deserved lots of credit, because their lives are often at risk every day in a rather thankless career. But this not sharing of information, how could that help solve a crime?

Intrigued by his knowledge of the case, she wanted to know if he had simply been talking with Rip Tyson, or did he have other sources? She balanced her paper coffee cup against the boat's rise and fall on the waves.

"I have a friend who's a Black Woods County Sheriff's deputy, and his agency worked on the case too. We talked about the murder a great deal at the time of the investigation," Cap explained. "I wanted to incorporate it into one of my criminal law classes."

They continued talking about the case awhile, and then Cap looked away. He had to let her know he knew. It would be deceitful if he didn't. "Rip told me about your husband. I'm truly sorry. It must have been very hard for you." He spoke with genuine compassion.

Her throat closed tightly for a moment. Unable to face him, she looked down as if she were studying the contents of her coffee cup. So he knew. It was not something she wanted to talk about. Finally she just nodded, incapable of speech at the moment.

Seeing her obvious distress, Cap felt a momentary pang of guilt at being pleased to know she was single. If he could have erased her sorrow he would gladly have done so. He couldn't bring back her husband. However, he might be able to change some things in her life. In that moment he certainly wanted to try.

Tia had no place to retreat on the boat, so she turned her attention to the divers, content to be an observer. She did not welcome any intrusion into her damaged zone. There were places in her life she was not ready to share. Maybe never would share again. The very thought of romance made her feel unfaithful in her heart to Jeff.

Still the afternoon went by pleasantly with much laughter and good-natured bantering among the group. When the boat finally pulled back into shore, Captain Nemo and Riptide Tyson asked her to have dinner with the group.

"I really can't," she began.

Cap interrupted, "Why not? Gotta get back to Woodsville and walk the neighbor's dog?"

Oh boy. She had set herself up for that one without thinking. That was before she knew Cap was aware of her status as a widow. She tried again to beg off, but the pair insisted.

The entire group ended up at an upscale biker lounge in the shore-side town, a place she would never have chosen herself, where the food was delicious, the atmosphere lighthearted and the conversation stimulating.

Cap tried his best not to stare at Tia. He was unsuccessful, but she never noticed as far as he could tell. He was thinking he had really started off on the wrong foot with her, both at the Old English House and then today on the boat. She rose to make her exit, saying good night to the divers and thanking him for inviting her.

"Wait, let me give you my card," he said, stopping her momentarily. Great, she probably thinks I expect her to call me, he thought, upbraiding himself for being so stupid.

She absent-mindedly stuffed it in the pocket of her blue jeans.

By the time she drove home and finally dropped into bed, she was thoroughly relaxed and sleeping soundly, long before her usual midnight hour.

For Cap, it was a different story altogether. Every time he closed his eyes, he could see Tia as she had looked on the boat, fresh and lovely, with that underlying wounded quality about her that made him want to shield her from further pain. See her as she had looked the first time he saw her at the restaurant when she'd threatened to call the police. So infuriatingly proper. So enticingly attractive. He'd quickly discovered she was a woman who wouldn't be approached or picked up easily, no matter how impressive the man might be.

And without being conceited, Cap had enough experience to know he was not unattractive. At least in some women's eyes. He'd had his share of female attention. Probably more than his share. He wasn't interested in female adoration based only on his appearance. There had to be some substance to the relationship beyond physical attraction or there was no relationship as far as he was concerned. He sensed that Tia was a woman who looked beyond the outward appearance. And that interested him. He was also well aware that she had little interest in him if any. Not at the

47

moment anyway. Not beyond his knowledge of the crime she wanted to investigate.

He would definitely have to change that.

Chapter 8 - Karla Brandon

Sunday morning, Tia opened her eyes, feeling more rested than she had in a long time. The sunshine and fresh air on the lake had been good for her after all.

Part of her wanted to go to church. A deeper part of her was still angry with God. She had not been able to reconcile the conflict. Without much thought, she decided to contact a mutual friend of Ben's and Rocky Miller's, since Rocky was refusing her phone calls. It was obvious that the state's star witness was not going to talk to her.

She called a man on her list of Krahl's acquaintances by the name of Beuford Brandon. Mrs. Brandon answered the phone. "We've been reading your articles, and waiting for your call," said the woman Tia was soon to know as Karla. "Why don't you come over, and we'll sit down and talk?"

Sundays were always particularly long for Tia, so she welcomed the invitation. After getting directions to the Brandon home on the south side of the city, Tia made the drive, enjoying a repeat of yesterday's sunshine.

She eyed the middle class neighborhood as she drove down the street to their address. The houses were small but well maintained. She could picture neighbors laughing over backyard fences, and cooking out together on barbecue grills in the summer while children tossed balls in the street. It was a place where decent, hardworking families lived, rested, and played.

Karla ushered her inside and poured her a cup of steamy hot chocolate. The warmth of the home and the beverage did much to chase the October chill from Tia's southern bones. So this was the place where Ben had spent much of his time, where he had brought Nancy for evenings with friends. It was comfortable, neatly kept, a place where people laughed and played their guitars together. A home.

Tia liked Karla at once, impressed by her calm, soft-spoken manner and her genuine concern. No emotions running high. Just deep disappointment at the outcome of the trial, and many lingering questions.

Like the others who knew Ben, Karla firmly believed that he did not kill Nancy, and she gave Tia several inconsistencies in Rocky Miller's behavior to think about as they talked.

"Rocky changed his story completely from the time he first talked to police and to us," she began. "First he was giving us a very detailed description of the shooter. Then a few days later, he tried to convince the police it was Ben. He even claimed Ben was shooting at him too."

Tia jotted down notes as she listened.

"My husband and I sat there in the courtroom watching as he changed his story time after time. We were shocked and outraged, but helpless to stop it."

Karla had a list of questions to point out Rocky's erratic behavior. "Why did Rocky call back to the Grill and ask if Ben was hurt? Why do that if he knew Ben was the gunman? Obviously Ben wouldn't shoot himself. It's clear that Rocky saw the gunman like he first said, and he really thought Ben might be wounded." She sat her cup down and continued.

"Why did Rocky go to the police station and give Ben a sympathetic hug? Why did he say Ben was firing a gun at him and then ask Ben to go trap shooting the next day? Do you really think he's going to say, 'Ben, I saw you shoot your girlfriend, and you were trying to kill me a night ago, but let's go shoot traps together today, buddy.' Come on!"

Tia thought that was about as likely as Bill Clinton keeping his clothes on in a bedroom full of enticing young lovelies.

"If he really believed Ben was trying to kill him, wouldn't Rocky be staying as far away as he could get? I know I would. But he went over to Ben's house within hours of the murder. He told us that he thought somebody was following him. He was very nervous. Why would he be afraid somebody was after him if he knew all the time that Ben was the killer?"

Tia jotted this down. Rocky was not afraid of Ben.

"Rocky also spent two or three hours with Ben to comfort him on the day of the funeral. That tells you something about how scared he was of Ben."

By this time, Tia was wondering if the investigators had bothered to interview Karla. She was very credible and had no reason to lie. As she spoke of her friendship with Nancy, it was obvious that Karla had every reason to hate Ben if indeed he was guilty of murdering her friend. Instead she was defending him.

Calmly and matter-of-factly, Karla continued pointing out Rocky's suspicious behavior. "His initial behavior shows Rocky clearly did not have the slightest fear of Ben or the remotest thought that Ben fired the fatal bullet. What made him change his story?" She looked at Tia with disgust in her eyes as she related her doubts.

Then Karla made a surprising revelation.

"Did you know that Nancy's mother, Cecelia, first thought Rocky was the killer? Shortly after Nancy's murder, Cecelia pointed at Rocky and said to his face, 'You had her killed didn't you!'"

Tia had not known this. "What would make Cecelia suspect Rocky?"

Karla looked at her cooling cup of chocolate and continued. "Cecelia knew that Rocky didn't like Nancy. Rip thought maybe he was jealous of her because Ben spent more and more time with her. Maybe Rocky felt like he was losing his buddy."

Immediately Tia thought of the gay man in the bar, but when she suggested that possibility, Karla shook her head.

"So how did Ben and Nancy get along?" Once again, she heard the same story. They weren't fighting. They got along great.

"Ben even bought Nancy's plane ticket so she could go with Cass to California to visit Cass' mom after the holidays. Why would he bother to do that if he was planning to kill her?"

Tia nodded. She was aware of the plane ticket.

"Then there was that mystery man. Rocky pointed out a car as it was leaving the parking lot and yelled, 'That's him!' A cop took out after him and pulled him over. Now get this. The driver was barefooted and didn't have a shirt on. He even asked the cop, 'Does this have something to do with the murder?' How could he even know there'd been a murder? Fred Speer hadn't arrived at the scene to broadcast the news on the radio."

"Barefoot? It was 28 degrees that night." Tia exclaimed.

Karla nodded with a knowing look in her eyes. "He told police that he took off his shoes so he wouldn't wake up his wife when he got home. He actually claimed he was out looking for drugs. The dumb cop let him go and didn't even bother to check his car. Didn't look for bloody shoes or a gun, or even the drugs."

Amazed, Tia sat her mug down with a clatter and exclaimed, "How could they have failed to check this character out?" She was incredulous. They had a guy half-dressed and barefoot on a freezing December night, leaving the scene of a homicide. And they didn't even check his car for a gun?

"Here's the clincher," Karla continued in a tone of disgusted resignation. "Just an hour later, when the officer realized he needed more information, he visited this guy's house. The guy comes to the door clean-shaven. It came out later in court from coworkers that he *never* wore a beard. So why the fake beard? Or was he even the same guy who had been in the car? Maybe someone else had been driving that car."

Tia shook her head in disbelief. What were the cops thinking? She wrote in her notes, Who was the barefoot man?

Still looking for a motive, Tia asked, "Was Nancy afraid of anyone?"

Karla thought for a moment. "I think she was afraid of Rocky. They were here one evening—Ben, Nancy, Cass and Rocky too. The guys liked to play their guitars and make music. We got together a lot. There was no drinking. Just fun."

Tia wrote as Karla continued, "Nancy and I were in the kitchen when we overheard Rocky saying something to Ben about how some women are like a raccoon scratching in the garbage can. You shoot 'em and they just keep comin' back."

"So what did he mean by that?"

Karla paused, and then continued. "Nancy looked at me and said, 'That remark was meant for me'. She didn't trust Rocky. He gave her the creeps. And she didn't really like being around him."

Tia flipped a page of her notebook, and then asked, "Anyone else that she might have reason to fear?"

Karla hesitated a moment, appearing to weigh her next words.

Tia repeated the question. "Can you think of anyone at all who might have had something against Nancy?"

Looking down her cup, Karla began, "Nancy has a sister, Amy. She was living with a boyfriend and Nancy thought he was bad news. Amy and this guy had a little boy, only a year old at the time. Nancy was threatening to take the child away from them."

Again taking notes, Tia asked, "Why?"

"They were both using drugs. They would drop the baby by Nancy's place on Friday nights and say they'd be back after awhile. Then they might not show up again for the whole weekend. Nancy had to baby-sit while they were out partying. Not only that, Nancy was threatening to turn Amy's boyfriend in for income tax evasion. Here's a detail that may mean something. The guy with the fake beard and shirt? He was driving a car registered to a relative of Amy's boyfriend."

A boyfriend doing drugs and fearing exposure for tax evasion. A sister afraid of losing her child. Could either threat be a reason for murder? Who knows what a drug-addicted mind might do?

Certain drugs linger in the system for years. What about a brain fried on heroin or crack cocaine? What could the longtime effects be on a regular user? Would he be capable of murder if threatened? But, no, Tia thought. The sister would never have stood for any deliberate harm to Nancy. Surely not. Unless . . . she . . . didn't know.

After thanking Karla for taking time to answer her questions, Tia gathered her notes, purse and headed the Bronco back to the apartment.

She had her next two articles for the series.

Who did Nancy fear?

And why was the driver barefoot, half dressed and wearing a fake-beard? Police had checked him out and obviously dismissed him as a suspect, but he certainly raised suspicions.

October 2003

Chapter 9 - The Watcher

He had waited. Bided his time. The watcher was tired of being patient. He wanted this job over with.

He'd had the woman in his sights so many times during the past few weeks. Even fired at her once but the bullet went wild. She'd never even noticed. The boss didn't want it done in the open. Too many witnesses. Too risky.

Why should he change his tactics now? Witnesses could be bought or threatened.

The woman never went anywhere except to her office, her news beat and back to her apartment again. He could have shown up there and popped her easily enough. But the boss wanted it to look like suicide. How was he going to manage that? Throw her in the river. That was the plan. But how do that without being seen?

He parked in front of a used car lot across the street from The Weekly News office, a convenient location because he wanted to trade the van in on a car anyway. Stepping out, he had walked only a few feet when he saw a bicycle cop headed his way. Not wanting to be seen, the watcher moved back to the driver's side and promptly tripped over a beer bottle lying beside the curb.

With an oath, he scrambled to regain his balance, tumbling instead to the sidewalk. Pain shot through his knee, but he got to his feet quickly. The cop was approaching him, "Hey buddy, you okay?"

The watcher merely nodded and turned to climb back inside the van, keeping his head down. Hell! He didn't need to be recognized hanging around her block.

Forget the river! He'd do it his own way, and in his own time.

* * *

Tia was disappointed.

As soon as the next Krahl story ran, her desk phone at the news office began to ring with supporters of Ben Krahl, thanking her for the article. Callers every day. But nobody with any new information. That's what she had been fishing for. Information.

"Someone out there always knows something," said James Bond as they sat down to lunch at Grandma's Café on South Spruce Road. Tia wanted to discuss the series with him in order to get a veteran law enforcer's perspective.

"These creeps get angry with each other. They need money. Sooner or later, one will turn in another for the Crime Stoppers reward, or they'll exchange information for a plea bargain," he continued as he picked up his fork and dug into a salad.

"I still don't think you're convinced that Ben Krahl didn't do it," Tia noted the skeptical look in Bond's eyes whenever she mentioned Ben's innocence, which was becoming more and more plausible to her with every person she interviewed.

Playing the devil's advocate, Bond responded, "Ben certainly had the opportunity to commit the murder. And anybody—ANYBODY—is capable of doing anything under the right circumstances."

"Maybe," she shot back at him, "but you just don't go out for a pleasant evening with friends, walk your sweetheart to her car, kiss her goodnight and then fly into a killing rage two seconds later."

Bond smiled patiently, "Tia, I'm a cop. Cops are trained to be skeptical." He took a bite of his meatloaf. "Any more threatening phone calls?"

She shook her head no, munched on her salad, put down her fork and started to argue once more but thought better of it. What could she say? Bond had spent over twenty years dealing with dirt bags, slime, the dregs of society. He had a right to be cynical.

"Tell you what," said Bond, sensing her frustration, "I've started working for a private investigation agency. Maybe I'll talk to my boss about looking into the case."

She picked up her fork again, flashing him a grateful smile.

Returning to the news office, she worked on her regular assignments the rest of the day and long past the autumn dusk, but her thoughts kept returning to Karla Brandon's observations. The woman was totally credible. Tia was certain Bond would think so too if he could have spoken with her.

"What are you still doing here?" Pat scolded as he walked past her desk. "Come on, let's go." He didn't like her driving home after dark.

As usual, he walked her to the Bronco and waited till she was safely buckled up. Then she waited until he was safely back inside the office before she headed down Tall Oaks Avenue. They were both cautious. The street had seen a rash of muggings and other crimes recently.

What a different street this was when night arrived.

The bars were lit up in gaudy pink and orange neon. Where the traffic had been scarce by day, it was bumper to bumper in the evening hours and moving very slowly. People crowded the walks. Characters she never saw during daylight hours.

The boss was right. This was not a good time to be here.

Maybe she should take Hawthorne Lane instead of driving past the naughty lingerie shops. She wanted to stop on the way home and grab a sandwich.

It wasn't until she had exited on Oak Street, searching for a café, that she noticed a van tailing her Bronco. How long had it been there, headlights bright in her rear mirror? It seemed a little too close. Her rear-view mirror bounced the beams back into her eyes, blinding in their intensity. She decided to turn off on a residential side street and lose him.

The van followed her.

Now in a darker and far less traveled area, she wondered if she had made the wrong decision. The sound of that threatening male voice on the phone immediately popped into her mind. She remembered the words and evil tone with chilling clarity. Back off the Krahl story.

Was she being followed? What did Bond say to do if that ever happened? Oh yeah. Make three left turns. She promptly did so. The van's headlights followed. Followed her. Right on her tail.

Making another series of turns, she realized she didn't recognize the streets in this part of Woodsville. Get back to a throughway. That was her immediate challenge. But the next street ended in a circle drive. Trees formed an eerie canopy of branches over the Bronco, their remaining leaves a sickly yellow in the headlights' beam. The limbs pressed low like the arms of some eager beast waiting to snatch her up in a terrifying sweep.

How to get out of here? Hurry. He's coming!

The van's tires squealed up beside her as she threw the Bronco into reverse, floored the gas pedal and screeched into an almost perfect 180-degree turn without knowing how she did it. Driving over some curbing she bounced back onto the street and shot down the block.

She could see the headlights turning as she rounded the next corner. Where were the connecting streets? Any of these residential drives could end in cul de sacs or loop back to the same point of entry.

The van was somewhere behind and could catch up to her at any moment. Which way to go? Another dead end could be disastrous. Relief flooded over her when she saw the traffic lights ahead on North Spruce Road.

She shot through a yellow light and out into the intersection, tires screaming their complaints. That's when she remembered her gas gauge registering very low fuel. She had hoped to wait until payday before filling up. Now she very much regretted that miserly decision.

What to do? Risk running out of fuel before she reached the safety of her apartment? Or stop and be vulnerable to whoever was following her while she filled the tank? There was a Mobil station at Brookside Shopping Mall. Well-lit, with lots of other drivers around. She should be safe enough. She hoped.

Nervously watching each approaching vehicle as she held the gas nozzle, Tia almost dropped it when a van pulled in. Then she let out a ragged breath, seeing a large woman at the wheel and beside her an equally large kid munching on a burger wrapped in yellow paper. From the roundness of their shoulders and triple chins, mom and son both were chow-hound champions.

No more vehicles pulled up as she paid for the fuel. By the time she finally pulled the Bronco into her slot at the Wood Hills Apartment complex, climbed the stairs and rushed inside, her heart was pounding less rapidly, but her knees were still weak.

Locking the door, she glanced out at the parking area from the window. No van. Then she dialed Carmen's number with shaking fingers. No answer. Bond? He wasn't home either. Who could she talk to about what had just happened? The need for some human reassurance was great.

That's when she saw Cap Nemon's card on the coffee table where she had tossed it after her outing at Lake Geneva. She had kept the card, thinking he would be an excellent source for stories on criminal justice. Tia dialed and while the phone was ringing she upbraided herself. What am I doing? He could even be a married man, and his wife will think I'm chasing after him.

Cap picked up the receiver just as she was talking herself into hanging up. Her jittery nerves felt enormously relieved just to hear a calm voice. It was like grabbing a life preserver after falling overboard in a rough sea.

Without further thought, she blurted out, "Hello Cap, this is Tia Burgess. I'm sorry to bother you, but I've just had a frightening experience."

"I'll be right over," he answered, hanging up the phone without another word.

Oh no. What had she done? She didn't want him coming over. She only wanted, *needed,* to talk to someone at the moment. Someone who could tell her everything was okay. That's all. Tia tried redialing his number to insist that he stay home, but when the phone kept ringing she knew he was already on his way.

It was hardly more than five minutes before the doorbell rang. She glanced cautiously through a curtained window to be sure it was Cap before opening the door. "How did you know where I live?" She demanded, thinking that this guy had some nerve tracking her down.

"I made it a point to know where you lived after our boat ride on Lake Geneva," he said tossing his leather jacket on the sofa.

Her eyes were not pleased, but Cap didn't notice. Instead he was observing how pale she looked. She'd been frightened more badly than her voice had betrayed.

He spoke gently, "Now let's get you some coffee, and you tell me what happened."

Tia didn't argue about the coffee. He saw her glance toward the small kitchenette and before she could move, he was filling the pot.

Okay, let him play Mr. Fix-it Man for a few moments. Then she would send him on his way. She had to admit she felt better with another person in the apartment. With his trim athletic build and muscular arms, he looked like a man who could handle any threat, probably even the ridiculous Karate midget that beat up John Wayne.

Soon they were sitting on the sofa, each with a mug of freshly brewed Folgers. Tia's hands trembled slightly as she spilled out her story, which sounded a little foolish to her, now that she felt more secure. "I'm sorry," she apologized. "It's probably nothing, and I overreacted."

"It's nothing to be ignored," Cap tone was serious. He looked her in the eye and advised, "You don't know what you're up against right now."

She didn't want to admit it. But a few moments earlier when she'd been driving alone with a van pursuing her through those dark and winding streets, she wouldn't have argued. "Look, I'm fine. Thank you for coming over, but I shouldn't have bothered you."

He was shaking his head, those sea-blue eyes looking genuinely concerned. "Don't apologize. The only way you could have bothered me is if you had not called."

Momentarily taken aback by his concern, which seemed a little overly personal, Tia was speechless.

"Now, did you get a look at the model of the van? The license plate?"

"No, he was behind me. I couldn't tell anything about it except that it was an older model SUV or a van of some kind."

"Maybe we'd better call the police," Cap suggested, but Tia was already shaking her head.

"What can they do? I can't give them any kind of a description. They can't chase down every van in Woodsville and ask—are you the guy who was following Tia Marie Burgess? And even if they could, there's no law against following someone."

She was clearly exasperated.

Cap used his most reassuring voice. "Let's just get a report on file. That way they have some documentation in case you're being stalked," he advised her.

The thought of being stalked had never occurred to Tia. It was an unwelcome thought. She slowly nodded her head. "Maybe. But not tonight. I'm really tired if you don't mind."

He recognized the cue. She wanted him to leave, but he wasn't ready. "I'm not leaving you. At least not unless you promise to call me if anything happens. Anything at all."

"I'm perfectly capable of taking care of myself," she answered, unwilling to admit that she might need anyone's help.

He could see that she was no longer trembling and that he was being dismissed, rather unsatisfactorily dismissed, in his estimation.

"Look, I'm going now. But if you don't mind, I'm going to call you when I get back to my place just to let you know that I made it home safe and sound. I'm sure you'll want to know if the bogeyman tries to get me."

Her eyes widened slightly, and he could see a glint of humor.

"Besides I'm really scared of the dark," he added.

A slight smile tugged at the corners of her mouth. "And I suppose you sleep with a Teddy bear for protection?"

"Of course. Doesn't everybody?" He rose to pull on his jacket, then checked the parking lot before he opened the door. "You don't have a dead bolt. I'll be over to install one tomorrow. Goodnight, Tia."

Before she could protest, he was gone.

* * *

On a darkened residential street, the watcher had climbed out of his van and walked to the rear of the now lop-sided vehicle with a flashlight. There he saw what he expected to see. The shredded and peeling tread on a very flat tire.

If passers-by had been watching, they probably would have roared with laughter to see him kick the tire. Twice. On the second kick, a sharp pain shot through his toe and radiated upwards to the achy knee. He cursed his luck, the van, the tire, the woman and even the pain. The string of obscenities that spewed from his twisted mouth would have earned him a place of honor in the dictionary of vile expletives.

Even more determined now to get this job done, he decided he would not wait another week.

Chapter 10 - "Okay Entertain Me"

True to his word, Cap telephoned a short time later, giving Tia just enough time to nibble a cold sandwich, change into a warm pair of pajamas and pull an afghan around her shoulders. She really wasn't in the mood to talk. Especially not to this man with his sea-blue eyes which portrayed soulful concern for her.

"So the bogeyman didn't get you?" She spoke in a mildly disinterested tone.

"Not a sign of him. But I'm still scared of the dark. Keep me company on the phone a little while," he cajoled her.

"I'm not going to be good company tonight," she answered, hoping to get rid of him quickly and—and what? She wasn't going to watch TV, and she didn't want to read.

Not about to be discouraged, Cap countered, "Okay then. Be bad company. I'm not expecting you to entertain me. How about I entertain you? I can be very amusing."

"Okay, entertain me, but I don't want to talk about the van anymore, and I'm not promising to stay on the line very long," she relented, although suddenly curious as to what Mr. Blue Eyes was going to say.

"Fair enough. Just let me put on my entertaining-and-charming hat." Cap was thinking of how he had used storytelling years ago to soothe his little sister whenever she'd been through an ordeal, a bicycle accident or a fall on her roller skates. He was hoping the same method would calm Tia's jangled nerves. "Ah yes. Here we go. How about if I tell you a fairy tale?"

A fairy tale? This was a novel approach, she thought with some surprise. If she had to guess what he might come up with as his idea of entertaining, she would never have guessed fairy tales. Cap Nemon was hardly predictable. She had to grant him that.

"Once upon a time there was a princess who locked herself inside an ivory tower to escape an evil wizard who had robbed her of her kingdom. This princess was incredibly beautiful. She probably looked a lot like you. Only not that beautiful."

Remembering his little sister always loved stories about herself as the heroine, Cap began weaving a similar tale. "The evil wizard was bald and had warts on his nose and rotten teeth and wore black robes covered with words like Packers are Losers." He imagined her lovely lips curving into a smile, or at least a half smile.

She half smiled. "That's a really evil wizard if he knocks the Packers."

"Now we get to the good part. There was also a brave knight who drove a Jeep and wore lots of shining armor whenever he wasn't teaching a class, and his job was to rescue the beautiful princess from the tower, because he had the only key."

"And who does the brave knight look like?" Tia stopped smiling. She didn't like the direction this story was going.

"Oh, he was very handsome. Probably looked a lot like me, only probably not quite that handsome. But he was definitely the bravest knight in the kingdom. In fact the evil wizard was terrified of this knight."

Tia pictured Cap in shining armor beating up a warty-nosed, bald wizard in a black robe.

"There is no way the evil wizard can defeat the brave knight, because Mr. Knight has the power of love on his side." Cap always referred to the power of love as the greatest power in his stories, rather than magic. He'd wanted his little sister to grow up knowing that. "The knight can defeat every dragon or wizard in the land, but he does have one little problem."

Keeping her voice cool, she suggested, "A brave, handsome knight with a problem. Let me guess. He's going to turn back into a frog?"

Now Cap was smiling. "Nope. Not this knight. He was never a frog. A nerd maybe, but he outgrew that long ago." He hoped what his little sister had always called his overpowering self confidence was not on display.

"Okay. So what's his problem?"

"He has to get the princess to notice him before the key will unlock her ivory tower and set her free."

"I see. Why wouldn't the princess notice him if he's so handsome? She must be sleeping, right?"

"I think so. Otherwise she would have been totally charmed by his bravery and good looks."

"Does this fairy tale have an ending?"

"Certainly. The princess will wake up any day now. She will smile at the brave knight, and he will unlock the ivory tower and set her free to go for a ride in his Jeep and maybe they will stop for a picnic."

Not this princess, Tia thought. She should let him know right now. "Maybe the princess has important things to do in her tower and doesn't want to go on a ride or a picnic."

Uh oh. A definite roadblock. Maybe his "charming" hat had lost some of its enchanting powers. Maybe he was wearing his "stupid" hat and didn't know it. Cap decided to try another topic, fully aware that he was talking to a young woman who'd had a very difficult time adjusting to widowhood.

"Okay, let's pick another subject. Tell me about your family. They still live in Missouri?" He was genuinely interested, wanting to know everything about her.

"Only my mom. We lost dad in 1999. Mom still lives on the farm. She doesn't do any actual farming anymore, but she keeps the place mowed and the fences mended. I have a brother living in California." Tia faked a yawn.

"I lost both my parents a few years back. I have a sister. She's modeling for an agency in New York, so I don't get to see her much." Changing the subject, he asked, "Do you like music?" hoping he could interest her in going to a concert with him.

"I like music, but I don't listen to it like I used to." She faked another yawn. "I'm starting to get drowsy. Maybe you could sing me a goodnight song."

"Your wish is my command, fair lady. Let's see . . .Old McDonald had a farm. E-I-E-O," he vocalized the kindergarten song with operatic enthusiasm.

Tia suppressed a chuckle, then laughed in spite of herself. "Rick Nielsen you're not," she informed him, speaking of the famed singer from Rockford. "You'll have to do better than that."

"Oh, I can do much better. How about poetry? The moon was a ribbon of moonlight, looping the purple moor."

She interrupted, "And the highway man came riding, riding up to the old inn door."

Ahh, a safer topic at last. He noted, "So you do like poetry."

"Sometimes," she faked another yawn.

"How about Edgar Allen Poe. Two roads diverged in a yellow wood, and sorry I could not travel both and be one traveler, long I stood and I looked down one as far as I could—"

She couldn't let him continue. "That's not Poe. That's Robert Frost."

"I knew you'd like Frost," Cap exclaimed enthusiastically, glad that he had her attention once again.

"How do you know so much about me?" and I know so little about you, she wondered inwardly. Tia was thinking this guy had taken the trouble to track down her address, had come to her assistance in a minor crisis and now was "entertaining" her over the phone. If there were a wife or girlfriend in the picture, she would surely be boiling by now.

"Maybe you should know something about me. I'm not big on walking the neighbor's dog, but I do like washing the car—especially when there's a beautiful princess scrubbing all the really grimy spots," he teased.

"I'm assuming you're not married then, or you would know better than that. The beautiful princess doesn't do the grimy spots," Tia answered with an imperious tone of voice.

"Oh yes you do. You've already told me that you wash the car for fun." He was pleased with the way the conversation was going now. She wanted to know if he was single. That pleased him even more.

"I do lots of things for fun besides washing my car," she announced, ignoring the implied compliment.

"Tell me what you do."

She didn't usually tell people about her book. It was a private project. "Don't you need to be doing something besides talking on the phone? Grading student papers or something? Maybe your roommate or your wife is expecting a call."

"I haven't had a roommate since I was in college. And I've never been married. All the beautiful princesses I ever asked just weren't interested in washing the grimy spots on my car."

Tia couldn't visualize a long line of beauty queens turning up their noses at Cap Nemon. Okay, she admitted to herself, he's an attractive man. A professional man. If a guy like this were still single at his age—30 something?—there had to be a reason why.

Then she remembered the hand-holding guys at the Irish Rose. Gay? Huh uh. Cap was all he-man, rippling muscles under his shirtsleeves, smelling of shaving cream and definitely attracted to the opposite sex. He'd already made that plain enough.

With his appeal, he must have women, including a bevy of dreamy-eyed college girls, throwing themselves at him all the time. He was probably a player.

Cap interrupted her thought. "And as for all the fun things you do, like walking the neighbor's dog, and going to the library, that sounds like great excitement to me."

He was teasing her. She knew he had a pretty good idea that she wasn't exactly a social butterfly. But she didn't want to give him an opening to ask her out.

The only guy she had agreed to spend an evening with—at Carmen's insistence and because he'd had an extra ticket to the Rockford Symphony Orchestra—turned out to be a real jerk. She had actually enjoyed the symphony. But Mr. Let's-Get-Physical had more than music on his mind.

She remembered his huffy words to her when he realized that she really did not intend to invite him in for a little sizzle on the sofa. "You're not going to make it in the dating scene with your attitude," he scowled.

"Neither are *you*," she'd told him in a firm voice as she closed the front door in his face. Tia wanted no part of a dating scene where men expected after-evening favors. Or any other dates, as she had so often reminded Carmen.

"Speaking of the library, I have some reading to do tonight," she began.

"Let me read to you. I've been told I have a great listening voice."

"Are you always so self aggrandizing?"

"Absolutely. I have to get your attention somehow, and I figure I can do it with my words easier than my gymnastic ability. Although my flying-leap-over-the-river is a pretty good stunt."

Tia shook her head. "You're incorrigible."

"Is that the same thing as irresistible?"

"Whatever you are, I'm going to say goodnight now."

Cap instantly changed the subject. He didn't want her to dismiss him just when he felt he was breaking through some of her polite-but-distant barriers. "Tia, don't hang up yet. Go look through your front windows and make sure there isn't a van hanging out in the parking lot, okay? Then come back and let me know."

She did as he requested, feeling a little silly. The parking lot was filled with only the usual, familiar cars. Back on the phone, she assured Cap that she saw nothing unusual, thanked him for his concern and stated firmly, "I'm perfectly capable of taking care of myself, so please don't concern yourself again."

He sensed her withdrawing into polite safety. "I guess that means you don't want to hear the second verse of *Old McDonald*?" He dangled a little bait.

"I admit it's been a long time since I've heard the entire song. But I think I'll have to pass. Goodnight, Cole."

So she used his real name instead of "Cap." That meant she'd removed herself a step back into formality. His charming hat must have fallen off. He hung up the phone and picked up a stack of student essays. A few minutes later, he put them down. He couldn't get the image of Tia, trembling and pale, out of his mind. Or the idea of the van following her Bronco. The creep! What did he intend to do anyway?

Who knew what twisted minds were out there waiting to force their messed-up view of the world on unsuspecting people? As a professor of criminology, he was very aware of America's most heinous predatory killers over the past 50 years. Serial rapist Albert DeSalvo, alias the Boston Strangler, had killed 13 women in an 18-month spree during the early 1960s in Massachusetts.

Ted Bundy confessed to 23 murders in the Seattle, Washington area and in Colorado during the 1970's. Bundy decapitated his victims and left their battered skulls abandoned on a desolate hillside. Satanist Richard Ramirez, the Night Stalker, went on a 15-month orgy of random break-in rapes in the 1980s leaving 13 Los Angeles women dead.

What if Tia had become the fixation of some deranged mind? But no. She said the caller had wanted her to back off the Krahl story, and the van's driver was most likely the same guy. She had touched on a nerve somehow.

Still, what if the van driver wasn't the same guy as the voice on the phone? She regularly reported the names of suspects arrested every week in Woodsville, Mackenzie Park and even Rockford, Illinois across the state line. Any one of these offenders could ostensibly have a grudge against her just for putting his name and charges in The Woodsville Weekly News.

She was a very attractive woman. Who knew what dirt bags were lurking out there hoping to get close to her? Like those wackos who stalk Hollywood stars. The more he thought about it, the more his imagination ran away with possibilities, none of them good.

Cap put on his jacket, grabbed his car keys and headed out. He wanted to make one more swing past the Wood Hills Apartments. After all, her number and address were in the telephone book. It wouldn't take a NASA scientist to find her.

Chapter 11 - Getting Past Formality

Cap rang Tia's doorbell three times early the next morning.

She had just pulled on a white sweater and blue jeans when she heard his noisy arrival. "What are you doing here?" she demanded after checking through the blinds to be sure of his identity before opening the door.

Cap thought she looked totally appealing, her face freshly scrubbed face, no make-up, hair slightly tousled. "Told you I'd be over to install a deadbolt," he gave her one of his lop-sided grins. The gesture of genuine concern and the charm in his voice touched her, caught her off guard.

"Here you are, my fair maiden," he handed her a sack of delicious smelling breakfast rolls. "I'm your knight in shining armor come to the rescue."

She took the bag of rolls, poured some coffee for Cap and a cup for herself, then waited while he made short work of installing the lock.

"There. Come try it out."

It was plain to Tia that he was enjoying his knight-to-the-rescue role. "It works fine. You didn't need to do that, but let me pay for the expense."

"If you insist. You owe me a walk on the Rec-path down by the river. I promise to be either laughably stupid or completely charming depending on your point of view. Fair enough?"

"Is there a third choice?"

"Superbly charming. That's the one I'm going for."

She almost shook her head no, but her mouth was saying, "Okay. Fair enough."

He helped her into her jacket and they headed out to his Jeep to make the short drive to the popular walking path. What was she doing? She promised herself this was the last time she was going anywhere with him. But she had to admit the fresh air and sunshine had done wonders for her after the Lake Geneva outing. She also thought there was nothing more beautiful than autumn along the Woody River near Enchanted Forest Park. She loved the tall cottonwoods, sweet gum, hawthorn and maple trees in fall colors, and most especially the magnificent bur oaks. By this time of year, they had already lost most of their colorful plumage, their skeleton branches now stark against the windless sky. Still the sun-drenched day was warm and the walk pleasant.

They passed a roller blader, a couple of joggers, two young women pushing baby strollers, and other walkers like themselves. Cap set a leisurely pace, enjoying the way Tia seemed to relax as they walked. "The river makes me want to become an artist," She commented.

"I could never paint. No talent for it. However, I'm good at the art of conversation, which I'm sure you've noticed."

Tia merely nodded, thinking he certainly was not lacking in self-confidence. Was Cap conceited? Probably. But not obnoxiously so. She had to admit she preferred a confident man to one who was so insecure he needed constant reassurance.

"How often do you come out here?" he asked. He liked the way the sunlight and shadow created a lacy pattern over her chestnut hair, ever changing as she moved beneath the trees. He resisted the urge to reach out and touch it.

"Not every day. Less often as the weather gets colder. My southern bones aren't ever going to get used to these Wisconsin winters." She didn't want to reveal her usual haunts and habits to Cap. One walk with him was enough.

"I grew up in Wisconsin, and I never get used to it either," he volunteered.

"Ever think about moving south?" she asked, mainly because she was looking for something to say.

"Sure. But I like my job at the college. I like the people I work with. And Rip at the Scuba Shop. Cap smiled down at her from his near six-foot frame.

She looked straight ahead, thinking he was adventurous as well as a professional man. The kind of man Carmen would have considered a real catch. There had to be lots of girlfriends in his history. Carmen would have asked him about past romances immediately and advised him on how to dress. She had the curiosity of ten cats and never minded asking tons of questions.

Without thinking first, Tia blurted out, "Why aren't you married?" and instantly regretted it. Why had she suddenly changed a perfectly comfortable topic to a personal one without any warning whatsoever? What was the matter with her mouth anyway?

"I almost was once," Cap was saying in an almost jovial tone, as if there was a joke in the story and the joke was on him. "It didn't work out. She was one of these modern, career-minded women who want to achieve goals and things. I wouldn't have minded that, but she finally told me she would never consider having children. That's an issue we couldn't resolve. Family is important to me."

Tia just nodded, thinking about the baby she had lost in the wreck. Family was everything to her.

"Hey you!" A dark-haired jogger waved as she approached. It was Carmen, resplendent in pastel pink jogging pants, matching zip-up jacket and pink tie around her dark ponytail. The pink of

73

her cheeks was not makeup, but the attractive natural blush of exertion.

Carmen, of all people. Tia knew she would be getting the third degree about Cap later in the day. She made brief introductions, very aware that Carmen was giving Cap the once-over with her Bambi eyes, appraising him as critically as she would a new car before buying it. With a radiant smile, Carmen stuck out her hand. She had sized him up on the spot and approved.

"Glad to meet you. Are you taking Tia to the October Fest tonight?"

Wouldn't you know it! The first question out of Carmen's mouth would involve a date. Tia froze, instantly wishing she were somewhere else—slogging across a crocodile infested swamp. Even having a root canal at the dentist's office. Either of those places would be better than standing here with Carmen arranging a date for her and Cap.

Cap smiled, turning to Tia, "I think that's a great idea. What do you say?"

"I'm sorry, but I have to wash the library—wash the laundry and go to the library," she stammered.

Cap's smile only broadened, charmed by the way she twisted her words whenever she was unsettled.

But Carmen was already insisting that plans could be changed. That Guitar Man was taking her. The four of them would have a fantastic time together and Cap should pick Tia up at seven and they could all drop by the Black Rose later.

Carmen, it seemed, was determined to drive Tia back to the point of sanity, and she was certain the best way to do that would be to introduce her to the right man. So it was all arranged. As they returned along the path toward Cap's jeep, he whistled a cheerful tune, "Darling, You Send Me."

After he drove her back to her apartment and waved goodbye, still whistling. Tia counted slowly, one, two, three, expecting the phone to ring. "Hello Carmen," she said picking up the receiver on number four.

"Oooh, he makes my liver quiver! Where did you find him?"

"Now hold on a minute, Carm. He's just an acquaintance. He's a friend of Rip Tyson's, and he's a professor of criminology at the college. A good source for a news story on crime."

"News, schmooz. He's a hunk! Don't tell me you haven't noticed," Carmen chided.

"Okay. He's sort of nice looking. But that doesn't mean I'm interested. You know how I feel about this subject."

"Yeah, I know how you feel. What do you need a man for? All you need is a parrot that talks, a chimney that smokes, and a couch that snores. But come on. He's not asking you to marry him. Just go to the October Fest with us and relax. You'll have a good time."

Tia sighed. "Looks like I don't have a choice."

So she was going to October Fest. She didn't want to go to October Fest.

She wanted to talk to Rocky Miller, and he was not answering her phone calls.

* * *

Cap picked her up at seven. Well actually, she noted he was two minutes early.

She wore winter white slacks and a matching sweater sprinkled with a few tiny rhinestones, "not enough to be flashy, and just enough to be classy" according to Carmen. She had brushed her hair back into a smooth bob and of course, Carmen helped her with makeup, "Just a little mascara, shadow and liner and, *voila!* Bambi eyes. You're gonna knock his socks off, *dahling*," she assured as she studied her skillful results.

The look in Cap's eyes when he arrived at the door would have pleased Carmen intensely. He thought Tia appealing in jeans and sweater, all soft curves and long, slender legs. Now she was stunning.

"I've never been to an October Fest before," Tia commented as he opened the Jeep's passenger door for her. "What do we do?"

"We eat. We watch the accordion players, and the polka dancers. We talk and laugh. And if you're really bored, I promise

75

I'll sing for you." He wanted to add that he would jump through hoops for her if he had to. Walk through fire. Anything to waken the smile in those haunted brown eyes.

"That should liven up the evening. Do you think the band can play *Old McDonald* with a polka rhythm?"

Cap slipped behind the wheel and buckled his seatbelt. "Maybe. But here's a better song. It describes you perfectly . . . Pretty woman, the kind I'd like to meet, no one could look as good as you... he sang, throwing an admiring glance her way on the last phrase, then started the engine and headed the Jeep out of the lot.

Tia looked straight ahead. "I can think of a song that describes me better. Karen Carpenter's *I've Said Goodbye to Love.*

Undaunted, Cap replied, "So you like the Carpenters? I know some of their songs. Let's see . . . why do stars fall down from the skies, just like me, they long to be close to you," he managed it just a little off key, tossing another glance her way.

She was growing somewhat uncomfortable with the conversation. "I remember some wrong sighter—song writer— who composed a song called, *I'll Never Fall in Love Again.*"

Cap tried to conceal his amusement at her verbal stumble. They were playing a game using song titles, sparring with each other to reveal their separate stands on their budding relationship. She was being stubborn, and he liked that. He was even more determined to see it blossom.

Tia intrigued him. She was charming, but didn't flaunt herself. Talented but working for a small, family owned newspaper instead of one of the TV stations where she could have shined. She was loyal to her husband's memory. He admired that. Faithfulness was a rare quality. Many young widows wouldn't have waited this long to have a string of new romances. From what Rip had told him, Tia was a woman of character.

She kept looking straight ahead, annoyed at herself for those embarrassing word mix-ups that seemed to pop out of her mouth every time he was around. She didn't want him to know the disconcerting effect he seemed to have on her.

They soon arrived at the entry gate, where they met a beaming Carmen, who introduced Joe Fox, her Mr. Guitar Man.

"So your name really is Joe Fox?" Tia asked, noticing the Fox symbol on his denim jacket, which apparently symbolized the band's name, White Fox.

Joe considered the question for a moment as if uncertain of his own name. "Nah. It's not Fox. But with a name like Fuchs, who wouldn't want to change it? People don't always pronounce it right."

Cap stifled a chuckle, pretending to cough. As they walked into the festival grounds, Carmen bubbled, "Joe's playing lead guitar with the White Fox band all over town right now. You ought to hear them. They're really hot."

Uh oh. Here was another evening she might be maneuvered into spending with Cap, Carmen and Joe. Tia pretended to be fascinated by the Polka band. This was her first and only date with Cap Nemon.

Their hair tied in gaily-colored ribbons, dancers in black velvet lace-up vests over white blouses and red skirts moved with surprising agility on ballet-slippered feet. Accomplished musician Mike Alongi played the accordion and the atmosphere sparkled, vibrant with celebrants enjoying the evening under the stars.

This last weekend of October was crisp with the promise of winter to come, but not too cold to induce shivering. Tia, as always, was content to observe the liveliness around her, present but somehow not an actual participant. From the safety of the sidelines, she continued to view others as they laughed, moved, and lived. Her own life had been on hold, frozen in a time she could not escape and could never really return to except in dreams. It was, somehow, a curious suspended animation.

The foursome wandered through a food court with offerings of Polish sausage, sauerkraut, and various other ethnic delicacies. Carmen stopped every few feet to greet friends and acquaintances, friends of friends and friends' mothers. Having grown up in Woodsville and establishing her own successful career, Carmen had a history here. She was part of the community. Tia was part of nothing. She accepted that. Even welcomed it. It was easier to devote herself to writing her book if there were no demands on her time outside the news office.

Later at the Black Rose, members of White Fox band gathered to play a few sets. She found herself enjoying their music from the fifties and sixties, even though certain songs triggered tender memories. A pang of guilt stabbed at her heart.

She could hear the psychiatrist's words. Guilt is a common reaction for the survivor of a fatal accident. First you feel guilty for surviving, and second for going on with the business of living. You experience guilt for enjoying anything again. Even the simplest pleasures of daily life from tasty food to a restful sleep can cause guilt, because the loved one is no longer able to have these simple pleasures. . . and you are.

Dr. Bradford was right. Tia was aware that her Great-Wall-of-Guilt defied logic. But recognizing the damaged structure of her soul did not furnish her the tools to rebuild it.

When the lead singer belted out *Pretty Woman*, she felt Cap's eyes on her. "Maybe I should go up to the microphone and dedicate this song to you," he suggested with mischief in his eyes.

"How about singing *Old McDonald*? They might hire you on the spot."

"You think so? I seem to remember you saying Rick Nielsen I'm not. So I'll have to impress you with my other talents, since singing is not one of them."

"Other talents?"

"Don't sound so surprised. I'm a very talented guy."

"Confidence seems to be one of your strong points." She knew he was bantering, not bragging.

"Of course. But only because I know I'll have to prove what I say. I don't expect you to take my word for it. Especially since I couldn't impress you with my singing. So here's what I'll do. I can make fantastic lasagna. I'll prove it to you next Friday evening. You bring the bread and salad."

It was an invitation in the form of a request. There was no way she was going to Cap's place for lasagna or anything else.

"No thanks. I have things to do," she said, rather abruptly.

"I'm not taking no for an answer, unless you happen to have an appendectomy or emergency bypass surgery," Cap was undaunted.

"Well it just so happens I'm on the doctor's surgery schedule. Gotta get this appendix taken out, and the week after I'm having a root canal, and after that a . . . a bunion-ectomy, so I won't be going out again for awhile."

"In that case, I'll bring the lasagna to you."

Tia shook her head no.

"I've had an interesting evening, and I'm glad I got to meet your guitar man," she said to Carmen, who was too enthralled with the musicians at the moment to realize Tia was about to make her exit.

"Now if you'll excuse me, I'm feeling rather tired."

Cap thankfully did not argue with her. He drove her straight out Woody River Drive to the apartment complex, where he insisted on checking her apartment for any possible intrusion before he left.

"You can't be too cautious," he advised. The single-bedroom, living-and-kitchen area combined did not lend itself well to hiding places. Still, he checked the bathroom, dropped down for a quick look under the bed, and even opened the narrow kitchen broom closet, while Tia watched, somewhat amused.

"I think I can handle any intruder skinny enough to fit inside that closet," she assured him. He was milking the van-stalker thing for all it was worth. Even so, she was glad for his caution. Skinny intruders in the pantry were not on her agenda tonight.

Her scalp still prickled whenever she recalled that thick, malignant voice in the night. The very receiver had seemed to crackle with static malevolence, no doubt a trick of her overactive imagination. She would be the first to admit her imagination worked overtime, but she thought that was probably a good thing for a writer.

During his search, Cap noted her apartment was sparsely furnished, no knick-knacks or decorative photos to give it a personalized touch. The computer sat on the small kitchen table, which was covered by neat stacks of paper and reference books.

A single floor lamp stood behind the small sofa. The only splash of color in the room was an inviting afghan of teals and rust hues, perhaps lovingly knitted by a kindly grandmother. She impressed him by her sense of orderliness, a slot for everything and everything in its slot. Spotless. Not even a dust bunny under the bed. Her place reflected a neatly ordered, strictly focused life—a life without frills, devoid of decoration or color. Empty of warmth and emotion? He'd have to change that.

She thanked him for the evening and for the deadbolt lock and then escorted him to the door.

"If anything disturbs you during the night, just call me. I can be here in five minutes."

"I'll be fine, thank you. Goodnight."

Fine? Cap thought she looked very vulnerable at the moment. How could she defend herself if some monster were really out to get her? Even the deadbolt was a farce. All an intruder had to do was smash out the window. He hesitated at the door, but she was stifling a yawn. She wanted him gone. He knew that.

"So, my fair maiden, I will call you as soon as I fight my way through the dark forest and slay the dragon on my way home. I'm sure you'll be waiting breathlessly to hear if I survive the ordeal."

"You'll survive."

Before she realized what he was doing, he leaned down and planted a quick kiss on her forehead. Then he was out the door.

She did not answer the phone when it rang a short time later.

* * *

The van driver had other things on his mind besides the reporter that night. He had a score to settle on the west side of town. He also wanted to spend some time with the dangerous new woman in his life. Hot tempered. Daring. She feared nothing and there was nothing she wouldn't do. He wanted to see her in action.

Loading his Tec-9 automatic assault weapon, he thought to himself, this time those bitches will get the message if the house gets cut in two by the bullets. Of course he didn't expect anyone to be home. They had been warned.

November, 2002

Chapter 12 - Susanna Krahl

The drive-by shooting death made headlines on the Monday after October Fest.

On her way to the office, Tia listened to the news on her car radio. Rockford police were already holding two suspects in custody. Like any big city, Rockford had its share of street gangs. Drive-by shootings were common and houses were riddled with bullets every week. Usually the gunfire was a warning to stay out of another gang's drug turf. The bullets were not intended to kill, but to intimidate.

This time a young mother had been fatally wounded with a Tec-9 automatic assault weapon while watching TV with her small children. Police believed the shooting was gang related.

Tia thought of the street gangs as servants of Baal, an ancient Semite god of pleasure, abandon and self indulgence, delivering temporary thrills that never satisfy, leading only to stronger desires.

Modern-day Baal worshipers filled police reports she read every day. Human beings were not as important to them as their own selfish pleasures or conveniences. Like that guy who was brought in for questioning after police found a body in his home. The fellow said simply, "I knows he's my brother, but that was my pork chop."

   * **(True story.)**

A pork chop? He killed his own brother for a pork chop? She'd asked James Bond in disbelief. Bond answered, "Oh yes. We've even had people kill each other over a pack of cigarettes."

Gang bangers usually came from dysfunctional families, their lives filled with difficulty. Of course, difficulties touch everyone—the most upright as well as the worst of the Baal worshipers. It was obvious to Tia that serving a god of pleasure eventually led to logical consequences. Addictions. Depression. Suicide. But what about those who were faithful to the God of the Bible?

This was her ongoing struggle. Logically, disobedience brings pain. But escape from pain is never a promise—even to the most obedient believer. Tia could not accept the idea of a vengeful God waiting to punish the smallest infraction of His law while capriciously refusing to bless those who diligently seek to please Him. Somewhere in between blessing and punishment, there had to be mercy. Peace. Maybe even joy?

She was not without hope. She knew God was there. She just couldn't find him at this time in her life.

Turning on Tall Oaks Avenue, She felt more than the usual pall of hard luck and depression hovering over the street. The business district should have been gaily proclaiming the coming holidays like every other business in town. Instead, the very buildings themselves seemed engulfed by mists of hopelessness swirling from a pall of gloom hanging over the street. People walked with heads bent against the wind, a hint of despair in their carriage.

But at the news office, ropes of fresh evergreen garlands swagged gaily across the entrance, yearly installed with the arrival of November. Pat O'Brien greeted her cheerfully.

"No calls from Elvis yet this morning," Pat smiled as he took her coat. "But you have Aunt Swoosie waiting for you to call her." Aunt Swoosie, a 60-year-old self-proclaimed psychic, loved to make predictions about the coming invasion of extra-terrestrials.

Tia dialed Swoosie to hear the latest. "I've been reading about that man, Ben Krahl, my dear," said Swoosie, who seldom actually read anything other than books on alien visitations to earth. Swoosie could tell you everything you wanted to know about the alien craft accident in Roswell, New Mexico.

She always added "privileged" information, believing she was communicating with one of the creatures who had died in the crash. Of course he hadn't really died. Just moved to another plane of existence. His name was Zar, and he advised Swoosie on everything from politics to planting petunias and even what brand of pantyhose to buy.

"So what do you think about the Ben Krahl case?" Tia asked, smiling. She liked the old lady.

"Zar is telling me that the real killer will be locked up in prison for another violent crime which happened near Halloween."

"Really. How can we get the real killer to confess?"

"He won't confess until some years have passed.

"Years? That's a long time for Ben to spend in prison for a crime he didn't commit." As she spoke the words, she realized she had become convinced Ben was innocent.

"Oh my dear, you just don't know. I've spent a lifetime on another planet and then come back to earth and the hands on the clock had barely moved half an hour."

"Wow!" Tia exclaimed. "Then Einstein was right about time and space being relative."

Swoosie giggled. "Einstein learned his theory from the extra-terrestrials you know."

"Your old friend Zar?"

"Of course. Zar is an excellent teacher. Ever since Nine-Eleven of 2001, he's been instructing our scientists on how to counter terrorist attacks. We have nothing to worry about dear."

"Well I am relieved!" Tia thanked Swoosie for her call and promised to talk with her again soon.

Her morning's assignments piled up until she was farther behind than ahead by noon. That's when Pat called her to the front office where she had a visitor. An attractive, middle-aged woman with prematurely graying hair was waiting, her face etched with concern. Tia instantly recognized a deep, inner anguish in the visitor, perhaps a reflection of her own.

"I'm Susanna Krahl, Ben Krahl's former wife," she said as she extended a hand. "I want to thank you and your editor for the stories you've run about his case."

Tia immediately had some questions for Mrs. Krahl, and after they exchanged a few pleasantries, she wanted to know if Ben was ever violent.

"Ben violent? Never."

"He never battered or struck you?"

"Absolutely not. He wouldn't hurt anyone or anything."

"So you believe he's not guilty?"

"I knew he didn't do it right from the start." Susanna insisted with a voice full of conviction. Tia was almost surprised to find this ex-wife as strongly supportive of Ben as any of his staunchest friends. Susanna described her former husband as a hard working, faithful and law-abiding man, a Boy Scout leader and a loving father. The couple had divorced over religious differences—not any philandering on Ben's part. It was an amicable divorce.

"He respected the law," said Susanna. "Years ago he got a DUI and his license was suspended. I drove him to work and back, until he got his license again. Ben absolutely would not drive because he felt it would be against the law."

"Was he an alcoholic?"

"No. Ben would drink beer sometimes in social gatherings, but I never saw him drunk after that one DUI. He learned his lesson."

Tia wanted to know, "Did drinking make him mean in anyway?"

"Never. He just became more mellow and relaxed."

Susanna expressed deep concern for their son, Jarrod. "How is having a father in prison for murder going to impact his life?"

Tia nodded. "I can imagine that it must be very difficult for both of you."

"I prayed so hard for the verdict to be not guilty, and..." Susanna's voice choked momentarily. She wiped at her eyes with a tissue. "This whole nightmare has really damaged my faith."

"Don't let it rob you of your faith," Tia spoke gently, laying a hand on the woman's arm. "Think about Joseph in the Old Testament. God knew how to get him out of prison. And please call me again if there's anything I can do."

Susanna grasped her hand, glad to have found someone with a sympathetic ear at last."

Back at her desk, Tia wrote down in her growing Krahl notebook, Ben was not a wife beater, and he respected the law. She had her next story for the Krahl series. Ben was not violent.

* * *

The watcher paced back and forth inside his cell. He was stunned. How could all his careful planning have failed so miserably?

His targets had been Viper Lords—not the woman in the house. She wasn't supposed to die. How could he have known she would be there that night? He put his head in his hands. The cops were charging him with murder, even though he'd had a good alibi. His big mistake was admitting he'd supplied the murder weapon. That made him an accessory. Stressed out, he stood up and began pacing, his eyes on the floor of the cell.

Jail was no big deal. He'd done time for possession of drugs. But hard time in prison? He hadn't counted on that. Didn't need it. Had to think of a way out of this.

Did he dare call the boss? His mind raced frantically, knowing that contacting Mr. P. could be deadly. It was expressly forbidden.

With his eyes on the floor, the pacing man banged his head sharply against the bars on his jail cell, unaware of the proximity. He looked startled.

Then he did it again.

And again.

Deliberately.

One jailbird hooted with laughter.

Another muttered, "You gonna be knowin' exactly how many steps you have in that cell by tomorrow."

Dallas, Texas

Chapter 13 – Mr. Phillips

"Please don't hurt me," the blonde woman pleaded when her captor entered the room.

He made a chuffing sound as he walked toward her.

Speaking in a heavily accented but silky voice, he asked, "What makes you think I'm gonna hurt you? Your boyfriend, he messed up big time, but you, little angel face doll, you're too. . . too fine."

The blonde stared at his eyes, looking for some assurance that he was telling the truth. She didn't see it. Instead she saw only a kind of appraisal as his eyes roved up and down her figure. It made her skin crawl. But maybe she could use it to her advantage. She had discovered her power over men at an early age and quickly learned to use it to get what she wanted.

The kind of men she knew always gave her what she wanted. Only it was never enough. This man was evil through and through. She recognized that. But he was still a man. And she could see he appreciated her beauty. That was the only thing she had going for her at the moment. She knew she had to win him over if she was going to survive this night.

Tossing her hair back over her shoulder so that her heavily-mascaraed blue eyes would be more visible, she gave him an inviting look. She regretted her rumpled skirt and hoped the perfume she always kept in her purse would mask the fact she hadn't been able to shower.

He walked toward her.

"How long you been here in this room? I told my guys not to mess with you. Are you hungry?" he asked, reaching out to touch her silky blonde hair. He appeared genuinely concerned.

She nodded, running just the tip of her tongue over her lips, hoping to draw his attention to her full, pouty mouth. Unaware of her ploy, the geek reached out for her arm. With a look of genuine regret, he commented, "I don't like hunger. It is too common in my country. That is why I come here. Hunger is a very bad thing. Come on. We're going to dinner."

Dinner? He's taking me to dinner? This was more like it, she thought, giddy with unbelievable relief. This man she had most desperately feared meeting for the first time wasn't going to kill her after all. After two days being held captive in this despicable, filthy room, he wanted to feed her!

He escorted her out the door and down an open corridor. She'd been blindfolded when the henchmen locked her in, and she had no idea where she was, but guessed from the room's standard appearance that it was an abandoned motel. An older Holiday Inn or Motel 6. God knew she'd been in enough of them.

No electricity or water. She'd been forced to use a bathroom that wouldn't flush and drink bottled water that had been there for who knew how long. Someone had left a bag containing a wilted ham sandwich in the room, but she hadn't touched it. She'd used all the blankets she could find to keep warm. Dallas in the fall could be chilly at times. But this was a comparatively warm night.

As he took her arm and guided her out the door, she could see other businesses lighted by various signs in the near distance. A couple of abandoned warehouses and three empty retail buildings stood nearby. A few blocks away she could see the familiar arches of McDonald's. Her prison was remote, but not in an area totally free of commercial traffic.

Maybe this guy owned the place. That could explain why nobody responded to her screams for help or heard her fists pounding on the boarded up windows. More likely there was no one near enough to hear her frantic pleas.

He guided her by the elbow down a flight of concrete stairs and helped her into a Cadillac, a roomy older model. She sat obediently and waited, crossing her legs and allowing her skirt to ride slightly above the knee.

After a drive through the outskirts of Dallas, branch banks, strip malls, grocery and convenience stores, they passed the Fighting Farmers football stadium and she recognized Flower Mound, a suburban satellite of the sprawling Texas metropolis. Where was he taking her?

He pulled the Cadillac up to a century-old, veranda-wrapped house which had been renovated into a classy eating establishment widely patronized by wealthier patrons who enjoyed freshly prepared selections rather than the frozen stuff served by the big chain restaurants.

The jerk actually opened the passenger door for her, playing the gentleman escorting a lady out for the evening, instead of some drug lord out to collect her boyfriend's money.

Poor, dumb Juan. What a dillweed. Oh he was undeniably a hottie for sure. A total chick magnet, and as hooked on her as any junkie was hooked on crack. But it was his fault that she was in this sticky situation. What had Juan ever done for her? Had he ever kept a single promise of big money? Not even one. The blonde suddenly decided he wasn't worthy of her attention.

Once inside the foyer, a tuxedoed waiter immediately escorted them to a private dining room lit by candles set in a golden candelabra. The single table sparkled with gold-rimmed goblets and place settings of delicate white china, also rimmed with gold, laid on a white damask cloth. Dancing lights reflected from the crystal chandelier hanging just overhead.

A bouquet of velvety, blood-red roses filled a Lalique vase sitting on a pedestal beside the wall. Candles also flickered from gilded wall sconces. Elegant. First class. This was the kind of place Juan had always promised to take her. Worthless promises. He hadn't delivered.

She suddenly despised him, more for failing to give her what she wanted than for causing her current predicament. She was starting to feel confident that she could get out of it in once piece. And if she played it right, she might even walk away with some of those big bucks Juan had stashed away. Her captor may be a toad, but he apparently knew how to treat a lady. She liked that.

"Your usual, Mr. Phillips?" the waiter asked.

"Of course, Alejandro. And the same for the lady," He spoke in a pleased tone. He might have been any Texas-oil man, wining and dining his latest romantic interest. He certainly looked the part. Flossin' like crazy, she thought. Every article he wore reflected excessive wealth and he wanted the world to know it. The expensive suede leather jacket, ostrich-leather cowboy boots, a diamond-studded presidential Rolex watch and three other enormous diamonds sparkling on his fingers.

The dipstick had plenty of dead presidents to spend. It might be fun to persuade him to spend them on her. Even if she had to go with him to South America or wherever he came from. She couldn't quite place his accent. Not Mexico. Brazil? Columbia? Right now she didn't care.

"Mr. Phillips? That's your name?" she questioned, after the staff filled their water goblets with sparkling water and their wine goblets with an imported wine. She thought it a good sign that he didn't try to hide his identity.

He chuckled and winked at her conspiratorially, "You can call me Mr. Phillips, little angel face girl." Clinking his wineglass to hers, he said, "A toast to the evening. I don't like it that you've been hungry. Hunger is a very bad thing."

Most of her anxiety began to abate, and her stomach growled noisily. It had been two days since she'd had anything to eat. Of course she hadn't had much of an appetite, but delightful cooking aromas wafted through the intimate dining room, waking her gastric juices with a sudden passion for food. Any food. Even that greasy stuff Juan loved sounded absolutely mouth watering.

She sipped her wine slowly, eyes wary and senses attuned to Phillips' every word, every change of expression, every subtle nuance.

Even though he liked her looks, there was something flat and deadly about those eyes. Subtle little alarm bells kept going off in her head. She told herself to remain on the alert.

However, the wine was delicious, and she relaxed a little. The waiter served celery root remoulade with scallops and caviar. In spite of her sudden appetite, she forced herself to eat slowly, daintily, smiling slightly at Phillips whenever he glanced up.

"Eat," Phillips ordered, his mouth full of caviar. "It's the best part of the evening. I always like to eat a good meal before business. Dessert too. And then a good cigar. My own personal label—imported. You smoke cigars?"

She shook her head, tasted the caviar, made a face, and Phillips roared with laughter. "What? Your boyfriend never treated you to a good meal?" Then he laughed again and helped himself to the serving on her plate.

"Okay," she said. "Maybe he isn't as first class as you are." She smiled and looked directly into his eyes. "Maybe I like first class men much better." She slipped a stockinged foot out of her shoe and rubbed it slowly against the inner calf of his leg.

Much more interested in stuffing his mouth at the moment, Phillips didn't appear to notice. The salad was escarole and herb with apple and pomegranates followed by a main course of pecan crusted beef tenderloin with juniper jus.

After the meal he ordered crème brulee and tiramasu. When the desserts weren't to his liking, the waiter removed them and brought out champagne glasses, fresh strawberries and a rich, chocolate dipping sauce.

"Bring her a vanilla pear mimosa," Phillips ordered, slurping noisily at the chocolate-dipped berries and leaving none for her. He watched her drink the rich concoction, satisfied that she was enjoying it, then suddenly got up and took her arm. "Come on, let's go."

Back in the Cadillac, she felt an icy prickle of fear when they drove away from Flower Mound. The roads grew darker as traffic thinned. She recognized the road to Grapevine Lake as they neared Sneaky Pete's bar. It was her boyfriend's favorite Saturday night hangout. Did Phillips know that? Of course he did.

"You're not a small time player, so why do you want to waste your time with my ex-boyfriend?" she hoped he would pick up on the "ex" part of the word.

He did.

"You may be through with him, Angel Face, but he's not through with you. That's why he's gonna be sorry he tried to mess with me."

Oh god. He was using her as bait. If Juan didn't fork over the shekels, she was dead meat. She'd drop the dime. Give him away in a minute if she only knew where he stashed the paper. She took Phillips' hand and placed it on her bare knee. "I can be valuable to you," she suggested in a husky voice. "I can get the money for you."

They were passing Sneaky Pete's bar now, driving down a narrow road toward a lonely boat landing on the water's edge.

"Ahhhh yes, that's just what you're going to do" he said with a silky voice. "The money, the money, the money. It's always about the money. I don't mind he keeps a little for himself now and then. But your boyfriend make a beeeg mistake."

His accent suddenly thicker, he explained, "One of my guys was down here to make the drop and got arrested with the bundle on him. Now your boyfriend owes me more than just the two-million-dollars."

He caressed her knee.

The road ended at what might have been a boat dock. Phillips stopped the Cadillac just near the water. He turned off the ignition and the entire scene went instantly black as if someone had dropped a dark blanket over the car. Not a single star shone overhead. No sign of headlights from a passing car. Her sense of isolation in the darkness was so complete, she might as well have been in a subterranean cave. Her scalp prickled. This wasn't good.

"C'mere little angel face girl," he pulled her toward him and kissed her full on the mouth. She moved her body against his, hoping to ignite and distract. Phillips disgusted her. Think about something pleasant, she told herself, and thought about killing Juan. Poor stupid Juan so totally devoted to her.

"Umm," she purred. Killing Juan. That would feel good.

"Come on," Phillips ordered. "We're getting out of the car." What was he going to do? Shove her in the lake? Maybe she could beat him to it.

He pulled her across the seat, out the passenger door, and positioned her with her back toward the water. She could hear waves lapping gently against the shoreline.

Then he took her arms and wrapped them around his neck. "That's right," he used his silky voice, when she pulled him tight against her. Play along with him, she thought. He's not going to hurt me. He needs me to find out where Juan hid the cash.

His hands dropped to her waist, and he kissed her again, his breath ragged. She didn't feel the surgical steel blade under her left shoulder blade until it penetrated her heart from behind. Phillips drove it in quickly, even as he deepened the kiss on the dying woman's lips.

Then he used the knife to carve out a little present from her still quivering flesh. It would be delivered to her ex-boyfriend, along with a lock of that unmistakable silky blonde hair. He planned to leave both souvenirs on the front seat of Juan's car, which was parked outside Sneaky Pete's bar.

Thinking of Jaun's expression upon finding it, he laughed out loud. Then he washed his hands in the lake water, changed out of his expensive clothes and wrapped them in a plastic bag. He shoved the body into the water. When police found her, they wouldn't have a clue. The wealthy Texas oilman, Mr. Phillips, did not exist. He'd be long gone.

Pulling his cell phone out of an inner pocket, he dialed a Woodsville, Wisconsin number. "Tell the peg-leg Mex I won't be back in town until after Christmas," he ordered, reaching for one of his favorite cigars. I have a little business to take care of while I'm vacationing in Nuevo Laredo over the holidays."

Then he flicked his lighter on and took a quick puff before exhaling slowly. Aah, it was a sin not to enjoy a good cigar after dessert.

November, 2002

Chapter 14 – Nate Cash

At her news desk, Tia read with keen interest a batch of letters from members of Nancy Jurowski's family, hoping they would give her some solid reasons why they believed Ben was the killer. She was ready to be convinced.

Instead, all she read were hate-filled accusations. "Why run this series in your paper? We cannot all be wrong. Ben is where he is because he killed our Angel daughter and sister, Nancy.

"Ben is a heartless, cold-blooded killer. He never cried one tear at her funeral or visitation. Now is that how a person acts who is supposed to care about her?"

Tia felt genuine compassion for Nancy's brother, sister and mother. She understood their rage. Dear God, how she understood it. Of course they wanted the killer in prison. Still, they didn't give her a shred of a motive. Not one single reason why they thought Ben would want Nancy dead, except for the supposed affair, and she wasn't buying that one. Even if it were true, it wasn't a motive for the murder.

Maybe it was time to interview a clinical psychologist—say Dr. Bradford, the psychiatrist she had consulted for her own grief counseling. Time to ask an expert why Ben didn't shed any tears. Of course, she already knew the answer. Not everybody cries in public. Her own tears had been slow in coming.

Grief is personal—and for her—a very private thing. She tried her best not to impose her sorrow on others, tried to smile and laugh at their humor. She supposed it was the same for Ben too. It's a fact of human nature that we tend to expect others to behave the same way we would in similar circumstances. When they don't, we wonder what's wrong with them.

Ben's "inappropriate emotions" had served the prosecutor well according to Karla Brandon. He made a point of speaking to the jury about Ben's "heartless, cold-blooded" behavior. Tia marveled at how a case can be made against a suspect based on his lack of appropriate emotion. How the most innocuous behavior can be so wrongly interpreted. Ben's nervous laugh over his son's Mickey Mouse tie at the funeral. A laugh instead of tears at the wrong time. Anger at the murder scene instead of weeping. A twenty-year-old lie about Vietnam repeated at the most damaging time in the investigation. None of that was that scientific evidence, but all of it helped to convict him.

Who sets the standard for just what "appropriate emotion" really is, she wondered. She dialed James Bond from the news office, and as always he was ready to answer her questions.

"How do people usually react after a loved one dies a violent death, James? Is there a typical response?"

Bond cleared his throat. When she didn't use the playful title, Mr. Bond, he knew she was all business. "Typical? I'd say not. Some people go into shock and are very calm. Eerily calm. I worked a homicide scene once where the body was stretched out on the floor. The mother was standing at the kitchen sink. She just kept on washing the dishes."

"Washing the dishes?"

Bond continued, "Yeah. I think she found some small comfort in doing her routine chores, maybe a sense of normalcy in the face of the terrible thing that had happened."

Tia jotted down notes as he talked.

"I've been in hospital Emergency Rooms where the dead victim's family just stands there, poker faced, and asks what they should do next. No tears. No crying or wailing. That comes later when it starts to sink in."

Then she asked him what he thought of her Krahl series so far, knowing how skeptical he had been from the beginning.

"I have good news for you, sweetheart. My agency is taking the case. I've got a friend working on it right now."

Tia breathed a long, ragged sigh of relief. Something like this was what she had been waiting for. In a voice filled with hope she asked, "Do you think they can turn up anything this late in the game? I mean, it's been almost four years."

"If Nate Cash is working on this case, nothing will stop him until he gets to the bottom of it," Bond assured her. "Let's have lunch today, and I'll introduce you. How about Grandma's Restaurant across from Forest Village Mall?"

"I'll be there. Tia hung up the phone, greatly relieved to know that at last, someone was taking a second look at the murder case.

* * *

The essential Dick Tracy. That was Nate Cash. He carried a "Colombo" raincoat, wore the standard fedora hat, and had a face carved by time into seams and friendly crinkles, every line telling a story.

His sky blue eyes had seen decades of purple winters and not enough yellow summers, and like those few who possess the ability to laugh rather than groan at the years, they twinkled with a hint of humor that made Tia want to share a good joke with him someday.

She sensed a gentleness lurking behind his crusty façade. She also sensed that Nate was a man with bulldog tenacity. If persistence was a stream, Nate Cash was the Mississippi River. Retired from the neighboring city's daily paper, where he had worked as an investigative reporter for a number of years, Nate had a solid reputation as a trustworthy and accurate news hound. And more importantly, the police trusted him. "If Nate tells me Ben didn't do it, I'll believe him," said Bond.

This weathered and determined former investigative reporter was going to find Nancy's killer. Tia could feel it in her bones.

They were seated at Grandma's Restaurant in a booth with a window overlooking a gorgeous forested area. Tia was unaware of the view. "So do you have an opinion on his guilt or innocence at this stage?" she asked Nate, eager to know.

If her conclusions this far were based on inaccurate or incomplete information, she would be the first to admit it. Until then, she couldn't shake the feeling that the jury had done exactly that—based their conviction on inaccurate and definitely incomplete information. This made her determined to dig out the truth, only she didn't have the resources or the expertise that Nate Cash and James Bond surely had.

Nate looked thoughtful. "It bothers me that the gun was never found, and the police couldn't prove he ever owned a gun," he said. Then raising his eyebrows in a puzzled expression, he added, "Still, he had the opportunity."

Back to that again. Opportunity.

Any of the eight or nine people who were known to be out in the parking lot that night also had the opportunity. Seeing her expression, Nate mused, "It bothers me that he didn't have a history of violence or bad temper. The best predictor of human behavior is past behavior. I'm not seeing any violence in the man or any motive at all for the murder."

"Have you talked to Rocky Miller?"

"No. He won't talk to me. I have talked with Rip Tyson and the Brandons. Ben's workplace associates and his former neighbors. All decent, solid citizens. Not a shady character in the bunch. If anyone had sinister people in the background, it was Nancy, not Ben."

Tia nodded in agreement.

"I also talked with Ben's brother-in-law. He says Nancy was stalked during the week prior to her death. A neighbor lady became suspicious enough to jot down the license number of the car. Unfortunately, she lost it. To my knowledge, the police never knew about the stalker."

Tia exclaimed, "Doesn't that make you wonder?"

Nate only nodded. They discussed a few more possibilities, before the private eyes insisted on paying for her lunch, and she thanked them.

"I'll look forward to hearing from you, Nate, as soon as you turn up anything. And I won't print a word until you give me the green light." Nate nodded. As one journalist to another, each knew their trustworthiness could not be questioned. It was an unwritten law for reporters working with police officers, elected officials and also with each other.

Back at the news office, Tia wrote up her story on Ben's "damning lack of emotion at the funeral," including a quote from the psychiatrist, who said just what she expected. Grief cannot be measured by a lack of public emotion. Dr. Bradford also asked her how she was sleeping.

"I'm okay," she lied, unwilling to admit her sleep was often disturbed by horrible nightmares. Then she reminded him she was at the office and had a deadline to meet.

The story flowed from her fingertips to the computer screen, easily and with conviction. Truth, it seemed, was on her side . . . for all that it mattered.

Justice may still be a long way away for Krahl, but Tia felt relaxed in a way that she had not been for weeks. At last, someone was going to help her find out what happened in the parking lot that night. She silently prayed that Nate would find real evidence.

If Ben really did pull the trigger, she wanted to know it, based on real, concrete evidence and not just supposition. If he didn't, she wanted to know who did.

November 2002

Chapter 15 - Wounded

Red haze spread over him, clouding Ben's vision. He was walking beside the killer, only the killer couldn't see him. Even when Ben knew the nightmare's events were totally garbled, he was caught in its inescapable grip, helpless as a rabbit in the claws of a hawk. He felt the terror of fleeing from the gunfire, the sudden shock of losing someone he loved. The horror of not being able to stop it

The street lamps, shut off by photoelectric sensors after midnight, had left the parking lot in blackness as dark as a cavern beneath a midnight sea.

Ben opened his mouth in a silent, futile warning. He heard Nancy's terrified scream again. Saw the muzzle split the night with sharp staccato blasts. The high-powered round from the .357 Magnum blast through Nancy's temple above her right ear, exploding in a burst of energy and instantly destroying her brain.

Like so many times before as a dream watcher, he saw her collapse to the pavement. The gunman fired again, one bullet shattering the storefront window, another pinging off a utility pole. Ben's conscious mind had not recalled those bullets, but they surfaced in his dream with surprising accuracy. If only he could see the face of the shooter.

Shocked silence as hushed as an empty tomb. The sirens and sound of tires shrieking to a stop. The rhythmic flashes of red and blue lights cutting swatches out of the black canvas of night over the death scene.

He moaned on his bunk and rolled over. Bars and locks could keep out intruders, insects and cold. But nothing could keep this nightmare from Ben's haunted mind.

* * *

Miles away in Woodsville, Tia tossed restlessly on her bed, trapped in her own recurring nightmare, a nocturnal horror she unknowingly shared with Ben.

An angry wind spit ice shards against the bedroom windowpanes. The sound of it called forth buried memories. She was in the car with Jeff. They were laughing in the face of the rain outside from the warmth of their togetherness within. They could see into the future only as far as the headlights' beam cut a dim swath through the storm-tossed night. But they trusted in the promise of tomorrow.

If only they could have seen far enough ahead in time. The headlights blazing into their eyes, impossibly bright. The jarring impact and awful shrieking sound of metal crunching against metal and shattering glass. . . Fingers clawing at a spider web.

No, not a spider web. It was the windshield splintering into a sudden, intricate pattern. Red fingers clawing on the broken pane. She woke with a start, sweat rolling off her forehead and between her breasts, still hearing the sound of fingers tapping the glass! Fingers tapping at the window?!

102

No! It was only the blast of ice-laden wind tapping a sudden rhythm against her bedroom windows. Her mind, like Ben's, under a mantle of sleep, had reached down into the place where painful memories lay buried for sanity's survival and had called forth details of the moment that had split her life in two definite periods—before and after the wreck.

This particular dream scene had been far more terrifying than previous ones. This time she had been driving the car that swerved over the centerline and into the path of the oncoming vehicle. With a gut-wrenching moan, Tia cried out, "Oh God! Was I at the wheel? Did I kill my husband and our baby?"

Tormented by her inability to remember, she climbed out of bed and stumbled into the bathroom, opening the medicine cabinet. There sat the prescription bottles, still completely full. Managing to get the childproof cap off the sleeping pills on the third try, she stared at the capsules.

For a long moment, she held the small plastic bottle in her hand. Maybe it would help. Maybe she could sleep again. Find that place of numbness where she wouldn't be torn by a certain song on the radio. Maybe her appetite would return. She might even be able to write that book she so desperately wanted to finish.

But no matter how many pills she took, it wouldn't bring Jeff back.

She slowly emptied both the sleeping pills and the antidepressants down the toilet bowl and flushed the handle. The prescription on the label allowed refills. Should she toss it too? What if the dreams and sleeplessness got worse? After a moment of indecision, she placed the empty bottles back inside the medicine cabinet.

Back in bed, she turned over and groaned into her pillow. Her sleep was yet to be interrupted by the ringing telephone.

A disembodied voice slithered through the wires, chilling Tia as she picked up the receiver. "You gonna keep on with that story, reporter girl? You gonna get yourself someplace you don't wanna be," the voice hissed as it wrapped around her mind, squeezing the last remnant of sleep into startled alertness.

103

"Who is this?" Tia demanded, sitting up in bed and glancing at the lighted dial on her clock. Three a.m.

No answer. Only a mirthless laugh causing tiny hairs on the back of her neck to prickle. If she had been a kitten, the fur on her back would have been standing upright. For a fleeting moment, she could see herself as a feline, all fluffed out with back raised like a Halloween cat. Then her anger rose up higher than the cat's arching back. The frightened kitten bared her claws. Speaking with a bravery she did not feel, she demanded, "Look, I don't know who you are or what you're trying to pull, mister, but you're the one that needs to back off!"

"I know what's going on there. You don't leesten. Could be it's already too late for you, reporter girl," the suggestive words hinted at things she could easily imagine as worse than a medieval torture chamber. Before she had a chance to speak, the line went dead.

Tia slammed the receiver down. Who was this creep? And what did he mean it's already too late? At that hour of the morning, she would not be rude enough to call anyone, but she desperately wanted to hear a reassuring voice. James Bond's voice telling her it was probably just. . .just who?

She reached for the phone, but thought better of dialing Bond's number, knowing she would be waking Bond and his wife and they would not appreciate the intrusion. Neither would Carmen, who kept early morning therapy appointments at the clinic and needed her sleep. She dialed another number instead.

"Ummm. H'lo," a sleepy voiced Cap answered.

For a moment, Tia remained silent. What was she doing?

"H'lo?" Cap repeated.

"Cap, it's Tia. I'm sorry. I…I shouldn't have bothered you."

Cap sat upright at the sound of her voice. "What is it, Tia? I'm here," he reassured her, already guessing that she had received another phone threat.

"Well please just stay there. Don't come over here," she immediately insisted. "I just—I just need to talk to someone a minute." An angry gust of wind rattled the windowpane, causing her to jump involuntarily.

"Okay, alright. I'm staying put." He assured her, "Talk to me." He was glad she had turned to him."

She hesitated, uncertain of what to say. It sounded silly to wake another person at this ungodly hour because of a stupid phone threat. They were common enough. She read about them in the police reports every week. The callers rarely harmed their targets.

Cap suggested, "Did you have a bad dream? I'm great at making nightmares go away."

Odd he should say that. He had no way of knowing that her sleep was sometimes plagued by nightmares. "I just had another phone call."

"Okay, so what did the creep say? No wait. Before you say another word, go check the parking lot from your windows."

Tia did as she was told. The lot was empty of any suspicious vehicles. Relieved but shivering, she crawled back into the warmth of her bed and picked up the receiver, glad to be connected to a calm voice, any voice, she told herself. Not necessarily his voice.

She told him what the caller had said, hoping he could persuade her that it was really nothing to be alarmed about.

"Tia, we don't know what this is all about," Cap said seriously, keeping his voice calm so as not to alarm her further.

She was glad he didn't ask why she'd been refusing to answer his phone calls. Or maybe he didn't know because he hadn't been calling? She knew she was being reclusive. But she didn't need another lecture about getting on with life now. All she wanted was someone to tell her there was nothing to worry about.

"What am I supposed to do?" she asked somewhat lamely.

"Well for starters, you could move in with Carmen for awhile."

"Oh no. I'm not putting Carmen in any danger because of me," she protested. Even as the words tumbled out of her mouth she realized that she was admitting the real possibility of danger.

"Okay then, why don't you camp out on my sofa? Nobody would ever find you here," Cap suggested.

Aghast at his suggestion, Tia began protesting firmly. Finally, Cap interrupted her. "Look, I'm not suggesting anything but a safe place for a few days, until the police have a chance to look into this."

"Yeah right. The police have their hands full with enough stuff every day. Burglaries and car thefts and robberies. You think they have time to go looking for a voice on the phone? Besides, he didn't even make a real threat." She was already convincing herself there was little reason to go the police. What could they do? She didn't want to admit to Cap that she had never bothered to file a police report after the van chase.

Cap decided to change his tactics. "Okay, okay. Maybe the cops can't do anything yet. But we don't want to wait until you get run off the road or hurt in some way before we do something, now do we?"

Tia considered for moment. What could she do? If someone wanted to hurt her, how could she protect herself? He started talking again, sensing his momentary advantage. "The least we can do is to make sure you have a gun for self defense. Do you know how to shoot?"

"As a matter of fact, I do," Tia answered. "I grew up on a Missouri farm, and my dad taught me how to handle a pistol in case there was a snake in the yard. We had rattlers from time to time."

"Good. Then just think of this scumbag as a rattler, and don't hesitate to shoot if he ever tries to hurt you. Next question. Do you have a gun?"

"No."

"Then we're going shopping in the morning. I'll pick you up at 8:30 in the morning," he announced. "No arguments. We'll do some shooting at the firing range. I taught my sister how to shoot before she moved to New York. I can probably give you some pointers too."

Before she could think of any possible objection, he added, "If you have a bad dream, call me again. I'll tell you another fairy tale story that's guaranteed to charm you back to sleep." Then he hung up before she had time to respond.

She turned over and pulled the comforter up around her ears, hoping for a few hours of uninterrupted sleep.

Cap switched off his night light, grinning to himself at the thought of seeing her tomorrow. This woman—this lovely, stubborn, blind-to-his-charm woman—was a total challenge.

He felt he was up to the challenge.

November, 2002

Chapter 16 – The Firing Range

Here she was, riding in Cap's Jeep after she'd promised herself she would never do so again. How did she get herself into this? A cold murder case. A mysterious, evil voice on the phone. A van following her on the darkened streets. And now she was actually on her way to buy a gun. A gun! Her mother would be horrified.

Tia didn't add to her list Cap Nemon's blue eyes and husky voice, a surprisingly tender voice that could be surprisingly soothing after frightening calls in the night.

"What kind of gun did you shoot on the farm?" he asked.

"A .22 rifle and a pistol."

"We're going to look at a .32 caliber snub-nosed revolver. I know a licensed dealer who has one for sale. Then we'll drive out to the shooting range and see if you can handle it."

"I'll handle it fine," said Tia confidently. I've got 20-20 vision and a steady hand."

She had dressed in slacks and a heavy sweater. It was sure to be chilly. However, after last night's sleet, the day had turned unseasonably warm, sunshine breaking through the clouds. Still, the warmth of the day could be temporary. Darker clouds already were rolling in over the Woody River, piling high above the trees.

They picked up the revolver and drove out to the firing range south of Woodsville. The area was actually a park-like setting complete with a few picnic tables. Cap opened the door for her. "Here we are. Let's see how you handle this. It's got a nice feel to it." He began to instruct her. Just like any man, Tia noted, as if only men can handle things like hammers, tire tools and guns. She expected the lesson to be as much fun as bobbing in hot grease for French fries.

"Okay, now aim for the target and squeeze, don't pull," he wrapped his arms around her shoulders, warm hands on her hands, helping her to aim the weapon. She could smell the clean scent of his shaving cream and feel the warmth of his breath against her ear. It made her uncomfortable.

Okay, let's get this over with fast, she thought, squeezing off the first round. The bullet struck the target, but off center. The force of the gunfire rocked her body back against his solid chest, but she quickly recovered her balance. He remained steady. Solid as a rock. The next time she did better.

"Bull's eye!" Cap congratulated her. He could see that her hand was steady.

Later, after she demonstrated she could hit the bull's eye four out of five shots, Cap was convinced. He liked her determination. She may be shaken by events, but she was not cowardly.

Paying no attention to the swollen belly of clotted clouds now directly overhead, Tia fired off the last round just as the unseasonable thunderstorm broke without the warning of thunder. Fat drops of rain pelted down and a streak of silver lightning darted over the treetops, a sudden wind bending their branches.

Cap and Tia ran for the Jeep. Nearly blinded by the stinging rain streaming down her face and into her eyes, she stumbled on the uneven ground and fell. As she struggled to gain her footing again, she felt strong arms under her knees, lifting her. Cradling her like a child, Cap carried her to a nearby picnic shelter. He sat her down on top of the wooden table and wrapped his leather jacket over her shoulders without removing his arm from the sleeve. She could feel his chest heaving slightly against her back, his muscular arm around her, and without thinking she leaned momentarily against him, glad for the warmth.

"Are you okay? Did you turn your ankle?"

"I'm fine. Just clumsy I guess." She answered.

Rain drummed loudly on the roof of the shelter and surrounded them with a curtain of gray, effectively walling them off from the world around them.

"Looks like we're going to be here for awhile or else make a run for it and get even more soaked," he observed. Then he added, "Actually I don't mind waiting it out with you beside me. In fact, I sort of hope it keeps raining for a while." And I hope you keep leaning against me just like this, his mind whispered the unspoken wish. He could feel her body against his, shivering slightly.

Suddenly very aware of the sweet scent of her rain-dampened hair, Cap didn't think. He just acted. Taking her chin in his hand, he tilted her face up to meet his lips. Totally unprepared for his kiss, and even more unprepared by the unbidden way her body responded, Tia pulled away from the warmth of Cap's embrace. "What are you doing?" she demanded, both startled and aghast.

"I'm sorry," he stammered, seeing the fire in her eyes.

"Don't kiss me and say you're sorry." The edge to her voice was threatening. The words hadn't come out right, but she was too flustered to clarify.

"I'm—I'm sorry," Cap stammered again. "I mean, I'm not sorry I kissed you. I'm sorry that it upset you." He was at a loss.

Seeing his perplexity, Tia softened a little. "Look Cap, I want you to understand tump-sing—something." The moment was too intense for either of them to laugh at her verbal blunder.

In a more gentle voice and with something like resignation, she explained, "I'm going to be as honest as I can be, and I want you to listen. I'm not ready for a relationship. Not with you or anyone else right now. You need to realize . . . I'm not—I'm just not a whole person at this time in my life."

Cap's eyes darkened as he looked into hers.

They seemed to bore right through her every defense. He spoke with a certain steely timbre she had not heard in his voice before.

"Listen to me, Tia Marie Burgess. You've been through a terrible tragedy. I understand that. But you've also locked yourself inside a prison of grief with bars on it every bit as real as the bars on Ben Krahl's cell. Sooner or later you're going to have to realize that. Don't throw away the key before it's too late." A sudden clap of thunder punctuated his words.

He stood up and lifted her off the picnic table, holding her body tightly against his, her feet completely off the ground. His lips hovered above hers, both threatening and promising as the wind began to whip around them, wildly passionate and full of fury.

"Kiss me Tia," his voice was husky. "Kiss me."

Her eyes had the look of the proverbial startled doe caught in the headlights.

Without waiting for her to respond, he kissed her again, claiming her unwilling mouth, conquering her resistance until she was breathless and limp, her body helplessly crushed against his while thunder exploded overhead and all around them.

It was a possessive kiss, a branding kiss. It infuriated her. How dare he! She struggled for release. "Put me down!"

Once more he kissed her, a punctuation of sorts, as if sealing the previous kiss, by which he'd claimed her as his own. Only then did he release her. Without a word, she turned and headed out into the downpour toward the Jeep. Cap followed, unlocking the passenger door for her while she shivered as rain dribbled down the back of her neck.

When he climbed inside, he infuriated her even more by whistling a tune that sounded vaguely like *Mean Woman Blues.*

How could he be so darn sure of himself? So cocky? The man had no compassion in him! No humility. Not a shred of understanding. Seething, she chose not to speak until they reached her parking slot back at the apartment.

In a stiffly polite tone, she said, "Thank you for your help today. But please don't walk me to the door." Then she insisted curtly, "And don't bother calling me again. Not ever again." She stressed the word *ever*, in a haughty, demanding tone.

It occurred to her as she spoke the words that it was she who had been the one to call him and not the other way around. Oh well. That was the message she wanted to convey, regardless of who had called whom.

Climbing out of the Jeep before he had a chance to exit and open the door for her, she hurried toward the stairwell without looking back, anxious to get inside.

Later that night when the telephone rang, Tia did not answer it. She didn't want to talk to Carmen. Or to Cap. Or to anyone. The phone rang again. Let it ring. If it was Mr. Evil Voice, she didn't want to know it.

The phone went silent after three more insistent rings. Tia turned over in her bed and put a pillow over her ears.

* * *

December, 2002

It seemed that Cap was going to honor her request not to call. She heard nothing from him, as November quickly became snowy December. Her Ben Krahl series was now on hold, since she had no new material at the moment.

But she was optimistic that Nate Cash would turn up something. The wastebasket beside her word processor at home continued to overflow with futile attempts at the book she could not write but would not abandon. No van followed her. No more evil voices on the phone. Life was routine again, and that was fine. There was satisfaction in the routine, and if there was no joy, at least there was numbness to pain.

However, Christmas was not a happy time. In the years since the accident she had driven back to Missouri and helped her mother, also a grieving widow, to make a holiday dinner for her brother, Andy and his wife and kids.

This year, Ellen had decided to fly out to California for the entire month of December at her son's invitation. Of course, Andy also had offered to send Tia a ticket, but she refused him politely, knowing that the expense would strap him. "I've been invited to Carmen's place, and her family is planning a huge Italian dinner. She often invites people who have no family nearby to her holiday dinners. It should be fun," Tia assured him merrily over the phone.

But when she hung up, she sighed. She was expecting that her boss would keep her busy at the news office. He seemed to know by some unspoken signal that she thrived on work. And withered without it.

After her gifts for Andrew's family and for Ellen were purchased, wrapped and in the mail, Tia had no further preparations to make. Once again, she had not decorated a tree or bothered to hang so much as a wreath on her apartment door.

When she arrived at Carmen's upscale condo on Christmas day, the colorful lighting and merry decorations delighted her color-starved eyes. She had forgotten how much she once loved making her own home merry and bright.

"Deck the halls with boughs of holly," Carmen sang as she answered the door, greeting Tia with a hug. Already, Carmen's sisters, nieces, nephews, aunts and uncles and a neighbor or two had gathered and were welcoming her with cheery nods.

Their merriment was as delicious as the eggnog. She found herself embraced by collective good cheer as warm as the Yule log burning in the fireplace.

"You look so beautiful in that Christmas-red sweater," Carmen commented enthusiastically as she lighted red candles in gold candlesticks on the table.

Tia thought Carmen looked especially festive in a red satin shell underneath a black velvet jacket and velvet palazzo pants.

She wore a holiday wreath in her hair that made her look like a Christmas tree angel.

Everyone began to gather around the beautifully appointed table when the doorbell chimed again. Helping to fill gold-rimmed crystal goblets, Tia didn't look up until the latecomer sat down beside her. It was Cap Nemon.

She had not seen or heard from him since that day on the shooting range over a month ago. She knew at once that Carmen had set her up. How dare Carmen do this to her! She barely nodded when Cap said hello.

But the merriment of the moment was overwhelming. Family and friends bowed their heads, offering thanks for the gift of God's Son, for the blessings of the year past and the one to come. Touched by their genuine gratitude, Tia joined in the singing of a hymn before Carmen's Uncle Tony carved the turkey. And of course there were delightful Italian dishes along with the traditional offerings, like the special meat-and-cheese pie with enough cheese in one slice to commit suicide by cholesterol. Who cared? It was delicious.

They raised stemmed wineglasses in a toast to family and friends. Cap touched his goblet to hers, but did not look into her eyes. Suddenly, she wondered if he had been just as surprised at her presence as she was to see him. Maybe he felt as unsettled as she did.

Well, she decided. Why let him ruin the day? She had not been at a table with such delicious offerings for a long time. And she was hungry for a change. "Who made this wonderful baked lasagna?" she asked after tasting the mouthwatering creation.

Carmen nodded toward Cap, her dark Italian eyes sparkling with merriment.

"I told you I'm a man of many talents," he grinned at Tia momentarily, and she was struck once again by the incredible blueness of his eyes. Then he turned back to Maria, Carmen's laughing, dark-eyed sister who seemed to be delighted by his attention.

Tia had to admit, the lasagna was very tasty, even if Cap had made it. After the pumpkin pie and a variety of other mouth-watering desserts, everyone gathered around the fireplace for hot cider or coffee. They sang Christmas carols again and exchanged small, token gifts.

From the corner of her eye, Tia could see Cap and Maria continuing their conversation. Maria laughed gaily. Although not quite as dazzling as her sister, Maria was still a very attractive woman. Was she married? Tia wondered, and then dismissed the thought.

Someone slipped a gift into Tia's hand. It was addressed to her from Cap. Inside the silver paper tied with lavender ribbons was a book of poems by Robert Frost. On the inside cover, Cap had written, "Wake up Sleeping Beauty. There is a road not taken. And you will find it soon."

She glanced at him across the room. He merely grinned that boyish lopsided grin of his and gave her a wink. It was maddening the way he seemed so darned sure of himself. Did he expect her to throw herself into his arms because of a book of poems? Forget that!

Carmen was planning to spend New Year's Eve at the First Night event across the state line in downtown Rockford, where White Fox was scheduled to play. Of course she invited Tia and Cap, but Tia declined.

She might have gone if it had not been for Cap. She was sure the music would be fun and the fireworks splendid, but the thought of his unwelcome kisses on the firing range still made her angry.

New Year's Eve arrived crystal clear with enough snow on the ground to race a team of sled dogs and enough marrow-chilling cold to remind Tia of Jack London's short story "To Build A Fire." She suffered from the cold more it seemed these days. Her hands were never warm.

She missed Missouri's milder climate. Especially now. She could almost see herself moving back. But oh how she wanted to write that headline: "BEN KRAHL INNOCENT." Then she might think about packing up and heading south.

She spent the evening alone, making only a single call to her mother, who wisely refrained from asking the usual questions and making the usual suggestions. Instead Ellen prayed a New Year's prayer over her daughter before hanging up. "I love you too, Mom," Tia whispered. "I'll be fine."

Outside, snowflakes floated as gently as the wispy veil of a bride. Across the state line Rockford sparkled with festivities and holiday lights. Cafés and theaters bustled with merry makers. Streets swarmed with bright-eyed youngsters swathed in layers of clothes, coats and mittens.

Costumed jugglers, crazy clowns, and a colorful Chinese dragon wound their way through the throngs to the rhythm of accompanying drummers. In the halls, orchestras such as Moonlight Jazz struck up lively dance tunes. Ethnic dancers twirled in colorful costumes. The popular Men of Our Times rock 'n roll band drew crowds of dancers and eager fans.

Alone in her Wood Hills Road apartment, Tia pulled an afghan over her lap and curled up with a book by Ann Rule, the former Seattle, Washington policewoman who wrote true crime novels. She sipped from a cup of hot tea and read into the late hours.

Cap Nemon, not far away in his own place off North Spruce Road., also settled in for the night with an Ann Rule book. The stroke of midnight announced the New Year's arrival without much notice from either of them. Barely a nod from Tia. A glance at the clock from Cap.

Thinking of Sleeping Beauty, he toyed with the idea of calling to wish her a happy New Year. She was alone in her apartment. He knew that. He'd driven by earlier in the evening. Reaching for the phone, he dialed the first three digits of her number. Then thought better of it and hung up the receiver.

Following Carmen's advice was going to be hard. But Carmen knew Tia better than anyone. So maybe he should listen and give her some time. Not much more time. He wasn't going to let her keep him waiting forever.

He stretched and poured himself a glass of wine, then lifted his glass and offered a toast out loud. "To Tia Marie Burgess, my lonely, winsome widow. You are going to find out that whatever healing you need won't happen if you're all alone. And I'm in your life to stay, whether you realize it or not." Then he swallowed the wine and grinned to himself.

She would not be spending another New Year's Eve without him. He was as certain of that as his own name. "Maybe you think I can't sing, but we'll make beautiful music, you and I, one day," he promised her. His grin widened.

January, 2003

Chapter 17 – Beginnings and Endings

"No I didn't go alone. Carmen went with me, and you'll never guess what happened" Tia explained to Pat with a grin of anticipation.

Pat and Lucy had tickets to a reception in Rockford for Rod Blagojevich, the successful young candidate taking over Governor George Ryan's office this January of 2003. Pat had asked Tia to go in his place and take a friend, as he and Lucy had already planned to attend a political event in Beloit, Wisconsin.

He raised his eyebrows, waiting to hear the forthcoming story. It was going to be funny. He could tell by the expression in Tia's eyes.

"Blagojevich was reading name tags so he could call everyone by name. And there we were wearing your name tags—Carmen's tag had Lucy O'Brien on it, and mine said Pat O'Brien. So what do you think she asks him while we're standing there side by side with the same last names?"

Pat had no idea. "Knowing our Carmen I wouldn't be surprised if she asked why he was wearing the wrong color tie with his suit."

Tia laughed. "Actually he's a classy dresser. No, Carmen wanted to know his stand on same-sex marriage. SAME SEX MARRIAGE! And there we were with these matching name tags! He probably thought we were partners."

Pat roared. He was pleased to see that Tia had enjoyed the occasion. She looked far too pale these days, and although he seldom sent her out on assignment after hours, he'd thought she would enjoy meeting the new governor. "So what was his stand?" Pat asked.

"Rod believes marriage is for a man and a woman. He didn't bat an eye at the question or the name tags."

Pat nodded. "Maybe he just thought you were sisters."

"Carmen says every time she goes out with me she gets a new name. Now she's Karen-Carmen-Lucy O'Brien Morrelli," Tia spoke with mock exasperation.

"Well, let's see what we can think of next." Pat added. When he walked her out to the Bronco at the end of the workday, he was genuinely pleased to see a little enthusiasm in her eyes. It was a good way to start off the year.

* * *

The year had hardly begun for the newly sworn in sheriff of Nuevo Laredo, when it ended in a hailstorm of bullets. Before he realized what was happening, three black Chevy Suburbans hemmed in his vehicle. He didn't have time to grab for his gun. The drivers opened fire with semi-automatic assault weapons. It was over in seconds. Esteban Dominiquez's bullet-riddled body lay slumped over the steering wheel.

The bold and confident henchmen climbed back inside their vehicles and drove slowly away, even as shocked bystanders stood frozen in open-mouthed astonishment..

The gunmen had just delivered a message to the governor of Mexico. Their organization was more powerful than any law enforcement agency. More powerful than the Mexican national army troops. Who would dare defy them? Dominiquez's' now-vacant job was not going to be a popular one, unless the next sheriff was willing to play their game.

The man known in Texas as Mr. Phillips drove a black Chevy Suburban across the border into Texas. He had unfinished business in Illinois. And in Wisconsin. Concern for his hungry country was driving him. It was time to get more funds transferred. And there was also that nagging little loose end.

He had already decided it was past time to care of her.

*Sheriff Dominquez died in Nuevo Laredo as described above.

* * *

In his cell bunk, Ben Krahl was sleepless. The New Year had come and gone without reason to celebrate.

Here in Green Bay Correctional Center, the monotony of routine was marked by such grand events as a meal with real bacon for the first time in years. Ben thought how nice it would be to eat a good meal. And even nicer to control the subject of his dreams. He had no choice in either matter.

If he could, he would dream of Nancy when they were together. He thought about the good times they had. There was that last Thanksgiving dinner with his son, Jarrod. They had been especially close, the three of them laughing and joking around with each other. If only it could be like that again.

Now Jarrod was getting married, and he would not be there to stand beside his son. There would be grandchildren he couldn't see except on visitor days. Grandchildren that must be told their grandfather is locked up in a place where bad people live.

Would his grandchildren think he was a bad man? Of course Jarrod had never doubted his innocence. Ben thanked God for that.

And he had many faithful friends who could never be persuaded that he had pulled that trigger. God, it was good to have friends who believed in you! Their faith in his innocence meant a lot. But faith couldn't change his years in the pen. Or the 37 more joyless new years he had yet to serve in this place. Long, monotonous years ahead, caged in with angry men, dull routine work and nasty food. He had no power to change even one day of the years stretching endlessly ahead of him in this place where bad men live, many of them getting out one day to continue unraveling the threads of civil order.

Ben groaned softly. He longed only for a chance to walk again in the sunlight with his son and maybe hold his future grandson's little hand one day. He was discouraged with the never-ending appeal process. But he hadn't given up hope.

Nate Cash was working hard on the investigation. Sure it was a cold case, but Cash was persistent. He would find out something. There had to be a break soon.

It was the gray side of a cheerless dawn before Ben slept again. He dreamed of a meal with real bacon.

March, 2003

Chapter 18 – Nate's Report

Nate Cash was dead. Impossible. Tia could not believe it.

She'd just spent an evening in his office that very week going over a summary of his investigation. After months of dogged determination, by early March of 2003, Nate thought he was getting very close to naming a suspect. And now he was gone. A sudden heart attack in his sleep!

Their laugh over a good joke was never going to happen. Another door had slammed shut in her life with the same terrible finality she had already experienced far too early.

Her heart went out to Nate's wife, daughter and son. She went home from the news office that night and wept before settling into bed, unable to stop thinking about her last conversations with Nate in vivid detail. Earlier that very week she'd met him once again at Grandma's Restaurant. It had been both an exhilarating and disappointing meeting.

"Ben Krahl didn't shoot Nancy Jurowski, but I can't prove it yet," Nate had told her.

"Yes!" Tia slapped the table. "I knew it!" She remembered the genuine perplexity in his sky blue eyes. How surprised and disappointed he was by the lack of response from the state's attorney's office.

"I've sat through a lot of court cases over the years. And I've covered lots of trials as a journalist. I've never seen a case bungled as badly at this one," Nate began. "You've got a murder with no gun ever found, not a shred of physical evidence pointing to the suspect, no motive and no credible eyewitness. Krahl never had a hint of violence in his background. No criminal record. There was no proof he ever owned a gun."

Nate's eyes were filled with disbelief. He had developed a detailed minute-by-minute account of what happened on the night of Nancy's murder, documented by phone records and security surveillance video cameras. He had even performed his own ballistics tests, proving that the second and third shots were fired from different locations from where Ben was seen simultaneously by witnesses.

He'd also developed a list of people who were associated with three violent street gangs—people who were there on the night of the Jurowski murder, subjects with histories of deadly violence, including murder, drug dealing and gun running.

"I believe one of these gang bangers killed Nancy and the others were involved," he had told Tia, his voice measured and filled with conviction.

Several weeks before his last conversation with Tia, Nate had turned over the summary of his findings to Black Woods County State's Attorney James Laloggia. Along with it was a letter stating he'd developed suspects who were now in prison, one of them for the drive-by shooting of Pamela Primm in October of 2002. He believed he was at a point in the investigation where he needed help from officialdom to continue.

"Maybe I'm just incredibly naïve, but I honestly thought Laloggia would reopen the investigation," Nate said the regretful words with incredulity in his voice. "I don't have the authority to question these suspects myself."

Anxious to know more, Tia asked him about the suspects.

"On that night at the Green Onion Grill, Nancy and Ben walked out into a den of rattlesnakes," Nate began, a look of keen disappointment and something else in his eyes. "There were drug dealers, gang bangers, killers and gun runners. There's no evidence the police ever questioned them or even knew they were there. Lord, you don't ignore the snakes in a murder investigation and go after the rabbit!"

He went over some of his findings with Tia, giving her copies of his report and a summary of his investigation. He cautioned her not to reveal the suspects' names, with a warning. "These are dangerous people."

Tia had not opened the large manila envelope containing the report.

She remembered all too well the evil voice on the phone which had left her shaken on two occasions. The very recollection made her pull her blankets more tightly around her, and turn up her night-light rheostat. Leave the investigating to the pros, she thought. She didn't want any more late night phone calls or vans following her. That hadn't happened since she'd put her Krahl stories on hold for these past few months, pending the result of Nate's investigation.

His envelope, marked "Confidential," was sitting in a drawer of her nightstand. Now was the time to open it.

Laloggia's office was not going to budge. When she'd run into him at the courthouse one day and asked him about the status of Nate's investigation, he'd admitted, "Yes, the Mackenzie Park investigators were not exactly thorough with their investigation." She recalled the almost sheepish apology in his eyes. However, Laloggia also was on firm legal footing by refusing to reopen the investigation. After all, the jury had found Ben guilty. Whether Ben committed the crime or not, he *was still guilty* in the eyes of the law. "I'm going to need a smoking gun before I have legal grounds to warrant a new trial," he had told her.

A smoking gun. The court didn't need a smoking gun to put Ben in prison, she thought. They didn't need any gun! Why do they need one to get him out? That's the way the law works?

"The criminal justice system is not perfect, but it's still the best system of any in the world," investigators and lawyers kept saying blithely, whenever she brought up the possibility of an innocent man in prison.

True, she agreed, but that still doesn't excuse a wrongful conviction, due to an improper investigation. There were far too many of those in Illinois. During Illinois Governor George Ryan's term of office, an astounding 13 death row inmates had been in headlines after evidence showed them to be wrongfully convicted, one of them only hours away from execution at the time his guilt was questioned. The poor guy's family had already picked out burial clothes. That's one big, disastrous legal error that could never be reversed, Tia fumed inwardly.

The Chicago Tribune began reporting a history of Cook County police "flaws," had implied tortured confessions, and investigations hampered by "tunnel-vision" as these stories continued to break throughout the years 2000, 2001 and 2002.

From Northwestern University's Center on Wrongful Convictions, Edwin Colfax had pointed out some very questionable police tactics (again implying tortured confessions). Colfax was quoted in the Chicago Tribune as saying, "If there was nothing illegal in these investigations, then what does that say about our system that we can have such a horrible result?"

Governor George Ryan called for a moratorium on the death penalty on January 30, of 2000, even though he had campaigned as a supporter of capital punishment. The death penalty at that time had been in effect in Illinois since 1977. Twelve men had been executed. How many of them were not guilty? Tia wondered with mounting horror at the thought.

As a result of Ryan's moratorium on capital punishment, a new state mandate came down that police should videotape interrogations and confessions in murder cases. Another package of reforms would allow judges to rule out the death penalty in cases that rest largely on a single eyewitness or informant. Ben Krahl's conviction rested on a single eyewitness, but the judge had sentenced him to 40 years—not death—so he was not among those who received Ryan's consideration.

Tia knew that people don't always live long lives in prison where medical care can be delayed and meals aren't prepared with the greatest nutritional value in mind.

Something as simple as a power failure can be deadly for a convict. During one bitterly cold snap, Illinois prisoner Charles Platcher was left in solitary confinement on a strip-cell suicide watch in Menard Correctional Center. He was given no clothing and only a single blanket. Apparently, no one bothered to check his cell during the power outage. When the Center's heating system failed, Charles died of hypothermia.

(*true story.)

How easy it would be to give up if no one cared whether you lived or died.

Some prisoners run out of hope and simply lose the will to live. How long would Ben survive?

Before he left office in January of 2003, Governor George Ryan fully pardoned four men and commuted the death sentences of 167 others to life, thereby emptying death row. Unfortunately, there was no DNA evidence to implicate or exonerate Ben Krahl.

Okay, thought Tia, maybe Ben is not going to get a new trial. And maybe the private investigation is not going anywhere now that Nate is gone. But he still has me, for whatever that's worth. She opened her nightstand drawer, pulled out Nate's large manila envelope, marked "Confidential," and began to read.

The night of the murder unfolded in vivid detail, carefully documented by Nate. He described how Nancy and Ben stopped by Rip Tyson's Christmas-tree lot that evening near the scuba shop. Ben and Rip were having a "few" beers while Nancy looked for the perfect tree. Ben wanted her to take all the time she needed, promising to buy her any tree on the lot. Nate surmised this probably meant Ben was enjoying a few beers with Rip in addition to indulging Nancy.

The couple drove back to her bungalow where he helped her set up the tree, then kissed her cheek and said he was on his way to deliver a present to her mother, Cecelia.

Does this sound like the actions of a man who is planning to kill his girlfriend? No, Tia thought. Premeditated murder was definitely out. Why bother taking the victim's mother a Christmas gift? Why bother buying an expensive plane ticket for Nancy if he intended to kill her? He would have had to be very conniving and unbelievably clever to plan the murder, adding those pleasant details just to make himself look innocent. Too clever to shoot Nancy in parking lot filled with witnesses.

Finding that Cecelia was not at home, Ben drove to the Green Onion Grill in Mackenzie Park where he joined his friend Rocky Miller around 8:30 p.m. The two had been friends for a long time and saw each other almost everyday, either working together at a part-time refrigeration installation business after their day jobs or just "hanging out."

This part-time work was significant in that Rocky had testified the reason he did not name Ben as the shooter at first was because he had been "afraid his business would suffer." In fact he did not own any business. It was part-time work by referral only, making his supposed fear groundless.

Once again Tia questioned, why would Rocky even hesitate to accuse Ben if he really believed Ben fired at him too? If my best friend turned a gun on me I'd want the police to know it immediately before the gunner had another chance to shoot me, she said out loud to the empty room.

Did Ben and Rocky drink together? Not often. The two most enjoyed playing their guitars and making music together. On this night, Nate indicated Ben and Rocky each drank "another beer or two."

How many beers had Ben downed before the evening's violent end? He had started drinking beer earlier at the Christmas-tree lot. Nate described him as glassy-eyed and "probably skunk drunk" by the time of the murder. Very poor planning for a premeditated murder.

A man clever enough to plan the shooting would surely have wanted to stay sober. After all, he would need a steady hand to fire the gun and go through the resulting interrogation that was certain to follow.

Ben telephoned Nancy from the bar and asked her to join them for a late supper. Of course she would be there. They were going together to his office holiday dinner the next night, and she wanted to talk about seating arrangements.

Nancy had asked Cass to come with her to the Green Onion. Tia once again noted the friendship of these two women. If Nancy feared Cass as a rival for Ben's affection, why bother asking her to come along? Cass stopped by Nancy's house to help her finish decorating the tree before they left together.

Tia could visualize Nancy driving her car to the Green Onion Grill, parking and pulling her coat around her tightly as she walked toward the restaurant.

The temperature had already dipped below freezing and would soon drop to 28 degrees by midnight.

The parking lot was full, the bar packed. Next door at The Game Place, nearly 200 teenagers and young adults were arriving to dance to DJ music and play video games. The Sandwich Shoppe, a few doors to the north and the Dollar Video on the west were also busy.

Around the corner of the L-shaped strip mall, employees of a telemarketing company were still making calls.

The whole area was hopping with activity.

Cass arrived and parked her car in the same row as Nancy's car, nine stalls down and almost directly in front of the Sandwich Shoppe. She hurried inside and joined Ben and Nancy at a table in the back of the restaurant.

Rocky remained seated at the bar. He seemed "fidgety" and was described as having "his nose out of joint" by the bartenders Nate had interviewed. What was bothering him?

Ben and Cass ordered drinks, but Nancy had only a single glass of beer.

The three ordered dinner and afterwards joined Rocky, Rip and another couple at the bar. Everyone was enjoying the evening, except maybe Rocky. "What's wrong with Rock?" Nancy asked when he walked away, presumably to visit the Men's room.

"Oh, he's just in one of his moods," said Ben with a shrug and a grin. Everyone was laughing at one of Rip's corny jokes. When Rocky returned, he walked over to Cass, leaned down and sniffed long and loud at the back of her neck, saying, "You smell good."

Tia knew from talking with Cass that she didn't like it when Miller acted flirtatious. After all, he was a married man. Miller and his wife were not yet divorced at this time. Cass took another sip of her drink and tried to ignore him. Everyone else seemed to be in high spirits, unaffected by Rocky's sour disposition.

Outside in the inky night, shadowy figures showed up on the surveillance video cameras as they crisscrossed the parking lot, using pay phones, walking to the Game Place in the strip mall and walking out again.

Dangerous people.

Tia's eyes widened when she read Nate's reports, which included police records on these people. Their run-ins with the law showed they were gang members from an underworld of drug dealing, gun running and deadly violence.

One of the vehicles in the parking lot that night was registered to a man with a homicide conviction already on his record. Another man later died in a gang-related shooting. Still another had gone to prison just last October for the drive-by shooting of Rockford woman, Pamela Primm.

Tia's eyes widened further when she read the rap sheets of these individuals. Any of them had already proved quite capable of murder. She recalled Nate's words, *"What were the police thinking? Good Lord! You don't overlook the rattlesnakes and go after the rabbit."*

Again she was impressed with Nate's thoroughness. He'd documented the time sequence from surveillance videos and phone records. At 12:15 a.m., mall Security Officer Ed Lock had been watching a suspicious character in a bomber jacket circling the parking lot for several minutes. The image of a shark circling its victim crossed Tia's mind. Ed decided to approach him. "What are you doing?"

"None of your f---n business," the man snarled.

"I said what are you doing?" Ed repeated firmly.

The man answered, "I'm waiting for someone in the bar," and kept walking.

Why didn't he go inside? It was freezing out there.

Ed watched the guy for awhile, anxious to go off duty at 12:30 a.m. He had a girlfriend waiting for him. After that, he didn't really care what the lurker was up to.

Later Ed identified a jacket in a catalogue as the one worn by the mystery man. It was a Dallas Cowboys jacket with a large, five-pointed star on the back. Significantly, this is the preferred attire for members of the Cobra Kings gang.

Shortly after 1:10 a.m., Rocky received the first of a sequence of calls on his cell phone (verified by Nate through phone records.) The call came from inside the bar. The second call coming from the bar phone to Rocky was made at 1:12 a.m.

It's a known fact that Rocky carried guns in his van. A waitress at the Green Onion was on the record, stating he had shown his firearms to her on one occasion. Ben had never owned a firearm.

At 1:13 a.m. a couple left the game place. They walked in the direction of Bill Haight's car, parked not far from Nancy's vehicle, moving in a direct line of intersection with Nancy's path. The woman, Jenny Trubb, was approximately Nancy's height and weight and was wearing a similar coat. She also had blonde hair, like Nancy. Both women were known to drive red cars. Could the shooter possibly have mistaken Nancy for Jenny?

It was a very real possibility, according to Nate's report. He'd uncovered some indirect links between Jenny Trubb and other people with criminal histories. At 1:14 a.m. the parking lot's streetlights blinked off by an automatic timer. Darkness settled like a blanket over the lot.

A shadowy figure could be observed on the video surveillance tape striding left on the sidewalk in front of the game place. Nate thought this figure might be the same character that Ed had seen earlier circling the parking area. Of great significance, that man's jacket and ball cap matched the first description Rocky had given of the gunman.

A third call from the bar phone was made to Rocky's cell phone at 1:19 a.m.

A pair of employees left the Game Place and walked to their cars in the row behind Cass and Nancy's vehicles. Tia read Nate's notation that despite close proximity to the shooting, these employees were never interviewed. Another police omission.

One of these persons later joined the Navy and was unreachable. The other one, Nate had learned, was a male stripper who had since relocated to Chicago. It was this person that Nate had been trying to contact on the day of his death.

Tia read on, fascinated with the report.

Ben helped Nancy into her coat, buttoned his jacket and they walked out together with Cass. Rocky already had walked out ahead of them, even though he testified at the trial that they all walked out together.

There is a parallel underworld in existence on the streets of Woodsville. By daylight, motorists and shoppers pass through its boundaries, staying on their own well-trodden paths, untouched and unknowing. By night, this world is filled with danger, drug dealing and violence, and sometimes, even the most innocent can become its victims.

Nancy was stepping into that world. A veritable "snake pit" of unsavory characters according to Nate's report. The darkness was thick. The night bitterly cold.

Nancy and Ben stopped at Cass' car for a moment to say their goodnights, then walked on. Cass unlocked the driver's door, turned on the ignition to warm up her car, and turned the stereo volume up. She had just completed two swipes with an ice scraper across her windshield when she heard Nancy's scream.

Facing in the direction of Nancy's car, Cass yelled, "What the heck is your problem?" Nancy stood nearer the back of her car and a figure beside the driver's door stood facing her, his arm outstretched, pointing a gun at Nancy's head.

Because of the darkness, Cass could not make out the shooter's face or features.

Tia made a note: This is significant because Rocky Miller said he was approximately 45 yards away—much farther than Cass—when he first claimed he saw someone he could not identify as being black or white because of the darkness. If he couldn't discern ethnicity, how could he suddenly decide it was Ben, he saw?

Terrified, Cass dropped to her knees instantly and tried to crawl under the vehicle in a desperate attempt to hide. Just a little over two months earlier, Cass's cocaine-addicted ex-boyfriend had been shot to death in a drug-related shooting.

All this violence in Cass's life. No wonder the young woman did not want to stay alone the next night. Another point Tia jotted down on her notebook—If Cass and Ben were lovers and planned the killing together, as prosecutors theorized she would have had no reason to fear the gunman. Yet, the Brandon's recalled how terrified Cass was at Nancy's funeral, "almost jumping out of her skin" at the sound of a car backfiring near the event.

Clearly, this was a woman in fear for her own life from someone other than Ben Krahl.

According to Nate's report, at 1:25:09 a.m. Cass heard four or five shots in rapid succession. She saw Ben's feet and legs near the back of her car . . . much farther from where the gunman was standing. She saw Ben moving as if dodging bullets.

Why dodge bullets if he were the shooter? So he's going to shoot up in the air and pretend to dodge bullets at the same time? Tia muttered to herself.

Ben testified that he had kissed Nancy goodnight and had walked away a few steps (one report says at least two steps and another says four or five) when he heard the scream and the gunshot behind him.

Inside The Game Place, Denny heard the sound of gunfire while mopping the floor at 1:25:09 a.m. At 1:26:27 a second gunshot shattered his storefront window. Denny dropped his mop and went to the doorway, clearly visible on the surveillance video.

He walked out and saw Ben kneeling by the body, then rising and moving to crouch by a utility pole, as if dodging gunfire. Denny did not see Ben with any gun. The surveillance tape shows it is 1:26:38, barely 12 seconds after the first bullet was fired.

Ben had twelve seconds to hide a gun that nobody ever found. Tia underlined that statement.

He didn't have time to toss it in his pickup, which was parked much farther across the lot, close to Miller's van some 45 yards away. He didn't have time to toss it inside Cass's car where she crouched in terror. Also, she would have heard the door being opened. And this would have been seen on the security videos.

So what did he do? Swallow the darned gun?

Rocky Miller dialed 9-1-1 at 1:26:49 a.m. (only sixty seconds after the shooting and said he was already several blocks away). He gave a detailed description of the gunman, as tall, thin, wearing a ball cap and leather jacket.

Tia noted Rocky was the only one who left the crime scene, other than the gunman.

Nate documented the driving time at fast speed in his own car to this location. It was nearly two minutes away. Did Rocky lie about his location? And if so, why?

Nate had considered Rocky's behavior very suspicious.

At 1:27:11 Ben and Cass burst through the door of the Green Onion grill, Ben yelling, "They shot my girl! Call 9-1-1!"

Nate noted the time—one minute eighteen seconds from the moment the bullet struck the storefront window. Denny met a "very emotional" Ben at 1:27:14 as he ran out into the parking lot. Ben, Rip Tyson, and Denny all ran to Nancy's body to check for a pulse. She was clearly beyond help.

The surveillance videos showed three vehicles fleeing from the parking lot.

From his cell phone, Rocky Miller called the bar at 1:28:34.2, asking, "Is Ben hurt?" Is Ben hurt? Why would Rocky even ask that question if he truly believed Ben was the one carrying the gun? Tia almost snorted in disbelief.

No, Ben wasn't hurt. The bartender told him that Nancy was dead.

Flashing lights indicated arrival of the first squad car at 1:29:54—just under three minutes after Rocky's call. Police vehicles arrived with sirens blaring and lights flashing. Tia marveled at the timeline, combining cell phone records and surveillance video cameras—at least eight of them, including one outdoor camera focused on the back alley.

Nate also included a notation: "There is an unresolved question as to whether additional cameras were focused on the sidewalk and the edge of the parking lot in front of the arcade and the neighboring Green Onion Grill."

He had traced and photographed wiring connectors and brackets. Each camera fed to its own videotaping machine and all were in operation that night, yet only four videotapes were ever logged into evidence.

Missing evidence? What happened to the tapes? And more importantly, why were they missing Nate wrote that he was "loath to infer police had deliberately withheld these videotapes or that the tapes contained the smoking-gun evidence concerning the murder of Nancy Jurowski."

He wanted official permission to interview the Mackenzie Park officers involved in the investigation that night. That permission was never given. The missing tapes clearly puzzled Nate a great deal, and even more so the glaring lack of officialdom to act on his report. He was deeply disappointed, and expressed his shaken confidence in the criminal justice system to Tia with incredulity in those sky blue eyes.

Witnesses at the scene described Ben as enraged, immediately blaming The Game Place owner for allowing drug dealers and gang bangers to hang out there, claiming "those druggies shot my girl!"

The game owner said Ben actually ran to a vehicle in the lot, pounded the driver's window and shouted, "Who did this?" The frightened occupants of the car drove away. One of the arriving officers observed Ben's anger and described him as "wanting to hurt somebody." The officer patted him down, handcuffed him and placed him in the back of his squad car in order to subdue him.

Patted him down. No gun was found on Ben. Ben never left the crime scene.

Prosecutors at the trial argued that he must have thrown the gun into his pickup truck (physically impossible because of it's location) or into Cass's car which was much nearer, challenging the juror's intelligence by saying, "Ladies and gentlemen, you *know* it had to be there."

Why did it have to be there ? Why did the investigators choose to ignore the witnesses who saw an unknown gunman fleeing?

When Tia had talked with Nate earlier in the week, he'd blustered, "It could have been argued just as effectively that the failure of police to report whether they checked the vehicles for the gun deprived Ben Krahl of evidence that could have helped to prove his innocence!"

Nate's incredulous exclamation still rang in her ears. "In all my years of covering trials, I've never seen a case like this—where sloppy police work was used to help convict a suspect!"

Tia felt his disappointment as she continued reading. Mackenzie Park police taped off the crime scene. From nearby Rockford, WROK news hound Fred Speer arrived on the scene. Affectionately known around both Rockford and Woodsville as "Spread Fear" because of the natural excitement in his radio voice, Fred snapped a photo of the body and interviewed police.

Fred later commented to Tia that it was "too dark to see Nancy unless you were standing very near to her body." Like Rip Tyson, Fred also doubted Rocky Miller's ability to see so well from 45 yards across the parking lot.

Rocky covered that doubt at the trial by claiming he recognized Ben's unique gait. But this story was never once mentioned in any police statement. Why should he be allowed to introduce this new twist never mentioned in reports, when the police were not allowed to testify they had searched the vehicles for a gun because they left it out of their reports? Tia snorted again.

Officers drove Cass and Ben to the Mackenzie Park Police Station to take their statements. Both their vehicles remained behind crime scene ribbon in the lot overnight. An officer drove Cass's car to the station the next morning. He testified at trial that he did not notice whether there was a gun in her vehicle.

Tia thought it highly unlikely that a trained lawman would fail to look for a gun in both vehicles at the onset of a murder investigation. She remembered the police chief telling her he had asked them to check Ben's truck after becoming suspicious. He thought Ben's anger was "inappropriate" for a grieving boyfriend. Once again she ran into the definition of appropriate emotion. Who can set a standard for behavior in the face of trauma?

Rocky arrived at the station in those predawn hours and gave Ben a compassionate hug. Tia raised her eyebrows again.

So, Rocky expects everyone to believe he sees his longtime best friend turn into a homicidal maniac without any previous emotional instability. Sees Ben shoot and kill Nancy. Sees Ben turn the gun and fire at him also—for absolutely no reason. Says he's terrified that Ben is going to kill him too. Yet Rocky walks up and hugs him less than an hour later?!

How could anyone take this man's story seriously? She sputtered with indignation.

Oh yeah. She was forgetting. Police have arrested murderers who killed their victims over a pork chop or a pack of cigarettes. Well, at least those guys had *some* motive. But for Ben to start shooting at the very people he loved most? He would have had to be in the grip of a sudden, unprecedented, psychotic fugue. An instantaneous Jekyll and Hyde transformation.

Whoever fired out of the darkness that night started a chain of events that shattered many lives. Nancy's many hopes and youthful dreams were blasted out of existence in one terrible instant. Her scream cut short. Her nightmare over before it began.

For Ben, the nightmare had only just begun.

March 2003

Chapter 19 – After The Murder

Rocky, Ben and Cass went to Ben's place after they left the police station that morning. Shaken and still very tearful, Cass sobbed, "I can't stay by myself tonight. The shooter may be coming for me next."

That was the first morning of Ben's nightmare.

Rocky Miller went home, but he called the next day and wanted Ben to go trap shooting. Ben was really not up for it. Miller later arrived at Ben's place, nervously looking over his shoulder. "I think someone was following me," he said to Ben (and later to Karla and Beuford Brandon). He stayed with Ben for a couple of hours to offer whatever comfort he could.

A few days later, Ben's nightmare grew even more intense. Rocky changed his original statement completely. Instead of a tall figure wearing a bomber jacket and shooting at Nancy, he claimed it was Ben he saw walking across the parking lot with his arm outstretched and then firing the gun. Rocky had been through the wringer from repeated interrogations. He'd failed his lie detector test. Like Cass and Ben, Rocky was stressed to the max.

Tia read the relevant questions which the polygraph report registered as answered falsely.

Was Ben the man you saw with his arm raised toward Nancy at the time you saw a flash and heard the gunfire? Yes. (a lie)

Did you see Ben Krahl fire a gun?

Yes. (another lie)

Before you walked out of the Green Onion Grill that night, did you know Nancy was going to be killed?

Yes. (another lie, which Rocky recanted on the stand at the post conviction relief hearing.) In that hearing, he said he never heard Ben threaten Nancy.)

Tia asked herself if Rocky had really known that was Ben's intent, why on earth wouldn't he try to stop the murder from happening? Why keep up such a front of loyalty to Ben? Why was he lying? The police had absolutely no evidence against him or against Ben.

What had caused him to change his story?

Nate's report pointed out that the very next day after failing the polygraph, a very nervous Rocky Miller agreed to make a pretext call to Ben while the state police investigators recorded it (the tape is referred to in court records as the "overhear" tape).

Rocky seemed to believe, or *pretended* to believe, he could get incriminating statements from Ben during the call. Tia had a copy of that tape included in Nate Cash's report. Until now, she had left it in the envelope.

Okay, it's time to hear this, she decided. She popped it into her tape player and listened.

Rocky Miller called Ben at his workplace and spoke in an edgy, nervous voice. He started the conversation with a comment. "Ben, Cass called me and asked me if I was still sane. Ben, I'm not sane no more. I've been upset ever since this happened. I have everyone in the world interviewing me and talking to me.

"The cops are torturing me over this, and I need my sanity back. I'm going crazy. I can't eat. I can't sleep. I've lost enough work.

"They're making me feel like a real big suspect, and I had nothing to do with it. And I need to know what to do to save you, *and* save me, Ben. I'm the only witness, and I've got everyone breathing down my neck."

Tia heard Rocky's voice rising with excitement and self-pity on the tape. That's when he started accusing Ben. "Why'd you do it?"

Ben answered in a calm, almost fatherly tone of voice, "Come on buddy, I was there."

Instead of calming down, Rocky's voice rose to an even higher pitch. "I know what I saw! I know what I saw! And I have to tell them."

Ben hesitated before asking calmly, "Then where's the gun?"

Rocky ignored that question, repeating that he had to tell the cops what he saw. Ben listened, apparently in shocked silence. Tia waited for his response.

Finally he answered with calm, measured words, "Well then tell them what you think you saw." His entire telephone manner, while being accused, indicated that he had nothing to hide. That he was shocked and disappointed at the accusation coming from his long time friend. Significantly, that part of the taped conversation was never played in the courtroom—a wise decision on the part of the prosecution, since it lent credibility to Ben's defense.

Rocky suggested the two of them should meet at a burger place after work to talk, but Ben had a better idea. "No, we'll go to the police station."

Ben was taking a very calculated risk to make that suggestion, if in fact he had everything to hide, Tia noted. Would a guilty man want to be confronted in front of police? She didn't think so. He did exactly what she would have done if she had been in the same spot. Let's get this out in the open. If you think you've got anything to prove what you're accusing me of, let's go tell the cops. I want them to know about it, because they're going to see how wrong you are.

The two men ended up at the State Police headquarters in the federal building in downtown Woodsville. That was the night. Fourteen hours of grueling, emotionally numbing, exhausting, brainwashing, mind-game playing, sanity-ripping interrogation.

Tia could picture Rocky and Ben grilled in separate rooms. She had read Ben's letter describing it. Cass went through an equally grueling seven-hour interrogation. Tricky questions can elicit incriminating responses. Interrogators informed Cass, "Ben Krahl has confessed to the murder." Even after she started to believe them, Cass maintained her original statement. "No, I did not see him shoot the gun."

Then they asked, "If you can't say for certain that he did it, can you say with absolute certainty that he did not?"

Cass finally answered, "Okay, if you tell me he did it, then I'll agree. She couldn't understand why they didn't arrest Ben at once, and she immediately stopped all contact with him.

Words from Ben's first letter came back to Tia's mind. "Rocky and Cass were each broken in different ways by the interrogation experience."

According to Nate, Cass later sought help from a counselor and willingly submitted to hypnosis, convinced by the police that she had repressed memories of the shocking event. If she was in denial about anything, she wanted to know it.

Later Cass came to the conclusion she had not repressed anything. "I saw the gunman near Nancy. I saw Ben closer to my car at the same time, so that's how I know he didn't do it," she said to Nate and also to Tia on several occasions. "Ben couldn't be in two places at once."

Tia wondered how easy it had been for Rocky to finger his best friend. It was obvious from these reports and especially the overhear tape that he was in the grip of a terrible fear. She remembered reading and underlining one of his statements in the police reports. The officer asked, "What are you afraid of Rocky?"

He'd answered, "Of not spending the rest of my life with my wife and my kids." Very likely he believed they were going to pin the murder on him.

Interrogators suggested sarcastically, "If Ben didn't do it, then who did? Maybe the Easter Bunny?" They also tried to get Ben to tell them Rocky did it, pointing out how Rocky acted very suspiciously, leaving the scene and calling back to ask if Ben was hurt.

Ben refused to say that Rocky was the killer.

Unfortunately, Rocky wasn't as generous to Ben. From the time he failed his lie detector test, he began pointing his finger at his best friend. Why would he lie if he had nothing to hide?

Rocky's wife also was terrified. One of the police officers had observed Mrs. Miller waiting in her car outside Rocky's workplace. He described her as "crying, trembling, biting her nails, and staring fixedly straight ahead." What had caused that kind of anxiety?

Tia read over the security guard's description of the mystery man circling the parking lot. He said the guy was wearing a bomber jacket with a star emblem on the back. The shooter also wore a bomber jacket, according to Rocky's first description.

Nate's report documented several gang members in bomber jackets at the scene that night by phone records and by the surveillance tapes. He had become convinced one of the gang wanted Nancy dead.

But who?

And why?

March 2003

Chapter 20 —The Innocent Don't Go To Prison

Nate's report was an eye opener. Tia wasn't able to digest it all in one reading. She took it with her to the news office the next morning, thinking that innocent suspects just don't go to jail. Like most people, educated by television cop dramas and crime novels, Tia had always believed that sooner or later, detectives always get their man—the right man.

However, Nate Cash and every cop in town said that the first arriving investigators had botched the job at the crime scene. One Woodsville desk sergeant had even commented, "Those guys could screw up a two-car funeral parade."

What she'd read in Nate's report the night before urged her to take up Krahl's story once more. She shoved the thought of threatening calls to the back of her mind. What could she write about next? She truly did not want to offend the state's attorney, or the Mackenzie Park Mayor with her less-than-glowing reports on the police investigation, trial and conviction. She liked both men.

They were dedicated to serving their communities and had done so in many exemplary ways.

The thought of Cap Nemon with his background in criminology had been crossing her mind during the past couple of weeks. It had been almost three months since she'd spoken to him.

With a blush, she thought of that stormy moment on the shooting range, but decided she had made herself perfectly clear she did not want a relationship. Cap had honored her request not to call. In fact, she hadn't heard from him since the Christmas dinner at Carmen's place, an obvious attempt on Carmen's part to play Cupid. Why else would she invite him? Oh sure, people without families were always invited to her holiday table. Or so she said. Carmen's little scheme hadn't worked.

Maybe Cap was seeing someone now. Maybe even Carmen's attractive sister? Tia told herself she hoped he was. Convinced she was in no danger of encouraging him, she decided to call from the news office, hoping to catch him at the college between classes.

"Professor Nemon," he answered, his voice all business and professional.

Tia brushed aside the usual small talk, coming straight to the point. "Cap, it's Tia. I have some questions on homicide investigations. I know you told me the Krahl investigation was flawed. What can you tell me about other homicide investigations that are historically known to be botched? I can call you back if this is a bad time."

Surprised and delighted, Cap tried unsuccessfully to keep the gladness out of his voice, "Criminology Professor Nemon at your service, Miss Reporter Ma'am."

She grabbed her pen to take notes. "Good, I'll only keep you a few minutes. I just need a couple of examples."

Cap grinned to himself and leaned back in his chair. He wanted to keep her on the line if he had to talk all afternoon. And he badly wanted to see her again. But he wouldn't mention that just yet. He'd play along with her and keep this a strictly professional exchange.

Assuming a scholarly tone, he began, "You know of course, the prosecution relies heavily on the actions and observations of the first officers at a crime scene. In some states the state's attorney is even held liable by the defense for any mistakes made by investigators."

"I never knew that."

Cap continued, "Those first 36 to 48 hours are the most crucial in a homicide. That's also the most vulnerable time for mistakes of omission or commission. Whatever suspect the investigators focus on in those first two days is usually the person they develop a case against."

Tia nodded, chewing on her pencil tip. She was thinking that several days had gone by before police finally charged Krahl. "So what if they focus on the wrong man?"

"If they focus on the wrong man—and if he can't afford an attorney who is sharp enough to find the police mistakes—he's more likely to go to prison than the guilty man."

This was important. Tia underlined the words and put a star in the margin. "Can you give me some documented examples of crime-scene investigations gone wrong?"

Cap reached for a textbook lying on his desk. "Sure. Of course the classic example is the O.J. Simpson case back in 1995. One detective wandered off and found the bloody glove all by himself. Nobody was around to witness where he actually found it. Then a forensic tech forgot to refrigerate a blood sample. Another detective kept a vial of blood in his pocket."

He leafed through the pages of the book, continuing, "Defense lawyers had enough ammunition to say the evidence could have been fabricated. That gave the jury enough reasonable doubts that they had to acquit O.J."

Tia remembered how the entire nation had been glued to their television sets during the celebrity football player's highly publicized trial. Too bad Ben hadn't been able to afford the Dream Team defense that won a not-guilty verdict for O.J. Lack of money. She groaned inwardly. Everything always comes down to money.

"So how am I doing?" Cap was enjoying the opportunity to show off some of his own background in criminology and, more importantly, hoping he could make himself valuable to her in some way, until she realized how very much she needed him in her life.

Blazes! The woman was driving him crazy. He felt some disappointment that she didn't seem to have missed him at all. Several times, he'd resisted calling her since Carmen's Christmas dinner. Instead, he'd called Carmen, asking for her take on Tia's feelings.

"Look, I know you like Tia. And the Lord knows she needs someone like you. But Cap, she's still in love with her husband. Nobody is ever going to take Jeff's place in her heart."

"I don't want to take Jeff's place," Cap answered without even thinking twice. "I want to make my own place in her heart."

Carmen paused. She liked that answer, and liked Cap's determination.

"Okay, then maybe you should know this. She has other issues. Did she tell you she's afraid she can't ever have kids?"

Cap swallowed hard. He'd already lost one woman because of his desire to raise a family. Was he really willing to risk getting into another relationship that might cause him that same kind of pain again?

"No. She didn't tell me," but there was never really a good time for her to tell him that, Cap realized even as he spoke the words. He remembered their conversation that day by the river when he'd told her how family was important to him. They were just getting to know each other. He could hardly have expected her to volunteer such personal information then.

Dimly hearing Carmen say, "Well, it's better you know it now, because that may change things for you." Cap silently agreed.

"Leave her alone for awhile and think about it. If she has any feelings for you, she'll come around."

And if you really want a family you better not risk loving a woman who can't give you one, Carmen wanted to add but kept her mouth shut. She could do that sometimes when it was important. This was one of those times.

Cap thanked her for the advice. During the past few weeks, he'd thought a great deal about this woman with the capacity for loving and laughing that he sensed was locked inside her. He'd thought long and hard about what his life would be like without having the family he had always assumed was in his future. And he'd thought about what his life would be without Tia Marie Burgess in it.

In fact he thought of little else. She was one woman he couldn't walk away from. What if she could never give him a family? That was important to him. How important? He wrestled with the question. He didn't know the answer.

When he heard her voice on the phone, he only knew that it had been weeks since he'd seen her and that was entirely too long. He'd already decided to end his waiting game and call Tia that very week. Now, here she was on the phone.

Was Sleeping Beauty starting to thaw a little? This time he would proceed with caution. He thought of those searing kisses on the firing range. The blaze of anger in her eyes. The storm of desire in his veins.

Cap dreamed of kissing her again, and in his dream her lips were willing. He was determined to make that dream come true, no matter how long it took.

"Give me some more examples," Tia asked, vaguely aware of thunder grumbling somewhere near.

"Okay, this is another classic case. In 1954, Doctor Sam Sheppard was tried for the murder of his wife. During the initial investigation, a crime-scene officer flushed a floating cigarette butt down the toilet bowl. That sounds so insignificant," he paused, also aware that a spring thunderstorm was loudly announcing its presence.

"Go on," Tia prompted.

"The cigarette butt was important because Sam and his wife were not smokers. It shows that someone else was in the house. There were also massive amounts of blood-splatter evidence, which got ignored or misinterpreted until years later. And you know the story. Sam went to prison for the next ten years until 1966 when F. Lee Bailey got him a second trial."

Tia had read that Dr. Sheppard had died in 1970, a bitter and broken man. She thought his story very tragic.

Comfortable with the conversation now, she felt glad she had tapped Cap's extensive knowledge as a resource. Of course she could have gone to the library but that would have taken hours of reading time.

Cap pictured her sitting on his knee as he expounded. Then he dismissed the pleasantly inviting thought. "Now it's your turn. What are you finding in your second look at the Jurowski homicide?" He asked her, assuming she was back on track with the Krahl story.

"I'm disappointed with the Mackenzie Park police."

Cap listened.

"They should have checked him out from the start, for his own protection. The spouse or boyfriend is always the most logical suspect, sadly enough. Because most murders are committed by someone known to the victim."

Tia put down her pen and notebook. "They didn't have any evidence against him. If it hadn't been for that stupid Vietnam lie he told! It cast doubt on everything he said from then on."

"You're talking about the story he'd been telling to impress Nancy's military father." Cap's voice took on a mock-serious tone, "Well, Tia, any guy who lies to make himself out to be a war hero always murders his girlfriend. Everyone knows that."

"Always," she picked up his satire, "Just think. Ben told that story for years. That means he's probably even a serial killer!"

"I never thought of that. A serial killer!" Cap exclaimed with mock excitement.

She almost chuckled, thinking about the headline she could write for a story like that one. "We should alert the city detectives to check all their unsolved murders. Ben has told this lie for over a dozen years, so he's gotta be guilty of crimes during all those years! You know what the prosecutor said. An innocent man doesn't lie. Police could probably clear their cold case files!"

Cap's tone of voice turned from playful to serious. "Any homicide detective focuses on four things during an investigation. Motive, opportunity, means, and physical evidence. They decided his motive was Cass Peters. Prosecutors couldn't prove it, but if they suggested it strongly, the jury would buy it."

Tia joined in with his analysis of the trial. "They said he had a gun. They never found it, but so what? Some people in Illinois have been convicted for murder without police ever finding a body."

A louder clap of thunder let them know the angry storm was much closer.

Cap reached for the mouse on his computer and clicked it to Shut Down. "Just by being there, Ben had the opportunity." Then he wanted to know, "What actual forensic evidence did the police have that pointed to Ben? Did they test for gunpowder residue on his clothes and hands to see if he had fired a gun?"

"Yes. He didn't have any gunpowder residue. They tested his clothes for blood splatters. He didn't have any. These tests should have been performed immediately, but they were done within a time frame that still would have gotten results."

Cap leaned back in his desk chair, groping for anything to keep her on the line. "Let's get back to motive. Who could have benefited from her death?"

"Nobody that I'm aware of. Ben had already paid back the money Nancy put into the house they were going to share. And she had moved out. He was free to see other women. He had absolutely no reason to kill her." She recalled Nancy's sister and boyfriend, threatened with losing their child, but dismissed the thought.

Picking up a pencil, Cap drew a huge question mark. "There has to be something you're missing. What did the twelve jury members see that you aren't seeing?"

"They saw a talented prosecutor cajoling the jury. Taunting them with words like *ladies and gentlemen you know the gun had to be there.* Pointing a finger at Ben and saying he lied from the beginning of the investigation. Although what a fifteen-year-old lie about Viet Nam had to do with a murder investigation is beyond

149

me. They saw the prosecutor waving a so-called confession in front of them. That goes a long way toward convincing any jury. Why would an innocent man confess to a crime he did not commit? Of course the jury had no idea of the grueling interrogation he'd been through, and when they asked to read a copy of his confession statement, it was withheld. I've read it, Cap. Ben never confessed to murder. But the jury thought he did."

Silently agreeing, Cap had just finished reading Stanley Cohen's book, "The Wrong Men," which documents one hundred cases of wrongful convictions across the country. Many of them due to false confessions and lying witnesses.

He summarized, "The jury believed Ben had confessed, and then good ol' buddy Rocky pointed the finger at him."

"That was the clincher. The eyewitness claiming he'd seen Ben holding the gun. Of course the jury never heard that Rocky changed his story sixteen times. That's prosecutorial misconduct if you ask me, and it's in the court records. I was there when the prosecutor admitted it on the stand at Ben's post-conviction-relief hearing."

"What bothers you most about the case?"

"All of it. I don't see any history of violence in Ben. He never owned a gun. Rocky's story is full of holes. I've been to that parking lot in the dark and there's no way I could recognize anybody as far away as from where he stood. I don't like it that Nancy was stalked during the last week of her life. I'm really bothered by the barefoot man with the fake beard. And the missing videotapes which could possibly have shown the shooter."

"Did the jury ever hear *any* discrepancies at all in Rocky's testimony?"

Tia was quick with the answer. "Here's one huge discrepancy. He said he first lied about the gunman being Ben because he was afraid it would hurt his business. Rocky never owned a business. He and Ben did some refrigeration work together after hours, but it was more of a freelance thing by word of mouth referral."

"Do you know how far Ben was from Nancy when she was shot?"

"Not far. Cass Peters was parked nine stalls away from Nancy's car. She saw Ben much closer to her car at the time she saw the gunman. That's how she knows he didn't do it."

Cap nodded as he listened. "And you believe Cass is telling the truth?"

"I sat face to face with Cass in Nate Cash's office for over two hours one evening right before Nate died. She's straight on. The only one who never changed her story—not a single time from the beginning," Tia explained.

She continued with an edge to her voice, "And I can tell you this. What they put that poor girl through for seven hours made her a basket case. They played games with her mind. Here, let me read Cass's statement from my notes. 'The cops convinced me I didn't see what happened, that my mind wouldn't allow me to believe someone I knew would kill, so they said I blocked out stuff. I don't think I blocked out anything. I saw the gunman, the flash, and I dropped to the pavement. I could see Ben's feet much closer to my car, and that's why I know he didn't do it.'"

Silence on the receiver, but she could hear Cap coughing slightly and a radio in the background occasionally crackling with static.

"Tell me more about Cass."

Tia was glad to oblige. "Police convinced Cass she'd failed her lie detector test. She didn't fail it. They told her Ben had confessed to the murder. He didn't confess. She wanted him arrested and refused to speak with him. She didn't know what to believe. In fact, she even underwent hypnosis later in order to resurface any suppressed memory. Why would she do that if she knew all along that Ben was the killer?"

The sound of rain began drumming loudly on the rooftop of her building. Tia remembered she should turn off her computer when the air was charged. She clicked the mouse to the shutdown command.

"Okay, let's look at the victim's mother. You said she believes Ben killed her daughter. A mother's intuition is not usually that far off."

"Cap, this mother did not suspect Ben until after police zeroed in on him. Until then she had found him charming. Of course now she hates him. Says he's guilty because he didn't show his emotions at the funeral."

As he listened, he still had a hard time believing that a jury would convict an innocent man. But he had to admit the prosecutor had a strong case, even without forensic evidence. A case built on lies, a so-called confession, and a suggested motive. He saw lots of room for serious reasonable doubt which had been withheld from the jury.

"You haven't written anything on Ben's case for a few months."

"No. I was waiting on Nate's report. Hoping that he would give Laloggia enough reason to reopen the investigation. Now that Nate's gone, and there's still no smoking gun, I'm looking into it again."

"Nate found some good stuff?"

"He has enough to point to more than one suspect. There's the gang members showing up on the surveillance tapes. There's the drug-link. There's the possibility of a mistaken identity. But Nate believed there was a link between the gang members and another murder. A drive by shooting of a Pamela Primm in Rockford last October."

"Any more threatening phone calls?" Cap was concerned but kept his voice casual.

"No. Nothing." She almost added, not since I haven't been writing anything on the Jurowski homicide, but thought better of it.

Thunder rolled and static crackled on the line. Cap was thinking it mirrored the electricity between the two of them if Tia would only admit it. She likes me, he assured himself. She just doesn't know it yet. Aloud he asked, "So what's your next angle?"

"I don't know exactly. I'm planning on reading the rest of Nate's report this evening. Maybe I'll find a springboard for another article."

"Here's something that might interest you. I've got my name on the visitor's list to see Ben Krahl this Saturday. He's been temporarily transferred to Dixon in Illinois for one of his many post conviction relief appeals. If you've never met the man face to face, you might like to go along."

"How did you manage that?"

"I'm going with Rip. He's been on Krahl's visitor list for a long time." What Cap did not mention was that he'd deliberately added Tia's name to Krahl's visitor list, planning to lure her into going with him to visit Ben. Her call to his office could not have come at a more opportune time.

Tia thought about it only seconds. She had wanted the opportunity to interview Ben face to face for a long time, but it was a long drive to the Correctional Center in Green Bay. A small percentage of Wisconsin convicts were temporarily housed in the nearby Dixon Correctional facility by agreement with the state of Illinois in order to expedite transports back and forth to the Black Woods County Courthouse during their court proceedings. Ben was going to be there a short time. This might be her only chance to meet him in person without having to make the long drive to Green Bay.

Since Rip was going along, it could hardly be considered a date if she joined the two of them.

A sudden thunderous explosion caused Tia to jump. Lightning played a hide-and-peek game in brilliant flashes outside the office windows. She knew she should get off the phone.

"Okay. Sure. What time?"

Pleased, Cap offered, "We'll pick you up at 8 a.m." He hung up before she could change her mind, and began whistling a tuneless melody, already thinking up a slightly devious plan for the next day. Only slightly deceitful, he rationalized with a mischievous twinkle in his eyes. She would thank him for it later, he decided. He smiled with anticipation.

Tia turned her attention to routine proof reading again and caught a disastrous typo—the reversal of the *t* and *i* in the words MARITAL ARTS Demonstration should have read Martial Arts Demonstration. She blushed at the mistake's implication. But her thoughts soon turned to the visit to Dixon tomorrow.

At last, she was going to meet Ben Krahl. What would she be able to see by looking into his eyes? What might she learn from talking with him?

March, 2003

Chapter 21 – Motorcycle Ride

The doorbell chimed at 7:55 a.m. Cap and Rip at her door already.

Tia grabbed her jacket and headed for the door, looking forward to the day she was finally going to meet Ben Krahl face to face.

"Good morning, your majesty," said Cap with a flourishing attempt at a courtly bow.

Buttoning her jacket, Tia answered, "Well it must take royalty to know royalty, so who are you? The King of Fantasy?"

"That's me. May I escort you to your chariot?"

"If any of my neighbors see you behaving that way, they'll escort you to the Janet Wattles Center over in Rockford," Tia advised with an arched eyebrow. She pictured Cap at the center where mentally ill patients receive treatment. Of course he'd be surrounded by adoring nurses catering to his every whim.

Undaunted, Cap took her arm and escorted her down the stairs to the parking lot.

There was no jeep. No Rip Tyson's scuba van. And no Rip Tyson.

Instead there was a Harley-Davidson Road King, dazzling in the morning sunlight bouncing off its silver chrome. "What's going on?" She asked suspiciously. Her eyes narrowed, searching Cap's face.

Avoiding her eyes, he answered nonchalantly, "Rip said something came up at the scuba shop, so I decided to come without him. And since the sleet last night seems to have washed away the last remains of winter, I thought maybe we'd take the Harley to Dixon."

For a moment Tia almost reconsidered. But the rare March morning was sun-washed with promise of an early spring day. And the rare chance of an interview with Ben was something she did not want to miss. Besides, she loved Harleys.

"Here's your helmet. Try it on for size," Cap was saying as he buckled her chinstrap. "You look sensational!"

"Then I'm taking it off right now," she answered, a warning against flirtation flashed in her eyes.

"Okay, you look . . . barely passable. Better? Now let's go."

"Are you a safe driver?" She asked, hesitating.

"The safest. I've been riding since I could walk, and I've never had an accident yet."

"Okay," she agreed, "But first let me go upstairs and put on a warmer jacket and boots."

After she was seated on the back of the Harley, she asked herself, what am I doing? Riding on the back of a Harley with a man who kissed me against my wishes, on my way to see another man in prison, a man convicted of *murder* at that. My mother would be horrified!

The Road King was fully equipped for a back seat rider, but considering the few times she had been on a cycle, Tia didn't feel secure without wrapping her arms around the driver. "Do you mind if I hold onto you?" she asked Cap.

That was like asking the cat if it objected to a dish of cream. Glad she couldn't see his Cheshire-cat grin, Cap only advised, "Hang on tight, Princess."

She wrapped her arms around him, immediately aware of the warmth of his body through her jacket sleeves, his muscles rippling and firm.

It occurred to her that he probably lifted weights or something to have such a tight, flat stomach. One of those guys who likes to prance around in Lycra pants and show off his washboard abs? No. He didn't strike her as vain. He struck her as solid and reliable. As reliable as the powerful motorcycle he handled so effortlessly. She felt intuitively that his character matched his physique.

Tia made a very deliberate decision to turn her thoughts away from Cap's muscles and his character. Instead, she turned full attention to the tree-lined scenic route along the gently winding Rock River. Towering evergreens, branches drooping gracefully into full skirts near the ground, made perfect shelters for woodland creatures. The oaks and red leaf maples were not yet putting forth their leaves, but she could imagine their graceful canopies of lazy summer shade over the roadway.

The warmth of the sun on her back, the cool air rushing past and the Harley's powerful grip on the pavement was invigorating to the senses of her frozen soul. Without admitting it, she suddenly felt starved for light, color and life.

As they neared Byron, Illinois Tia watched sunbeams silvering the usually murky river. Flocks of geese and ducks floated lazily, and a morning fisherman was already drifting in his boat.

The Harley rolled at a pleasant speed past the Byron nuclear power plant with its ever-present twin columns of steam rising into the skies. Whenever she saw those clouds, the unwelcome thought of living so close to a nuclear power plant intruded.

Depressing thoughts vanished as Tia's mind turned to the history of these winding river bends and forests haunted by the memory of the legendary Sac and Fox tribal Chief Black Hawk. He roamed the forests of Illinois during the 1800s, unwilling to give up his territory to the ever-encroaching floods of white men.

Black Hawk and his band from the village of Saukenuk (today known as Rock Island) had refused to depart from their homeland in 1804 after then president-to-be William Henry Harrison tricked most of the Sac and Fox tribes into signing away their tribal territory.

Like every other tribe desperately clinging to a vanishing way of life, the Sac and Fox suffered for Black Hawk's decision. His ultimate surrender marked the last of Indian Territory in Illinois. Tia recalled the words he had written, "My reason teaches me that land cannot be sold, The Great Spirit gave it to his children to live on . . . but such things can be taken away."

Her editor always referred to the chief as a bad guy who liked to raid other Indian camps. What had old Blackie ever done to deserve the 50-foot monumental statue of himself on the banks of the Rock River near Oregon? He looked very regal in stone, tall and imposing with his arms folded underneath a blanket and his stony face peering out over the waters from a high bluff.

A deer leaped across the road several yards ahead of them and disappeared into the woods. Cap slowed the Road King, ready to stop if the deer's companion should also leap in front of them. "Look, there's another deer," she heard Cap saying. She caught just a glimpse of cream-colored legs under a white tail as it bounded into a thickly wooded slope.

She enjoyed the ride and it ended all too soon for the both of them. When they arrived at the Dixon Correctional Facility, surrounded by wide expanses of grassy fields, gun-carrying guards searched them for weapons. Tia and Cap displayed their ID's.

Once inside the compound, they went through the same procedure again. After placing purse and jackets inside separate lockers, a prison guard ushered them through several barred gates and into a commons area where prisoners sat drinking sodas or coffee. A uniformed matron showed them to a separate interview room walled by glass and then sat down with them.

There he sat. Ben Krahl. Dressed in a bright lemon-yellow prison jumpsuit. The man she had been writing about and thinking about for months of her life. The man who dominated his many loyal friends' thoughts with the belief that he was innocent and that they must do something about it.

The first thing she noticed was his colorless skin as pale as mushrooms in contrast with the bright yellow jumpsuit. His silvered hair was thinning. His short-cropped beard was almost white. Rip Tyson had warned her that Ben needed dental care, but the prison's dentist simply pulls teeth and does not repair them. Otherwise every lowlife in town would want a prison sentence just long enough for the state to pay for his dental work.

Ben greeted Tia with a grateful handshake. After Cap explained why Rip had not come along, he merely listened as Tia and Ben sat and talked. She was very sorry to tell him that Nate Cash was dead. He dropped his eyes. He'd already heard. Nate's death was the end of an avenue of hope for him. Too many of Ben's hopes ended in despair.

Their talk turned to guesses about who might have been the shooter and why. Ben really had no ideas. He was as clueless as the police reports had stated. It was frustrating.

Finally she asked, "What do you think went wrong at the trial?"

Ben looked at her with eyes as colorless as his hair. Everything about him reminded her of a pale shadow rather than a man of flesh and blood. In a tired voice, devoid of anger or accusation, he explained, "A lot was left out that should have been said or done."

Folding his hands on the table, he continued, "No clear motive for the murder was ever established. Only suggested. As you well know, the state doesn't have to prove a motive. Just the opportunity and the means. The state's attorneys were convincing with their ludicrous suggestions." Ben imitated their sneering voices, "We don't know if Ben and Cass were sleeping together, but we know she spent the night at his place after the crime."

He smiled wryly. "The opportunity? Well anyone in the parking lot had the same opportunity. And the means? I never owned a gun. The state never proved I had one. The fire department scoured the area and never found a weapon."

Reasonable suspicion can be a persuasive tool, Tia decided.

"I went with Cass to buy a dress for Nancy's funeral. How could I have guessed that would lead to suspicion of an affair? I didn't buy it for her. She paid for it with her Visa card. And how could I say no when she asked to sleep on my sofa that night? She was emotionally wrecked as much as I was. Terrified the killer might be after her."

He paused, cleared his throat and looked Tia in the eyes.

"When you're dealing with raw grief, you don't think in terms of what other people might suspect. Besides, if the affair had been an actuality, it would have been incredibly stupid of us to spend the night together immediately after Nancy's death. Why rouse suspicion by falling into each other's arms the very night of the murder?"

Tia silently agreed.

Continuing his analysis of what went wrong at the trial Ben said, "Rocky Miller drew a diagram for the jury to see. He marked the spot where I was supposed to be standing when the gun fired. That mark placed me at least fifty feet from Nancy at the time of the shooting."

Tia looked aghast. "But Dr. Blum said stippling around the wound showed the gun was fired from six to no more than 24 inches away."

Ben nodded, and continued calmly, "Rocky also swore he was absolutely certain that I was wearing a green baseball cap and a bomber jacket. My attorney had my cap and jacket with him right there in a plastic bag, and I nudged him and told him to show the jury my cap."

"And?"

"Mine was white—not green."

"So? He didn't show them your white hat?"

Ben shook his head.

"Why not?" she asked with a degree of astonishment.

Shrugging his shoulders, Ben answered, "Don't know. That was reasonable doubt, to my way of thinking. Nancy was shot above the right ear. Rocky drew diagrams for the court claiming I was aiming at her left side—shooting some 50 feet away. There was no way I could have been the shooter from where he said I was standing! Even if I'd been left handed."

The facts didn't matter. Ben could see that now.

"Ben, I'm considering writing some more articles about your conviction," she said hesitantly. She might be an amateur with no investigative skills whatever, but how could she abandon him now? He looked impassive, his head lowered.

Changing the subject she asked, "How did you meet Nancy?"

His mind flashed back to that night. "It was at a sports bar in the Mackenzie Park Mall. I was playing darts when Cecelia Jurowski, one of the regulars at the place, introduced me to her blonde and smiling daughter. She looked up at me with the most amazing blue eyes I've ever seen. But I was very aware that Nancy was much younger, I figured our age difference was too great."

"And?"

"Cecelia just kept after me, asking what difference did age make. She finally persuaded me that 14 years was really nothing."

Ben explained that his marriage to Susanna, Jarrod's mother, had recently ended—amicably enough—but still the shake up of break up was working its unsettling effects. He remembered how nervous he'd been to meet Nancy's dad and how he had desperately wanted Mr. Jurowski's approval. And that led to the Vietnam story.

They rehashed some issues—the inappropriate tie his son wore to the funeral, his damning lack of tears at the funeral. Ben couldn't really tell her anything more than she already had in her notes. He had been walking away from Nancy. The shooting happened behind his back.

When time was up, she shook his hand and said she hoped something would come of his next appeal. She knew Crane was working on it.

161

But she could see resignation in Ben's eyes. He was tired. He looked old. Every day that passed for him behind bars was a day he could never recapture. A day without the love of family, friends, and the pleasure of working and building a future. It occurred to her that both she and Ben had lost a future they could never recover. There was a definite link between the two of them.

Cap and Tia left Ben behind, both feeling very discouraged as they walked back to the Road King. "I can't think of anything more nightmarish than being locked up for something you didn't do," said Cap, his hands on her shoulders, turning her to face him as he helped her with the buckle of her helmet's chinstrap.

If he noticed the unwept tears in her eyes, he didn't say anything. "At least he's not on death row," Tia muttered. "That would be worse."

She swung her leg over the Road King's saddle and the Harley chugged to life. Once more she wrapped her arms around his chest. Cap liked the feel of those arms around him. Liked the way her jeans hugged those long, slender legs. Darn! He just plain liked everything about her.

They were quickly out of Dixon, since the prison was on the outskirts of town. Then Cap surprised her by turning down a different road and soon they were winding through rolling, wooded hills. Must be the alternate way back to Wisconsin, she thought, once again enjoying the blanket of sunbeams and the coolness of the rushing air tousling her ponytail underneath the helmet. It seemed only a few miles later, when Cap turned the bike into White Pines State Forest Park.

They wound through a forest of blue spruces and white pines, rolled down into a hollow beside a babbling brook and pulled up next to a picnic table. Cap dropped the kickstand. While removing her helmet, Tia inadvertently pulled her scrunchie loose from her ponytail. Chestnut hair tumbled loosely around her shoulders and she shook it free of tousles.

She'd been attractive with her hair tied back, but Cap thought she was an absolute knockout now. He envied the sunbeams allowed to touch her hair, knew that if he got close enough to

162

caress those silky tresses he'd be kissing that tender mouth again. He dared not risk being told to buzz off like the last time. Not after feeling her arms around him twice in the same day.

That doesn't count, he told himself. She just felt insecure riding behind him on the Road King. No it was more than that. He sensed that she was starting to trust him at least a little. He wouldn't shake her confidence again.

The next time he kissed Tia, it would be with her permission, he promised himself. If he could just get her to spend some time with him she would realize that life still had a lot to offer her. Namely himself. He hung his helmet on a handlebar and started unbuckling a saddlebag.

"What are you doing?" she asked with a suspicious edge to her voice.

"I thought we might get hungry, so I packed a little lunch. Just some sandwiches. Have you ever been to White Pines? Beautiful isn't it?"

She had to admit the place was charming. However, she well remembered the last time Cap had brought her to a picnic table. She did not want a repeat of that too-close encounter.

He was unwrapping sandwiches and pouring from a thermos of coffee into plastic cups. "Sugar and cream?" he offered.

"You think of everything don't you?"

"Just one more thing," he pulled out a blanket and headed toward a spot near the brook. Tender shoots of green were showing through the wintered yellow grass where he spread the blanket. Afternoon sunlight slanted through the bare branches, striping the ground with alternate ribbons of blue shadow and yellow light.

"Bring your coffee," he said as he knelt on the blanket. The brook was indeed babbling merrily beside the sun-dappled grass, a welcome sight after the long Wisconsin winter. From an overhanging branch, an irritated squirrel shook its tail and barked a warning at them. Settling on the sun-and-shade-striped blanket she took a bite out of her sandwich.

"This is tasty," she munched.

"My own sandwich filling. I make it up with secret ingredients guaranteed to put the roses in your cheeks."

"Uuuum." She nodded, suddenly aware that she was very hungry. She was also thinking about the man they had just met for the first time. She wanted Cap's impression. "So what did you think of Ben?"

"He's not smart enough to be the cold-blooded, calculating, premeditated murderer the prosecutors portrayed him to be."

She immediately seized the thought, "Premeditated. That's the word that blows my mind. He could have taken Nancy anywhere that night and shot her without a parking lot full of witnesses looking on. He was taking a huge risk to do it in front of so many people," Nancy mumbled as she took another bite of her sandwich. "How smart was that?"

Munching on an apple, he watched her as she pondered the case aloud.

"Nate conducted his own ballistics test you know. He found the bullet that struck the game arcade's storefront window was fired a hundred feet away from where Denny saw Ben crouching only a second or two before. That alone shows the shooter had to be some person other than Ben."

Cap could see her passion for the injustice of this case. He felt it too. She was as infectious as she was beautiful. But she was still impervious to his charm.

"Enough about the Krahl case. Let's talk about you. How have you been?" Her cheeks were rosy rather than pale at the moment. He thought the blush became her.

"I'm fine, working on a writing project and staying busy at the news office. I've got my hands full right now."

She was dodging him again. He'd hoped Carmen was right. That she would miss him if he just backed off and gave her some time to herself. Suddenly very aware that Tia had not missed him—would never miss him unless he could somehow make himself valuable to her agenda. Cap decided he would have to do just that.

With a lop-sided grin and humor in his eyes, he teased her in a mock-serious tone, "Tia, I know you've missed me terribly these past weeks. I honestly don't know how you've stood it, going this long with seeing me."

He could see the almost-laugh in her eyes.

"I've managed to survive," she answered, thinking to herself, oh, no, here we go again. Even so, she was amused.

"You wouldn't admit you missed me, but I'm going to make it up to you. We can't have you suffering from Cap-deprivation, now can we?"

She half smiled in spite of herself, more at his bravado than anything. The man may not be completely conceited, but he was definitely self-assured. "I'm sure you have lots of admiring fans," she countered, "I wouldn't be so selfish as to take you away from them. I'd feel so guilty. All those deprived women sighing and moaning for your company."

"Yeah they do that all the time. Well, from now on you're at the top of the list, Sleeping Beauty. The others will just have to sigh and moan. Besides, we need to work together to find out who killed Nancy Jurowski. Not that I don't have confidence in you. You're as determined as a bird is to fly. But I can go places you can't go. Places you shouldn't go."

"Like where?"

"Like the biker bar for instance where some of those gang bangers hang out. There are some real tough characters who hang out there. I wouldn't want you to set your little booted foot in that place on certain nights. Who knows if the driver of that mystery van might be a regular there?"

Tia was thinking of Nate's reports and the rap sheets he had included. Venomous gang members. Dangerous drug dealers. Violent gunrunners. She would rather meet a ravenous, giant rat fed on Byron-nuclear-plant waste than any one of them. But Cap? Maybe Cap could be of some help.

He was watching her enormous dark eyes and sensing a momentary advantage, he stuck out a hand and said, "So what do you say? Let's work together. Shake on it partner?"

She hesitated a moment. What did she have to lose? He was right. He could go places she wouldn't go. And she certainly had no better ideas at the moment. "Okay," she nodded, "but we're keeping it strictly professional."

"Done!" he agreed.

He waited as she licked the remains of her sandwich filling off the tips of elegant fingers, then shook her hand firmly. It was hard to let go.

Okay, she thought with a sense of relief. She and Cap may not be professionals, but they were all Ben had at the moment.

Now if only they could somehow find the smoking gun or get the confession from the real killer. She knew the trail was cold. So cold it was moldy. But Tia wasn't ready to give up, in fact, she was just beginning.

Chapter 22 – Drug Deal

What had she seen in Ben Krahl's eyes?

Were they the eyes of a murderer? A Baal worshiper who lived for his own pleasure and thought nothing of treating others like Dixie cups to be disposed of when he was through with them?

Was he the lust-crazed lover who wanted Nancy out of his life so he could continue a torrid love affair with her best friend? Had Nancy really been a jealous, clinging vine who cramped his style so offensively that he had to kill her to get rid of her?

No. Tia had seen none of those things. The morning after the motorcycle trip, she was thinking that if Ben resembled anyone, it was the taller, balding comedian on the TV show, *Whose Line is it Anyway?* when the phone rang.

"Good morning partner. I want to see where the vehicles were parked," Cap said, fully intending to hold her to their agreement to work together. "You've got to show me that bullet hole in the utility pole." He would have said anything to get her out with him again on this gorgeous almost-spring day.

"Cap, I'm really busy," she answered, trying to avoid him once more.

"Come on, Tia. You're the only one who knows the locations of the vehicles. I can't analyze the crime scene without your help."

Reluctantly she agreed, but she would drive her own car.

"No way. I don't want you out in that parking lot in your Bronco when we don't know if the stalker van might be lurking around. I'm picking you up in ten minutes."

How do I get myself into these situations with Mr. Blue Eyes, she asked herself once again after buckling the seatbelt in his Jeep. This outing was probably going to be like talking to a shadow. It is plainly there but has nothing to say. What could Cap learn from seeing the bullet hole?

He was whistling a tuneless ditty that sounded a little like *I Got You Babe.* Tia ignored the implication.

The morning sun's climbing rays were already sending the coolness of the night running for cover. Early spring freshness and tender new growth budded timidly throughout the Enchanted Forest Park area along the river. Cap was hoping to talk Tia into another picnic on its shores as they parked in the area of the Mackenzie Park strip mall near where Nancy's car had been parked. She pointed out the bullet-shaped dent in the utility pole.

"That was from a high-powered gun," Cap ran a finger over the dent. The bullet had not penetrated the pole. "What kind of gun did you say killed Nancy?"

"It could have been a .357 Magnum according to Dr. Blum, but he wasn't certain. Investigators said this pockmark could easily have been from an earlier time and there was no way to prove it was directly linked to the Jurowski homicide."

"A high-powered gun fired in a busy mall parking lot. Don't you think police would have had reports in their records if that had happened on another night?" Cap mused.

Tia was looking at the scene. "Cap, this utility pole was very close to where Cass had parked her car that night. It looks to me like the gunman was firing at her. And probably at Ben too."

Cap shook his head in an attitude of exasperation. Nothing made sense in this case.

Police believed Ben killed Nancy, dropping her with the first bullet, and then kept firing the gun upward into the air—for no reason whatever—while dodging imaginary bullets. It made far more sense to Cap that a gunman was firing toward the witnesses in order to cover his getaway.

They walked back to the Jeep and were buckling their seat belts when Cap looked up and zeroed in on the guy standing in the parking stall directly in front of them. "Look at that. He's thinking he's so cool."

Tia saw a slender black man standing next to the driver's side of a white van. He had reached down inside his baggy sweat pants and was pulling out a large, clear plastic baggie filled with a white powdery substance. Mr. Cool glanced furtively right and left, then slipped the bag through the driver's window. After waiting a moment and nonchalantly checking the area once again, he pulled out a second baggie. The baggies were not just sandwich size. They were quart size or larger.

"Wow!" Tia whispered. "Something tells me that's not powdered sugar."

Mr. Cool obviously was not aware that the vehicle in front of him was occupied by two people observing his very covert activity. At that moment, he glanced in the direction of the Jeep. Uh oh, Tia's heart pounded. She imagined his eyes penetrating the windshield, boring like twin drill bits straight into her mind to determine whether she was aware of him.

And then what?

Tia dropped her eyes, feeling a momentary chill of alarm. This was not exactly the place she wanted to be at that moment. If someone had asked her—do you want a front row seat to a big-money drug deal going down in the parking lot this morning?—she would have said no thanks, this is my day to wrestle alligators.

But here she was sitting in Cap's Jeep with a drug dealer staring straight at her, wondering just what she had seen. She averted her eyes, whispering, "Cap, he sees us. What do we do now, smile and wave? Ask for his autograph?"

"Why don't you just slide over here and put your arms around my neck like we're boyfriend and girlfriend?" Cap suggested calmly. "We don't want him to think we were watching."

Without a moment's hesitation she did as he suggested, locking her arms around his neck in a nervous embrace. From the corner of her eye she had glimpsed Mr. Cool walking their way before she buried her face against Cap's shoulder.

"He's coming! He's coming towards us," She whispered urgently, her heart pounding more rapidly. Thoughts of Nancy's bloodied corpse flashed vividly through her mind.

"Just stay put," said Cap, his breath warm against her ear.

"We've got to make this convincing. I'm going to kiss you, with your permission of course," he added, noting that the drug dealer was walking away from them, already visible in the rear view mirror heading for the Sandwich Shoppe. Their romantic ruse had evidently worked.

But Tia didn't know that.

"Okay," she whispered, anxious to thwart any suspicions that the dealer might have. After all, a woman had been shot to death, probably in this very spot where they were now sitting. Cap brushed his lips very gently across her cheek. He waited for a response, but Tia was taut as a fishing line with a shark on the hook. Then he felt her body relax just a little.

He moved his lips to her ear and whispered, "I think he's behind the Jeep."

"What's he doing?" she whispered urgently, wondering just how desperate a dealer might be to protect himself. "Is he getting your license number?"

In truth, the man had already disappeared inside the Sandwich Shoppe. Cap was enjoying the moment so much he couldn't resist extending it. "Sh-sh. I don't think he's convinced yet. We better make this look like we're so lost in our embrace that we couldn't possibly have noticed anything else."

This time he moved his lips slowly against hers. And this time he felt the tension in her body began to ease. She was actually responding to him, not woodenly as before. She was almost kissing him back. Her lips sent an electric surge through his veins sweet enough to light up a Christmas tree.

Call it escape from a stressful situation or a defense mechanism, but at that moment in Tia's mind, she was kissing Jeff, reliving a tender memory from her past. This was the night of their homecoming dance at Southern Missouri State University, when he had first kissed her and struck a note in the depths of her heart. It was the beginning of a melody that she wanted to hear for the rest of her life. A melody that promised a full symphony of love, laughter, children. Somewhere in her heart, she still yearned for the music of that night, felt incomplete without it.

The memory was so real that when she opened her eyes, she was almost astonished to see Cap Nemon's blue eyes instead of Jeff's shining back at hers. The jolt back to reality angered her. Drug dealer be darned, this was not happening! Tia released her hold on Cap and quickly slid back to the far side of the passenger's seat.

"I think we should go now," she said quietly, looking straight ahead.

Cap started the Jeep and began whistling. He was getting used to the routine. Sleeping Beauty may still be locked in her ice tower, but she was definitely starting to thaw out a little. The taste of her lips lingered on his own.

He'd kept his promise not to kiss her again without her permission, even though he'd resorted to a slight deception. A necessary deception after all. The drug dealer actually could have caused them serious harm. Besides, she would thank him for it eventually.

Cap was already looking forward to the next kiss.

When Tia got back to her stark and uninviting apartment, she did something she had not been able to do for a long time since the accident. She sat down in the middle of the floor and wept.

171

Not great, heaving sobs at first. Just quiet tears that trickled then began streaming down her cheeks in little rivulets dropping off her chin.

Finally, the dam broke. She was swept on a tide of emotion bursting through the tight web of self-control which had kept her numbly functioning since the accident. Unwept tears flowed from the bottom of her soul, washing out some of the pent up sorrow, anger and guilt that had pooled there so long.

She was not aware of how long she sat weeping. It may have been hours. But when the last sob finally heaved her sagging shoulders, she felt a release. On a deeper level, the long-postponed healing had begun.

She got up from the floor, took a shower and washed her hair.

Chapter 23 – Somebody Knows

After her crying jag, Tia spent the weekend cleaning her apartment. She decided it looked a little drab. Maybe it was time to hang a picture and set out some decorative vases. A bouquet of cut flowers on the table would be nice.

By Sunday evening, she surveyed her touches of color with a pleased expression. She even hung a wedding photo of herself and Jeff. They were smiling, so very joyfully. She was pleased that looking at it made her smile instead of cry.

Back at the office on Monday, Tia turned her thoughts once more to where she might go with her Ben Krahl series. She realized she was at an end. No new sources. She sent up a silent prayer to Heaven. What do I write about now?

And then amazingly, she received three possible leads by unexpected phone calls to the news office—one, a beauty operator at The Cutting Edge in the strip mall where the Jurowski murder had taken place. The woman thought her ex boyfriend had done it. She was suspicious because after the murder he suddenly had the money to buy a brand new vehicle, even though he was out of a job. He also hung around with members of the Cobra Kings. That got Tia's attention. Cobra King members kept showing up in Nate's report. They were in the parking lot that night.

Another woman, Terry Raymer, called to say she had seen a gunman running through her yard late that night, probably just moments after the shooting. Significantly, the man she saw also was wearing a leather bomber jacket such as Rocky had described.

Miss Raymer had never bothered calling police because she figured they had their man at the time, but after reading the Weekly News series, she'd begun to doubt it. Tia was excited about Raymer's call, first because it fit with Nate's theory that the gunman could have run through the Sandwich Shoppe and out into the alley behind the mall. Second, the woman's house was located in the block directly behind the place. If Nate's theory were true, Raymer had seen the killer.

The most chilling call came in to the news office only a day later from a former acquaintance of the Jurowski family who did not want his name revealed. The man described a casual conversation he'd had with Nancy during the week before her death. "Nancy said she was involved in investigating something at the bank where she worked," he began. "That conversation has been bothering me a lot lately. She told me something didn't add up. When I asked her to explain, she said she wasn't at liberty to talk about it."

Tia's eyebrows went up. Something didn't add up at the bank where Nancy worked. A week later she was dead. "What do you think she was talking about?"

The caller answered, "I always figured she had uncovered something illegal going on. Embezzlement maybe. I never doubted that somebody had her bumped off before she could blow the whistle."

Maybe that added up to the long elusive motive. Darn! If only she had more details to go on. The caller wouldn't even give her his real name. Said he was "scared."

The whole thing stinks, she thought. Even when she tried deliberately to look at the police reports and trial records from the assumption that Ben was guilty, all the conflicting details just did not compute.

She desperately missed Nate Cash. If only there was someone, a person of respected authority to pick up the investigation.

However, her friend Bond's words spurred her on. Somebody out there knows something, and someday someone will talk.

James Bond was right.

*All the above were actual phone calls to a reporter who worked on the crime on which this story is based.

Chapter 24 – Sycho's Letter

The letter arrived at the news office from the Department of Corrections at Menard, Illinois. It was addressed:

To The Reporter who is investigating the Nancy Jurowski case.

Tia figured it was from another convict asking her to look into his case as she had done for Ben Krahl. More than a few had written to her with complaints about the judicial system, hoping to get her newspaper on their side. The Menard convict's letter lay aside until after she sorted her daily mail. When she finally opened it, the handwritten letter on notebook paper sparked intense interest:

"My name is Jerry Skare and I go 'Sycho.' You should already know me, considering that you have mentioned the leader of the Cobra Kings in your paper. I'm locked up for the murder of Pamela Primm, and you've written about me, but not by name."

Tia scrambled in her mind for the brief mention she had made of a Cobra King member possibly connected to the Jurowski homicide, Lynn Jordan, a woman known to have been contacted on the night of the shooting death. She had not mentioned gender or names. The writer implied she was referring to him. She read on.

"I've got fifty, long, happy years to do for the murder of Pamela Primm. I got locked up in 2002, along with a co-defendant who is as innocent as hell. The only reason she confessed is because I threatened her that she'd end up the same way as Pam if she didn't.

"Now I have decided to give the full truth about what I did on the night of Oct. 30, 2002, and what I made Lynn Jordan confess to doing. She got fifty years for a murder that I committed.

"You probably wanna know what I know about the murder of Nancy Jurowski. Well, I may and I may not know something. It was a dark, dark night in the parking lot where she got killed. But you're smart, and it seems you're getting close to the truth. Only time will tell.

"I'm sending you a copy of my affidavit that's going to the judge, another guy who helped me to put an innocent person in prison. Or is it two innocent people in prison? Who knows anymore?

Maybe I'll hear back from you."

Skare included a sworn and notarized affidavit stating it was he who had killed Pamela Primm. He also confessed to threatening Lynn's life and the lives of her children if she did not confess to the murder.

Wow!

Tia put down the letter, then picked it up and read it again. What did she have here?

She vaguely remembered the night of Pamela's shooting because it happened right after October Fest. She didn't give much space to the story because the crime had happened across the state line in the jurisdiction of Illinois.

Was this guy on the level? Anybody can say anything, especially if he has an agenda. But this guy apparently didn't want anything except to clear Lynn Jordan's name. Why now? He evidently thought Tia had been referring to him as the unknown killer in her Krahl murder series. He certainly hinted he was at the crime scene. "It was a dark, dark night."

Had she kept the bait out long enough to get a real bite on the line at last? Now if she could only reel him in. The names of the players were in Nate Cash's report. The link to the crime scene was there. According to Nate, a call to Lynn Jordan's home had been made from the bar on the night of murder. From Rocky's phone.

She fired back a carefully worded letter to Mr. Skare, and held her breath. His second letter arrived within days. On the back of the envelope he wrote, "I've got the world in my hands!" Just as a gunman has the power of life or death in his hands, it seemed Skare now had the power of freedom or prison in his hands for Ben Krahl.

He asked her to call him "Sycho," a different spelling of the word "psycho," because it "fit his persona" and had been his nickname since he was age nine. Skare politely thanked her for writing. Then he wrote:

"On Nancy Jurowski's death, you don't have any direct leads. I already know that. How I know that is the question. Answer? There is only one person alive who knows what happened to Nancy, and that person isn't ready to reveal the truth. But I will tell you that Ben Krahl is innocent.

"He's a victim of circumstances and a cop-out for the mayor, running for chief of police at the time, so he could close Nancy's case. Being innocent doesn't mean shit to the legal system! The late Nate Cash was the best at his job, and I believe he's the only one who has come close to the truth. Now I'm the only one left alive who knows what really happened that night."

Tia grabbed one of the pages from Nate Cash's suspect list, checking again for Lynn Jordan or Jerry Skare's names.

Members of Skare's gang showed up on the surveillance cameras at the game place around midnight. Was he there too?

He sounded well adapted to prison life. And if what he said were true and not sarcasm, he even enjoyed it. Sycho wasn't asking for a bargain if he turned state's evidence. He wasn't asking for time shaved off his 50-year sentence.

In fact, Sycho Skare was actually incriminating himself farther by confessing to murder. Why? He wanted Lynn Jordan back on the streets for a reason.

Tia faxed a copy of his letter to Ben's defense attorney. Then she decided to visit the courthouse to look up the records on the Pamela Primm murder.

After driving to downtown Rockford, finding a parking place with a two-hour meter and then locating the court records, Tia sat down to read through witness statements taken by police on that October night of violence.

It was a revealing and dreadful look into the twisted mentality of gang bangers, a much closer look at what their lives are all about. Many of their statements were conflicting and revealed just what kind of evidentiary work investigators had cut out for them that night.

Like everyone else in Rockford and Woodsville, Tia knew street gangs existed. Their violent deeds made news from time to time, bubbling up like lava from a hotbed of underground volcanic activity. She knew life on the streets was far from glamorous. But she never realized just how close the members actually lived to the edge of danger.

They were so young. Tia often wondered how mere girls could get caught up in such violence. Now she was reading the answer. The mug shot showed Lynn Jordan, pretty, wide-set eyes, full pouty lips, long wavy dark hair parted in the middle. She was described as tall at 5 ft. 9 in., and had pierced her ears five times each. One eyebrow was pierced. A rose was tattooed on her right leg beside the name "Billy." She also had the name, "Sycho," tattooed on her right ankle.

Lynn was the unwed mother of two children and had falsely claimed to be pregnant with Sycho's child at the time of her arrest. She admitted to having alcohol and drug problems.

Ah yes, the drug connection, Tia noted. Lynn began drinking at age 13, and started treatment for addiction at age 14, and

Harriett Ford

dropped out of the program. She was in her early 20s when charged with first-degree murder.

Tia found a mug shot and description of Jerry Skare. So this was Sycho. His face in the file photo was not extraordinarily evil or cunning. Only 19 at the time of his arrest, he looked pudgy at 5 ft. 6 in. and 195 lbs. with a shaved head, droopy eyes and prominent, heavy brows.

Sycho Skare also liked tattoos. He had a "C" on his right ear and a "K" on the other, presumably marking his allegiance to the Cobra Kings. Tattooed on his back was a serpent with hood extended and wicked fangs bared to strike. A pair of horns and a six-point star were tattooed on the left hand, another six-point star and the name "Sycho" appeared on his neck. On his abdomen were the letters "S S."

In his statement to police on the night of his arrest, Skare began, "My name is Jerry Skare and I go sycho. I'm in command of the Cobra Kings gang."

Was that bravado or simply an admission of fact? He named Lynn Jordan his girlfriend in the report. She referred to him as her "main squeeze." The pair told the same basic story to a point. It began two days before Halloween in October of 2002.

Sycho and his "folks" (fellow gang members) had somehow gotten word on the streets of "a one-legged Mexican in town with a lot of weed."

One-legged Mexican? Tia mused wryly, somebody had charged the guy an arm and a leg for drugs but he could only afford half a load. She continued reading Sycho's statement:

"We copped some weed from the lopsided Mex to be sure it was good stuff. That night we put on hooded sweatshirts and I loaded my .380. We broke into the Mexican's place, and I held the gun to his head while my folks ripped off the place. We took about $40,000 in cash, thousands of dollars worth of gold and silver jewelry, and over 400 pounds of weed. The next day one of the Viper Lords confronted Lynn and slapped her around because of the robbery."

From that point, the war was on. Before dark, Sycho and his buddies drove down Liberty Avenue, looking for the gang member who had dared to put his hands on Lynn. One of the Viper Lords was sitting on a porch. When he saw the vehicle approaching, he pulled a gun out of his "hoodie" (a term used to describe a hooded sweatshirt) and fired at their car.

Sycho hit the gas pedal, screeching out of the area, but he was already planning revenge. Nobody was going to make him look like a "bitch."

Tia could visualize the night. It was a moonless, wind-driven October's eve. Sycho and Lynn both said they had spent the afternoon "drinking, blowing coke and playing pool," according to their separate statements. They began planning a return visit to the Viper Lord who had dared to fire a gun at them. Sycho's original story to police was that Lynn, after drinking into the evening, finally decided to take matters into her own hands.

He loaded his Tec-9 and then bet Lynn forty bucks that she wouldn't shoot up the house. She answered, "You know I will."

Sycho waited at Little Caesar's Pizza restaurant while Lynn drove away in the van. Police found a receipt for the pizza in his pocket, the time coinciding with Primm's death.

Lynn's first account to police was that she drove, "stopped the van in front of the Primm house, rolled down the passenger window and began firing the Tec-9 at the house as a warning."

It was a night of mind-numbing terror for the victim's family. The woman inside the house, Pamela Primm, wasn't supposed to get hurt, Lynn stated in later court records. "I called the house and warned her not to be home that night."

As Tia read other witness statements from court documents, she saw that some of the youngsters inside the house had actually identified Sycho as the passenger firing the gun. One in particular, a young girl had no doubt about seeing Sycho Skare holding the Tec-9. She knew him well. He was her uncle.

Police recovered 21 casings from the assault weapon. In his third letter to Tia, Sycho wrote that he had fired all 34 rounds, but some of the casings fell inside the van. That's why police found only part of the casings.

He added that he "couldn't shoot easily enough from the passenger window," so he exited the van and fired away in wild abandon. "I didn't want to stop firing. I could hear chunks of wood ripping away. It was a rush. I wanted to cut that house in two with bullets."

Sycho's intended targets actually were three of the Viper Lords gang. None of them were inside the residence that night, at least as far as Tia could tell from police statements. As gunfire peppered the home, a bullet struck Pamela Primm in the head right before her children's horrified eyes.

Lynn described her reaction, "I was trembling even with the alcohol and cocaine in my system, while I sped the van away from the house." She didn't know that Pamela had been killed. "I begged Sycho to rent a motel room for the night. I was afraid of what the Viper Lords would do to us."

If what they said were true, Tia noted, here they were, loaded with the one-legged Mexican's cash, thousands of dollars worth of gold and silver jewelry, all the weed they could ever smoke and they were afraid to sleep in their own beds. Live by the gun. Die by the gun.

Lynn and Sycho didn't have time to rent a motel room that night. The police picked them up instead. During the interrogation, police seemed to know that Lynn was lying about her part in the shooting, finally asking, "Lynn, are you gonna take the rap for Jerry Skare?"

She answered, "I've done it before."

Tia could imagine Lynn's willingness to go to jail for her man. But at that time, Lynn obviously didn't know that she would be facing 50 years in prison for murder or that Pamela had been killed.

What a shock it must have been when her sentence came down. Lynn later wrote a pleading letter to the judges: "I thought the whole thing was about gunfire, not murder. I was coerced into confessing."

Tia recalled Sycho's affidavit saying he had threatened Lynn, "Tell them you did it or you and your kids end up just like Pamela."

At this point, Lynn did not have a lawyer. All she had was a convicted murderer deciding, after nearly a year, to confess that he was the one who actually fired the gun. That was little better than nothing. Who was going to believe Sycho? She read through the conflicting statements. She re-read Sycho's letter.

No wonder Rocky Miller had said he was afraid of not spending the rest of his life with his family! It was easy to imagine someone like Sycho threatening him, "You and your wife and kids will end up just like Nancy if you don't tell them Ben did it."

Why else would a man turn on his best friend and send him to prison for 40 years? Word on the streets and the biker bar was that gang members had threatened Rocky and his wife. Now it seemed more believable than ever. One question still had no answer. Why would Sycho want to kill Nancy?

In her next letter to Sycho, she decided to banter with him, teasing a little. She wrote, "Okay Sycho. Call me Dirty Harry, because it fits my persona. You can make my day. Tell me what you know."

C'mon, Sycho, Tell me where that smoking gun is that killed Nancy Jurowski. That was her unwritten message.

Chapter 25 - Refreshed

Songbirds warbled outside the window. A yellow sunny-side-up orb filled the expansive blue plate stretched overhead, a breakfast plate that must belong to a hungry giant ready to swallow up the last drop of winter and spit it back to earth in the form of spring blossoms.

Tia felt sunshine in her bones where winter had dwelt far too long. The night had passed, restfully, dreamlessly. She felt refreshed, and it was a welcome feeling. She tied back her hair which had grown longer over the winter and examined her spring wardrobe, all the while humming a tuneless melody. This would be a fantastic morning for a walk on the Rec path.

Sycho Skare had not answered her "Dirty Harry" letter yet, so where did she turn now to keep the series running? She decided to hit the library downtown instead, hoping to find out more about wrongful convictions and how they were solved.

Choosing her most comfortable jeans, sweater and tennis shoes, Tia headed out. She was still humming when she drove down Woody River Drive beside the swan lagoon across from Enchanted Forest Park. On an impulse she swung into the park entrance and parked the Bronco. The flowering crab apple trees were covered in blossoms, some white, some pink and others red. The cottonwoods wouldn't be blooming for a few more weeks, but there was enough color along the river to make an artist want to grab his brushes.

Mornings like this didn't come along too often. Maybe she'd park and walk from here to the library. Then she saw it. Cap's Jeep. And Cap opening the passenger door for someone. A woman.

A startlingly, beautiful woman. He offered her a hand. Tia stayed in her Bronco, a plethora of mixed emotions washing over her. She watched as the pair, both wearing comfortable jogging suits, headed for the Rec path and fell into an easy trot beside each other. She had to admit they made a striking couple. The woman was tall and slender. A mane of shiny dark hair cascaded down her back. She wore it loose and flowing. She was laughing and Cap threw an arm across her shoulders with an affectionate squeeze.

For a moment Tia sat in the Bronco, confused by her reaction. Walking on the Rec path no longer appealed to her. Well, what if he did have a girlfriend? She had made it plain to him on several occasions that she was not interested. He had a perfect right to a romantic interest. Every right.

She started the Bronco and headed for the library, unwilling to admit that some of the sunshine had just gone out of her day. Soon enough she had a pile of books on a table and was reading selected pages.

Who was that woman with Cap? The question kept popping into her mind, but she shook her head and kept reading a book on wrongful convictions. She was amazed at what she found.

Suspects lied. Even the innocent ones. Police lied. Witnesses lied. In the case histories of Gary Gauger, Sonia Jacobs, and so many others, cops and even lawyers had lied. It would take the wisdom of Solomon to separate lies from truth in the courtroom. It took the science of DNA evidence to undo most of the lies.

Gary Gauger of McHenry County in Illinois had become one of 13 amazingly lucky death-row convicts in Illinois to be released, and one of four to receive a full pardon from Governor George Ryan before he left office. There was no forensic evidence against Gary, no motive for the brutal slayings of his parents, and no weapon ever found. Just like Ted's case.

Northwestern University of Law professor Larry Marshal took Gauger's case, and found that there was never enough evidence to arrest Gary, let alone try him. The facts of the crime did not fit the investigators' hypothetical scenario.

Most of the dismissed cases had been exonerated due to the science of DNA finally coming into its own. But there was no DNA evidence in Ben's case. The court wanted a smoking gun before they would give him a new trial.

Where was she going to find it? Even with all she had managed to scratch up, Tia still had no scientific evidence. Just a ton of reasonable doubt. However the court hadn't had scientific evidence either. Just a ton of reasonable suspicion. Or was it even reasonable?

Sycho wasn't telling her anything that could be proved. Even if he confessed to the murder of Nancy, it was doubtful anyone would believe him. Certainly not without that smoking gun.

By the time she closed her notebook, she had a headache.

* * *

Tia ran the story on Sycho Skare's confession to the murder of Pamela Primm, leaving out any reference he made to Krahl's innocence. Maybe he would tell her where the gun was and ballistics tests could prove it fired the fatal bullet. What a headline that would make.

Response to the Krahl series was disappointing. Nobody, it seemed, cared anymore what happened to Ben Krahl. The Woodsville Police were starting to roll their eyes when she brought them a paper. No doubt they thought she was beating a dead horse.

Cap still called her from time to time, but she avoided talking with him for more than a moment or two. She was certain that Mr. Cole Nemon was far from lonely, remembering the exceptional beauty she had seen with him on the Rec path.

How was she going to keep the Krahl series alive now?

Come on, Sycho! This is Dirty Harry talking. Make my day and spill the whole story. He was her best hope at the moment. However Sycho enjoyed playing power games. He had fifty years to do in prison.

He was in no hurry.

June, 2003

Chapter 26 – The True Killer

Settling in once more with the television, her usual companion before bedtime, Tia got a call from Carmen, excited by the new development in the paper.

"Have you heard from Sycho again?"

"Sure have. This time he called me Dirty Harry and said he likes my sense of humor."

Carmen snorted. "Oh boy. I'm Karen-Carmen-Pat O'Brien and now you're Dirty Harry. What did he say about the murder?"

Tia picked up the letter and read aloud, "You don't have a single lead to go on. Why I know that? There is only one person left alive who knows who killed Nancy, and that person isn't ready to talk yet."

"Wow. He knows doesn't he? Let's tell him we're sending some tough guys to Menard stretch his neck and pull off his fingernails until he talks."

"Carm, even if he did tell me the name of Nancy's killer, who's going to believe him? They'd say he's just a crazy convict who would say anything to get his name in the paper."

"I don't think he killed her. Didn't you say he was only 17 when Nancy died? How could he have become such a hardened killer at that age?"

"It happens. There was a boy who murdered a Rockford woman in 1986. He was only 15 when he stabbed her 50 times with a survival knife because he wanted her new red Camaro. The court found him guilty, but mentally ill."

"Maybe Sycho's off the beam too. You don't get a nick name like that for nothing."

Tia examined the notebook paper. He'd traced his hand on the paper. Written across the outline were the words, "The hand of the true killer."

Carmen declared, "He's teasing you. Keeping you guessing whether he might confess and free Ben Krahl, or just leave him in prison."

Tia agreed. But that didn't mean everything he said was a lie. "He's incredibly cunning. Listen to this. He wrote how he went to several restaurants earlier on October 30, 2002—the day Pamela Primm got shot— looking for a café that hadn't yet changed over their cash-register receipts to daylight-savings time."

"What for?"

"Think about it. October 30 was when daylight-savings-time ended. Sycho wanted a receipt in his pocket in order to establish where he was at the time of the shooting."

"Wow! Clever. Who would have thought of that? Hey, that makes me think of Aunt Swoosie's prediction about a Halloween murder connected to Ben's case. Didn't you tell me she said the real murderer was in prison and wouldn't confess until several years went by?"

"Oh, yeah. I'd forgotten about that. She did say something like that. But you know Swoosie. She changes her predictions to fit whatever is happening. Kinda spooky though isn't it?"

"Did you talk to the police about Sycho's letter?"

"I did. Deputy Chief Nick Rinaldi said his detectives had worked hard on the Primm murder case and there was no question Lynn was the shooter."

"Did they find Lynn's fingerprints on the Tec-9? I thought Sycho told you he was the only one who ever touched it."

"Why would he resort to such an obvious lie, easily disprovable? He seems to believe his testimony will free Lynn. And he wants her free. Says her kids need her."

"He wants her back on the streets so she can pop somebody for him. I don't trust him. He's using you for his own purposes, Tia."

"Sycho doesn't expect to get out of prison. He has nothing to gain by confessing to Pamela's murder. In fact he's incriminating himself even more."

Carm hesitated a moment before blurting, "I still say that police artist's drawing of the suspect Ricky described looks exactly like a client of mine, Clyde Mooney."

"Do you think Mooney did it?"

"No, silly. Clyde's a used-car salesman in McKenzie Park. He wouldn't kill anybody. Did you ask Sycho about the gun?"

Tia picked up the handwritten letter again and read: "The gun that killed Nancy is in the river by the dam. You and the private eye, Nate Cash, had it figured out."

"In the river. Let's get Riptide to dive down there and fish it out!" Carmen's voice exploded.

"Rip would do it in an instant. But the law won't allow any diving by the river dam. Too dangerous. I asked the sheriff and he says the only thing to do is wait for a drought when the water is low. How often does that happen. Could be a decade."

Tia shrugged hopelessly. Then she picked up Sycho's letter. "Carm, listen to this. He says, 'You already know who killed Nancy. But nobody will ever know why she had to die. I can tell you this though. She wasn't the only one who was supposed to die that night.'"

Carmen listened, then asked, "You always figured that. But who else? Not Ben. He was too close for a bullet to miss. What about Cass? Didn't you say her cocaine-addict boyfriend had been gunned down just a few weeks earlier? Maybe Cass knew things she wasn't supposed to know."

"I've thought of that. And Rocky Miller. Ben said he thought the gunman was firing at Miller.

"Was Rocky doing drugs?"

"I asked Ben about that. He didn't think so, but he did comment in one of his letters that Rocky Miller always seemed to have plenty of money for toys—boats, cars, guns—even though both of them were far from wealthy."

"Maybe Rocky was a dealer?"

"What if he was? No matter where I look for a motive, I can't find one unless it was possibly a gang initiation thing. The Gang Unit cops talk about how wannabes have to commit an offense to get into the gangs. Members have to do more serious crimes in order to move up."

"Even kill?"

"It happens. Remember that gunman that shot Rockford Officer Sheri Glover? But I don't think Nancy's killing was a random thing. There are just too many sinister persons lurking in her background. The drug link isn't direct, but it's plainly there. As plain as a shadow in the rain."

"I don't like it. You writing to a Cobra King. He's got gang buddies out on the streets that he can contact. Who knows what he might do? You could be in danger."

I wrote him a friendly letter today and didn't mention Nancy's death until the final line. Told him I finally figured out who killed Nancy. O.J. Simpson did it!"

Laughing, Carmen asked, "Where did you come up with that one? He's got to get a real kick out of your letters."

They talked of other things. Carmen filled Tia in on the latest with Guitar Man She avoided any mention of Cap, figuring Tia would tell her if there was anything worth mentioning.

Later that night, a restless Tia tossed in her bed, thoughts of Sycho, Nancy and Ben Krahl twirling through her mind, causing her head to ache. Enough! She got up and turned the TV to the old movie classic channel for some diversion. There was Jane Wyman being kissed by an actor with his back to the camera. Jane turned away, a very dissatisfied look on her face. The camera panned to the actor—Rock Hudson. No wonder Jane was dissatisfied with his kiss. Poor woman. Did she know he preferred men? Finally, Tia dozed on the sofa. She might have expected her dreams to be filled with violence, guns and drug dealers.

Instead Cap Nemon paid her a dreamland visit. A very pleasant visit.

Chapter 27 – Cap and Collynda

June melted into July like butter in a saucepan. It was Tuesday, a warm lemon-yellow morning, as Tia worked at her desk, still thinking of Cap and his dream visit. Finally, she decided to call him. She wanted to find out if he'd been able to get any information out of the biker bar where the gang bangers hang out in Mackenzie Park.

"Well, well, well, if it isn't Sleeping Beauty," he answered, the gladness in his voice unmistakable.

"And you're the knight in shining armor as usual," she parried. "But look, Cap, I'm onto something here and I need your help."

"I'm all yours," and you're mine he promised silently, even though you don't know it yet.

He's a hopeless flirt, she thought. Taking Miss Rec Path out and flirting with me at the same time! He probably saw her in some restaurant and helped himself to a chair at her table. Probably turned on the charm with that lop-sided grin and those gorgeous blue eyes.

The poor woman didn't have a chance. Now she's crazy about him, and he doesn't care that he's breaking her heart every time he eyes another pretty face. What a jerk!

"You're incorrigible."

"Is that the same thing as irresistible?"

She changed the subject, unwilling to let him know she was irritated with him.

"Have you read the story I wrote about Sycho Skare?"

"I read every word you write, Tia. You know I'm your most loyal fan. And I don't have to tell you these Cobra Kings are dangerous characters. You could be stirring up a hornet's nest, my little Cold Case Coquet."

"I've used different names in my letters. Sycho Skare doesn't know which one is the real me. I signed my last letter Dirty Harry."

"Dirty Harry?" She could hear Cap stifle a chuckle. "Dirty Harry?" The chuckle turned into an outright, sidesplitting belly laugh.

"Well, why not? He's playing games with me, telling me the name Sycho fits his persona, so I decided to communicate on his level," Tia explained. "Besides, I want him to make my day and tell me who killed Nancy Jurowski."

Cap's hearty laugh brought an unwilling smile to her lips as she began to appreciate the humor of her situation. "Dirty Harry, huh?" he chuckled again. "I can't think of a name more opposite of your persona. Sleeping Beauty fits you much better. But I'd rather let Sycho think you're a salty old woman with lots of wrinkles and gap teeth."

"Here's what I need. Can you talk to some of those characters at the biker bar and find out if they know Skare? I want to know if he had any connections to Nancy. And if he was there on the night of her death."

Struggling to control his amusement, Cap agreed. "I can do that." He burst out laughing again. "When Dirty Harry met Skary.

194

Sounds like a great title for a movie to me. Want to come along with me to the biker bar, Dirty Harry?"

"Sure. I'll just put on my biker leathers, walk in, hop up on top of the bar, put my hands on my hips and say, howdy boys. This is Dirty Harry talking. Any of you bad dudes want to tell me who killed Nancy Jurowski?"

Cap pictured Tia's slender legs in black leather biker's pants, a black leather lace-up bustier emphasizing her narrow waist, and black high-heeled boots, a dangerous costume, totally out of character for her. And total desire. Especially when she took off the helmet and that long chestnut hair cascaded around her shoulders and down her back.

"They'd tell you anything you want to know," Cap assured her playfully. Then he added somewhat forcefully, "There's no way I'd let you go anywhere near that place."

Does he really think he has anything to say about where I go? Tia fumed inwardly at the possessiveness in his words. She decided to cut the conversation short before she blurted out something she might later regret. "Thanks for your concern. So let me know what you find out, if anything."

She hung up the phone, still a little huffy. A few moments later she found herself wishing she could go with Cap. A ride on that silver Harley Road King would be so pleasant on a warm July evening.

She imagined the two of them wrapped in starlight, her arms locked around Cap's waist, as they road on a ribbon of moonlight looping the purple. . . oops. Wrong poem.

Wrong scene. Wrong time. What the heck was she thinking? She shook her head.

But she couldn't help wondering if the Rec Path brunette was riding behind Cap these days. Probably. Of course she was. What woman in her right mind wouldn't want to go riding with Cap Nemon?

And there was the heart of the manner, Tia realized.

She hadn't exactly been in her right mind. Not for a long time. But she was going to get there.

Oh well. She had better things to do. The car really needed washing.

Wednesday night in church, where she had started attending once again, Tia glimpsed Cap in a pew on the opposite side of the chapel. "I didn't know Cap came to this church," she whispered to Carmen seated beside her.

"That's because you've stayed away so long. I've seen him here lots of times," Carmen answered. "Who's that lady with him?"

Tia didn't know for certain, but she could see the unmistakably long, dark hair tied back under a picture hat. Miss Rec-Path beauty, she thought, as she turned the pages of her hymnal. When the service ended, Carmen suggested, "Look, the festival on the Rec Path ends this Wednesday night and one of the guys in Joe's band has been dying to meet you. What do you say we pick you up and all go together?"

Everyone in Woodsville would be heading south to Rockford for Mr. Fourth-of-July Joe Marino's popular parade, music and fireworks display. Woodsville couldn't possibly compete, so they staged the Woody River Fest, early in the first week of July.

Crowds were small enough to make it a pleasant attraction for those who wanted to avoid the throngs in the downtown area during Rockford's hugely popular celebration.

Carmen recognized the look on Tia's face. "C'mon. We'll have fun. If you don't like him you can tell him you're engaged or something. But you can still enjoy the food and the music."

"Sure, why not?" Tia surprised herself, "but I'm driving my Bronco, so I can leave whenever I want."

Carmen reluctantly agreed.

The walkways beside the Woody River were filled with families, babies in strollers, kids carrying cotton candy, toddlers perched on dad's shoulders and skeptical teenagers determined to remain unimpressed but hoping to impress other teenagers.

Joe, Carmen, and Brett Hanson were ushering Tia from food stand to food stand. She laughed at their jokes and contributed to the conversation but found her eyes wandering every time she saw a tall, dark-haired man in the crowd.

It almost startled her to realize she was actually looking for Cap. Did she really want to find him? Not with the slender beauty she had seen at his side on two separate occasions. Jogging together and going to church together implied a close relationship.

Brett was pleasant enough, polite and mannerly, even good looking. He was also disappointed that Tia seemed to have little interest in watching him perform with White Fox during the band's next six weeks of bookings. That alone told him he was not likely to see her again, but he wasn't giving up.

The foursome had stopped to watch the River Nymphs performing water stunts on skis at Enchanted Woods Park when Carmen suddenly began waving. "Look there's Captain Nemo! We've got to go say hello to him," and she took off before Tia could stop her.

Carmen returned holding Cap by the arm and chatting animatedly. "Look who I found," she smiled as if she had just grabbed the latest American Idol. Cap was grinning too—at Tia— obviously pleased to see her.

At that moment Brett stepped up and took Tia's elbow possessively. "Uh, Cap, this is Brett Hanson," she stammered uncomfortably. "He plays music with Carmen's band-friend in the White Fox boy—boyfriend in the White Fox band."

For just an instant she glimpsed disappointment flash across his blue eyes. Then Cap smiled, extended a hand and greeted Brett. "Cole Nemon, but everyone calls me Cap."

They exchanged pleasantries while Tia stood there miserably, wishing she had not agreed to come with Bret.

"Oh, Tia, I have someone I've been wanting you to meet," Cap turned to her. "Can you come with me for moment?" Brett reluctantly allowed Tia to leave, promising to catch up with her.

They walked between random rows of lawn chairs or blankets on which sat groups of girls in hip-hugging shorts, midriff-baring jeans and crop tops. The Britney-Spears look was everywhere this summer. Woodsville teens and even their mothers were showing as much skin around the middle as possible—mostly rippling middles that should have been kept covered.

Cap remarked, "If those bare-belly gals ever decide to go swimming, it won't be skinny dipping. They'd have to go chunky dunking."

Tia's grin pleased him. He liked making her smile. They were going to share lots of laughter in years to come, he told himself, thinking he'd just have to steal her away from her new boyfriend.

Standing beside the snow-cone stand was Cap's lady friend with the mane of luxurious dark hair. If Hollywood actress Catherine Zeta-Jones ever needed a double, this woman could easily pass for her. Tia's heart dropped somewhere below her knees. It took grit for her to smile pleasantly.

So, he's going to introduce me to his girlfriend, she thought with both puzzlement and disappointment. Why?

"Tia, this is my sister, Collynda. She's given up modeling in New York and is looking for work in the Woodsville area. I've told her all about you."

All Tia heard was the word "sister." Suddenly her smile became genuine and she extended a hand.

"I'm so meet to glad—glad to meet you. I believe I've seen you at church with Cap," she blushed. Here she was reversing her word order again. Why did she always do that in front of him? Cap's sister! Of course. He'd told her about a sister who modeled in New York. She'd forgotten all about it.

Some huge part of her was very glad. In fact, when she thought it about it later, there was no part of her that wasn't absolutely delighted.

His sister!

Collynda greeted her warmly. "You're as lovely as Cap said you were. If you ever want to model in New York, you could land a job with a blink of your eyes."

Tia smiled again. "Not if I had to compete with someone as beautiful as you. Why did you leave?" She couldn't imagine anyone leaving such a glamorous job.

"The usual boring reason. A failed relationship. If I could ever find a man that has even half the integrity of my brother, I'd never let him go," Collynda patted Cap's shoulder with affection. "Of course Cap's conceited, but he's not arrogant, so I can forgive him."

They chatted about the zero-job market in northern Illinois and southern Wisconsin, and Collynda laughingly suggested she might apply at the news office.

"I'm great with a camera," she assured. "I'd love to be a photo journalist. You must have all kinds of fun."

At that moment Brett Hanson found them and once again took Tia's elbow possessively. She introduced him to Collynda as a friend and a musician.

Brett stood there, dumbstruck, staring at Collynda's flawless face. He barely managed to stammer a hello. She quickly put him at ease, asking him about what kind of music he played.

He stammered "We p-play—we do the fifties and sixties rock and roll stuff."

"Oh, I love the oldies! Maybe I'll get to hear your band sometime," she exclaimed with genuine enthusiasm

"We're playing a set later tonight," Brett offered, "Would you like to stop by the Black Rose? I can get you a front row seat."

Collynda seemed perfectly willing. She was rattling off a list of her favorite songs, and Brett was telling her his band played them all.

Tia turned to Cap. "I'd forgotten you have a sister," she ventured.

"I've been trying to get you two together. I knew she'd like you. But you don't stay on the phone long enough—not even for me to tell you what I found out at the biker bar." Suddenly all ears, Tia took his arm and ushered him aside to a less crowded area, leaving Brett and Collynda lost in conversation with each other.

"What have you found out?" she demanded in a hushed voice.

"The bartender does know Jerry Skare. They did some jail time together. He wants you to be careful. Sycho is known to write letters to people on the outside and find out personal information—stuff like when they're going on vacation. Then he writes to his gang members and sends them over to burglarize the house while it's empty."

Tia looked at him expectantly. "And?"

"And there *is* link between him and the Jurowski family, a relative who's a gang member. The gang banger has a daughter who is the mother of Sycho's child."

"I knew it! But what does that prove? If only Nate were still alive. He could tie this all together and wrap it up. Does the bartender have a theory about why anyone would want to kill Nancy?"

"All he can do is guess. He says Nancy was killed because she knew too much."

"Nothing more?" She asked him hopefully.

"I wish I had more to tell you. That's all I have at the moment," he explained, thinking he had never seen her look so animated. And something about her was different, less guarded. He couldn't quite put his finger on it.

Then he noticed that Brett and Collynda had disappeared from sight. "I'm afraid you'll have to forgive my sister. She has that effect on guys, but I promise she won't steal yours."

"He's not my guy," Tia blurted all too quickly. "I only just met him tonight, and I drove myself to the River Fest." Shut up mouth, Tia cringed inwardly. Why did it suddenly matter to her that Cap should know she wasn't seeing Brett?

Cap breathed an inward sigh of relief. So she wasn't really dating the guy. He'd felt a stab of keen disappointment at seeing Tia here with Brett, especially since she'd been so adamant about not being ready for a relationship.

Something had definitely changed in her attitude toward him. Whatever it was, he liked it, and his grin broadened even more as he realized that she actually wanted him to know Brett's status as a non-boyfriend.

"Well, so. . . shall we just walk along . . . together, and maybe we'll run into them?" Tia suggested hesitantly.

"Better yet, why don't we just walk along together and hope we don't," he took her arm. "I can be very entertaining."

Tia smiled. "More fairy tales?"

"I've given up on fairy tales, since my last one didn't impress you much."

They strolled through the crowds, pausing at different artists' displays, admiring the paintings and wood carvings, discovering their taste in art was very similar.

"You like paintings of trees that actually look like trees," he said as she nodded. She didn't object when he took her hand and they wound their way through the booths.

After a brilliant crimson sunset, blocked mostly by giant oaks and smaller trees lining the Woody River, Tia thought she should be finding Carmen and Joe. "I suppose everyone will end up at the Black Rose, including your sister," she suggested. Cap agreed, and they headed toward the popular downtown spot where they rejoined their friends.

Once again, Tia found herself seated beside Cap, listening to music that stirred tender memories. Except this time she didn't feel the familiar tightness in her throat.

The beauty of her love for Jeff would always be a part of her. Only now it was something to be recalled with more joy than sorrow. At last, Tia had begun to experience thankfulness for their time together rather than the anguish because it was over.

When White Fox played *Unchained Melody*, she decided it was time to go, but not because of tender memories. This time it was simply that the hour was late. The band took a break, and Tia made polite farewells.

Brett offered to see her to the Bronco, but Cap insisted he would be glad to serve as Tia's escort. "Besides, I really need someone to keep an eye on my sister," he teased, seeing Brett was only too eager to remain beside Collynda. For her part, Collynda appeared equally pleased.

Carmen's eyes twinkled with amusement. This was going even better than she had hoped. She liked the color in Tia's cheeks and the light in those once-haunted brown eyes. She liked the way Cap looked at Tia, and more especially that Tia was looking back.

It was all she could do to keep from giggling out loud. "See you later, Tia," she waved, then grabbed her fork and exclaimed, "*Mangia, mangia!*" to Joe, Brett and Collynda as the waiter served dessert.

Cap and Tia walked back along the Rec path as far as the swan lagoon, laughing about the way Brett had reacted when he first saw Collynda. As they reached her Bronco, she surprised Cap by looking up at him, brown eyes mischievous under velvety lashes. "So when am I going to get a ride on the back of your Harley again?"

She spoke in an almost flirtatious tone. "Any time you want to!" He exclaimed, greatly pleased that she was opening a door to him at last. He wanted to lift her in her arms and carry her to the Road King right that moment. Ride away with her to some enchanted moonlit glade and cover her sweet mouth with tender kisses. Do everything in his power to convince her that she belonged with him. Belonged *to* him. This was a woman who knew what it meant to be committed. Faithful. The kind of woman he wanted.

Instead he just stood there drinking in her fragrance, her smile and the way she looked up at him. It was the first time he had seen her eyes without that impenetrable veil covering her emotions. Instead there were hints of shyness, teasing, admiration and something else shining through. He couldn't put a name to it, but whatever it was, he liked it.

He liked it a lot.

Tia extended a formal hand by way of a goodnight. Instead of a handshake, he brought her hand to his lips in a courtly gesture. "My lady, how about if I pack some sandwiches and we go riding tomorrow after you leave the office? I know this fantastic place for a picnic supper near Lake Geneva." He was unwilling to wait until the weekend to whisk her away.

"I, uh, I think I should check my social calendar first," she teased, pretending to look at a pocket calendar inside her purse. "What do you know, I'm free!"

Before she could escape, he planted a quick kiss on her forehead. "I'll come for you at six."

She waved to him with a dazzling smile that made his heart turn flip-flops as she pulled out of the parking area. Cap wondered if she had any idea of the effect she had on his heart, or the rest of his anatomy for that matter.

Good grief, woman, do you know how long I've been waiting for you to smile at me like that?

All he could think about was seeing how those beautiful eyes lighted up when she'd learned Collynda was his sister. Carmen had been right. Let her think about the possibility of another woman in the picture. Then her true feelings would show up, whatever they might be. Of course Carmen had known all along who Collynda really was. She just hadn't bothered to mention it to Tia.

Clever girl. Cap thought he would have to send her a bouquet of flowers or some chocolates later. Certainly before the engagement announcement.

But first things first. He could wait until Thursday to take Tia riding. Or could he? Would he be rushing things to call her tonight? Maybe. But she did say she was tired, and it was getting late. Tia would have to go to work in the morning.

Okay, he could wait. But in the meantime the thoughts of having her arms around him again on the Road King made his heart pound with anticipation.

Heading back toward the Black Rose to retrieve his sister, Cap whistled cheerfully all the way, something that sound vaguely like, *You Smile and the Angel Sing*, a long-forgotten tune from his parents' older than moldy collection of big band records. He was certain he could hear singing from somewhere.

Chapter 28 - Kidnapped

.

What am I doing? Tia asked herself, amazed at her sudden boldness toward Cap as she headed the Bronco away from Enchanted Forest Park. I practically threw myself at him. Asked him to take me riding. Just came right out and asked him, of all things!

Oh well, at least I'm rid of Brett Hanson, she decided with relief, then smiled to herself thinking how Carmen would approve of this sudden change of plans. Tia suddenly laughed out loud, recalling the way Collynda had completely bedazzled the dumbstruck musician. Noticing her gas gage sitting on empty, she pulled into the Mobil station at Brookside Mall.

She had just finished filling her tank when the gun barrel jammed hard against her ribs and a male voice ordered, "Don't scream. Just do as I say."

Every hair on the back of her neck prickled with alarm. Tia recognized the malignant voice instantly.

"We're gonna just get inside your little Bronco, reporter girl." He steered her to the driver's side with his arm around her shoulders and the other holding the handgun to her side. She had no choice but to get in. He followed, shoving her clear across to the passenger's side and then started the Bronco, all the while keeping the gun jammed under her ribs.

Paralyzed from the surprise and shock of what was happening, she sat motionless, incapable of reacting for the moment, afraid to think what he wanted with her. She completely forgot about the handgun lying inside the glove box.

"You thought you got rid of me, didn't you? I took a leeetle job-related vacation, but I been reading your little newspaper every week. You don't pay attention to warnings like a good girl, now do you?" His voice was silky, as if speaking to a pampered pet. She couldn't place the accent, not exactly Spanish, but close.

Suddenly he jammed the handgun brutally into her ribs and snarled, "I told you to back off the Krahl story!"

Tia bit her lip to stifle a cry of pain. "What do you care?" she demanded, suddenly finding her voice.

"You're gonna find out soon enough," the man promised in the same silky tone he had used a moment earlier.

She turned her head to get a look at her captor. The brim of a slouchy hat drooped over his face, so she could see only the lower half at the moment. He wore a pullover shirt and faded denims— no name brand clothes, nothing out of the ordinary until she got to his boots. They were genuine ostrich leather—the expensive kind.

"Who are you anyway?"

"You don't want to know."

Wednesday, July 2, 2003

"Where are we going?"

"You ask too many questions." He pulled the Bronco to a curb in a residential block and stated, "We're gonna get out here. Just do as I say."

205

Mr. Evil-Voice pulled her roughly out the passenger side door and shoved her to a dark colored, older model Cadillac. Tia fell across the broad front seat as he shoved her inside. She sat up and immediately tried to find the door handle. There was no handle.

Evil-Voice chuckled that same malevolent throaty sound that reminded her more of a dog's growling. She realized with a shock that he had prepared this vehicle for her. With a practiced move he grabbed her wrists and lashed them together tightly. Then he shoved a wad of fabric between her teeth and tied it in place.

"Down on the floorboards," he ordered. She had no choice but to obey.

Okay. Think. Count the turns. Memorize the way he's taking us, she instructed herself out of desperate need to do something— anything.

They crossed the Woody River at some point. She could tell by the sound of the pavement, the same sound she heard every time she crossed the bridge on her way to the Post Office.

She knew when they left the main streets by the lack of street lamps shining through the car's interior. When he finally stopped the Cadillac, she knew they were in an older, poorly lighted neighborhood. Then she heard the sound of a screechy garage door opening and. rattling as it closed behind the car.

The darkness was smothering. Tia felt claustrophobic, as if she were inside a close, black cavern.

Her captor pulled her out of the car and moved her through the inky garage to a door and into a narrow stairwell. The stairs were rickety, steep and narrow. They climbed past two landings. Then he unlocked a door, shoved her through it and down a narrow hallway to a pull-down ladder that led to a trap door in the ceiling. With the gun hard against her back, she climbed up to a narrow attic room.

Once inside the small area he shoved her to the floor.

"Now then. We're going to decide what to do with you. You didn't leesten. I don't like little girls who don't leesten." His accent was even thicker now, as if he had no need to keep up a pretense.

Tia said nothing. She tried once again to get a look at her captor, but the slouchy hat shadowed his features. She was choking on the gag, and desperate to catch her breath. "Ummmm!" She pleaded.

He hesitated, then he ripped the gag out of her mouth.

"Now, you gonna find out what it's like not to do as you're told," he purred once again in that silky voice that goose pimpled her flesh.

"Who are you" She demanded, finding the temporary courage of defiance.

"Nobody knows who I am. But you gonna wish you never met me. The cops think I'm a small-time drug dealer, and that's good. I even do a stint in their jails from time to time just to keep them happy. . . and also to keep myself informed. I have guys in jail that need to be reminded of . . . certain things. The cops don't have any idea how big I am."

"So you're Mr. Big Stuff, huh? Then why do you care what I write in a little weekly newspaper?"

"Maybe I don't care. Maybe I just don't like you nosing around in my business."

"You know who killed Nancy Jurowski don't you."

"Who pulled the trigger is no matter to me. Finding out why is another thing altogether. That Jurowski woman—she knew too much. You keep nosing around, pretty soon you gonna know too much."

Tia started putting two and two together, recalling that Nancy had worked in the bank and had been in charge of transferring funds to overseas accounts. Had Nancy run across some drug lord's money laundering scheme? Is that why she had to die?

"You think I was going to expose your operation by questioning who really killed her?"

Mr. Evil-Voice chuckled. "You don't have any idea what you're playing around with. Jurowski didn't either, but she knew enough to make her dangerous."

"They'll come looking for me," Tia announced firmly, with a certainty in her voice that she didn't feel.

"Yeah, they'll come looking," the maniac smirked under his slouchy hat. "They gonna find you. Maybe they gonna think you decided to end it all. My guy's been watchin' you. He knows about that shrink doctor you been to. All we have to do is leave them a little goodbye note."

He was untying her wrists as he talked.

She was thankful for that. The cord had been so tight it had cut off circulation. She rubbed her hands together, while her mind raced ahead.

"You think you can make my murder look like suicide? The cops won't buy that. Look at these marks on my wrists. There's probably a good bruise on my ribs too from where you jabbed me with that gun. They'll know it wasn't suicide."

Evil-Voice laughed. "The marks will be gone in a day or two."

"What makes you think I'll write a suicide note?"

"You'll write it if you want a quick death. I'm expert. I know how to make you beg for death, without leaving a mark on your lovely body."

He stressed the word lovely and laughed. It was a laugh that raised the tiniest hairs on Tia's arms. She didn't want to think about the implications of his statement.

"Or I can take out your friend, that Morelli woman too. It's up to you."

She knew he wasn't making an idle threat. This man had every intention of killing her, slowly or otherwise. He knew she would cooperate to protect Carmen.

"Now you gonna wait, and think about how bad you been. You can scream all you want. Nobody gonna hear you. I'll be back." He used an exaggerated Arnold Schwarzenegger accent when he spoke the last three words. Did he think she would laugh? Tia didn't bother.

"I'm leaving you a sandwich and some bottled water. I don't like hunger. Hunger is a very bad thing in my country. Not like Sicily where my father was from. Of course I didn't have family privileges since my mother was not born there. That's okay. I make my own family. You eat."

She saw him take a key ring out of his pocket and open the door. After closing it behind him, she could barely hear the clicking of triple locks and the faint, muffled sound of his footsteps disappearing as he descended the attic stairs.

She leaned back against the wall, breathing heavily. Don't hyperventilate, she told herself, trying to inhale more slowly, willing herself to exhale after holding her breath to the count of ten. She made it to six, while her eyes darted wildly around the closet-sized room.

The low ceiling formed steep angles overhead. A single naked light bulb hung at the apex, burning weakly. If ever there had been a window, it was sealed over. The place was as dry as mummy dust and the air was suffocatingly stale. It also reeked with the strong odor of stale urine and something else. A sweetish scent of some kind. Marijuana? She could only guess, having never been around it.

The walls felt unbearably close. She remembered a short story about a prisoner of the Spanish Inquisition who had been locked inside a torture room with mechanical walls capable of closing in and crushing him to death. At that moment, she knew how he must have felt.

She also felt a terrible connection to Ben Krahl, locked inside his own prison for the past three years. In a sudden claustrophobic attack of panic, she threw her body against the door, pounding, kicking and shouting futilely for help, her heart galloping wildly inside her chest. Five minutes later she collapsed to her knees, exhausted, her knuckles bruised and bleeding. Tears of frustration streamed down her face and she crumpled in a forlorn heap on the yellowed and peeling linoleum.

The door was solidly reinforced. The rattletrap stairs had seemed so rickety when Evil-Voice ushered her up that she marveled they hadn't fallen through. But this room was not rickety.

She imagined her attic prison to be in one of those boarded up, abandoned two-story homes on Woodsville's decaying west side. The walls were probably reinforced as well as the door. If anyone was nearby, they would not hear her shouts for help. Obviously, Evil-Voice had prepared this room for her, and who knew how many others he had brought here previously.

Had he tortured his victims here? Killed them? Was she in a death chamber? She muzzled that thought from chewing at the perimeters of her sanity.

"Help! Is anybody there?" Tia's desperate voice bounced off the walls once more, muffled by some kind of heavy insulation. She listened, straining her ears to hear something. Anything. The silence was fathoms deep, as soundless as an empty asteroid hurtling through centuries of space and time.

Evil-Voice had told the truth. He was going to come back and find her waiting helplessly. Nobody else would come. This room was going to be her tomb.

No. He wouldn't leave her here. He'd dump her body somewhere else. A number of chilling possibilities, each one more macabre than the next, flashed through her frightened mind like previews of horror movies.

"I will live and not die," she said aloud. Her voice was shaky but determined.

Tia sat up and leaned back limply against the wall. She knew the weakness she felt was temporary, just the initial adrenaline rush leaving her body. But it was a consuming exhaustion nevertheless. She felt as weak as a caged butterfly.

The light bulb continued to burn a sickly yellow, but she sensed darkness gathering like a presence. Silent shadows lurked in the corners, provoking childhood fears of creatures lurking under her bed. Monsters waiting in closets for the right moment to grab her and tear her to pieces. Waiting for the lights to go out.

But those had been childhood chills. Evil-Voice was not a mythical monster. And she was no longer a child.

Here she was, Tia Marie Burgess, mild-mannered investigative reporter for the Woodsville Weekly News, locked in an attic prison that had most likely been used for torturing other victims.

She might as well face it. She was no Lois Lane and there was no Superman coming to her rescue. Evil-Voice was coming back to kill her . . . or worse.

Dear Lord! She was not stupid. She had been cautious, not careless. How the heck had she gotten herself into this nightmare? She sat there, unable to control her thoughts after her burst of futile exertion. Unable to avoid thinking about the chain of events that had set this dreaded scenario in motion.

The senseless murder of a decent young woman. The conviction of the wrong man. Her growing interest in the case. The past unfolded on the memory screen of her tortured mind with startling clarity.

Was this what it felt like before you die? A cruelty beyond understanding had torn her life apart in a single shattering accident, and she had been helpless to stop it. Now she had a window of time. There must be something she could do. She hoped for some kind of gentle guidance to show her what action to take. No, not gentle. Loud and clear, please Lord. She prayed. She waited silently for what seemed a long time.

There was no guidance forthcoming.

Sleep overcame her as she waited. The deep, dreamless sleep of exhaustion.

Thursday, July 3, 2003

Chapter 29 – The Attic

Tia awoke with a groan and immediately searched her watch for the time. *Lord, how long have I been asleep? He might be coming any minute.* In a moment of desperation she started to hyperventilate once more, then talked herself out of it.

Breathe. Count. Slow down.

Her attic prison remained unchanged. No magical doorway had appeared while she slept. No escape hatch in the floor or ceiling. Her breathing returned to normal while she talked herself into a forced calm.

Okay, she thought with some determination, she would not be paralyzed into inactivity. A realization hovering at the edge of her awareness for the last two years began to unfold with sudden clarity.

Tia saw clearly how events of the past often become excuses for failing to live in the reality of now. Many live their whole lives trapped by memories, forever blaming a tragedy, an abusive relationship, divorce or other unfortunate circumstances for their lack of achievement or fulfillment.

The history of a soul cannot be erased. No deletions. No corrections. But that writing does not have to determine the soul's future. She had lived far too long in the past, trapped by the paralysis of grief and guilt.

Her tomorrow would not matter if she did not start a plan of action now. She might have only a few more hours left. But what to do? Anything was better than nothing. She was not about to give in to the apparent hopelessness of her situation, and merely wait for her tormentor to return.

That's when she noticed the bottled water and the brown paper sack by the door. Tia quickly opened one of the bottles and gulped down the water. She had already swallowed when the thought struck her. What if Mr. Evil poisoned it?

No. Not if he wanted her death to look like suicide. Inside the sack was a wilted sandwich wrapped in paper. She unwrapped it and stared at the contents. Ham and cheese. Should she eat it?

He was coming back to kill her, but he wanted her alive when he returned. Why? Some diabolical reason. Maybe he was stupid enough to think he really could stage a convincing suicide. She munched down on the stale sandwich, deciding she would need her strength.

Slowly she became aware of the stench of urine, growing stronger with the heat. Dear Lord, her own? Admittedly she had been frightened enough to lose control, but her slacks were dry. How many others had been locked in this room with no provision for nature's call?

She realized she desperately needed relief. Glancing at the faded and peeling linoleum floor, she noticed a stained and rotted spot in one corner and stepped toward it, drawn by need.

Her nose told her this was definitely the spot where someone else had made a toilet. The odor made her nauseous. Up came the contents of her stomach spilling on the rank floor with a noisy splatter. Tia heaved twice and then once more.

She caught her breath, her attention riveted. It was the *sound* of her gore striking the floor. The first two times it had splattered. The last time it thunked.

Was the flooring rotten? Could she force her way through it? She started to get down on her hands and knees but thought better of it.

Bracing herself against the wall, she stomped the floor with the heel of her sandal, working her way by the sound of solidity toward a more hollow, rotted area. The flooring groaned under her assault.

Friday, July 4, 2006

Cap was growing increasingly alarmed. He had called Tia's apartment after giving her time to get home from the news office on Thursday evening, just as they agreed. After several unsuccessful attempts to reach her, he drove by her place on Wood Hills Rd. No lights shown from her apartment window.

While keeping a watchful eye out for the mystery van, he had driven by Tia's place often enough to know that she wasn't in the habit of going to bed early. He also knew her editor seldom gave her evening assignments. Where could she be?

By Friday morning he was alarmed enough to call the Weekly News office. He introduced himself to Pat O'Brien, asking to speak to Tia, and discovered Pat was just as worried as he was.

"Tia didn't show up for work yesterday. That's highly unusual. She never misses a day, and if she were going to be absent for some reason, it wouldn't be like her not to call me," Pat explained with concern.

Both very alarmed, the two men agreed to call each other at once if either of them heard from Tia. After hanging up the phone, Cap headed straight for the Woodsville Police Department, his body taut with spring-coiled tension. He knew that police don't usually take missing person reports seriously until after three days, but he was hoping the city cops knew Tia Burgess well enough to realize her disappearance should be looked into.

She was a reporter who hadn't shown up for work. She had been threatened and stalked by some jerk. Something was seriously wrong.

The front desk officer agreed. He sent Cap straight upstairs to speak to Sergeant Don Blocke, who listened patiently. Cap told him the story of the threatening phone calls.

"You say she hasn't had one of these calls since last fall?" Blocke asked. Heavy lidded eyes underneath the shiny brim of his officer's cap gave his puffy face the appearance of being either very bored or very sleepy.

"It may have nothing to do with her disappearance, but then again it might. I just know that it's highly unusual for her not be at work, and I'm certain she's in some kind of trouble," Cap blurted once more, not bothering to hide the alarm in his voice.

"Does she have family members in Woodsville?"

"No, her mother lives in Missouri and her brother's in California. Her best friend is a physical therapist. Carmen Morelli. I called her on my way down here. Carmen hasn't heard from Tia either."

Blocke, his paunch slightly hanging over his belt, did not look up from the notepad he was writing on. He spoke in a maddening monotone, "We don't usually start looking until three days have passed, but I'll have a man check her apartment to see if anything is missing. For instance, if her clothes and suitcase are gone. Or if there's any sign of a struggle, but I'll have to get authorization for a welfare check."

"That could take hours. Maybe I'll just go see the landlord and explain things to him and ask for a key," Cap was ready to take matters in his own hands.

"Negative, Mr. Nemon. If there is something there, you could destroy evidence. Let me handle it."

Cap nodded reluctantly.

"I will tell you this," Blocke acknowledged with a tired sigh. "Her Bronco was found this morning over in Rockford. A traffic patrol officer stopped some kids on a DUI charge. They admitted they had grabbed the vehicle for a joyride after they found it parked on a residential street in Woodsville around 1 a.m. Thursday morning. The keys were still in the ignition."

"What! That means she never made it home after she left the park Wednesday night," Cap quickly filled in the details of the last time he had seen Tia, his alarm growing by the minute.

Blocke took a few notes, and then instructed Cap to go home and wait, assuring him he would call as soon as he had any information.

Right. Go home and wait. Like I could do that, he thought as he walked down the stairs and out onto the sidewalk. Tia was in real trouble and he had to find her.

Black rage welled up at the thought of anyone harming her. His eyes narrowed while he drove straight to the street where Blocke said the Bronco had been taken.

After knocking on a few doors to ask residents if they had seen or heard anything on Wednesday night, he soon realized he was wasting his time. Nobody wanted to talk to him. Even if they did know something, nobody wanted to get involved.

Finally in desperate frustration, he gave up and drove home. Later that afternoon he called Blocke's number.

"Yes, we checked the apartment. Nothing seemed out of order," the detective said in that same monotone voice.

"Mr. Nemon, are you aware Mrs. Burgess was seeing a psychiatrist?" Blocke asked.

"No. But I know that she went through a lot after her husband was killed in a car wreck. Maybe she was seeing him for grief counseling or something."

"She was taking antidepressants and sleeping pills. We found empty prescription bottles in the bathroom."

"I don't know about anything about any pills. What does that have to do with anything anyway?" Cap demanded, suddenly irritated with Sergeant Blocke's matter-of-fact attitude.

There was a pregnant pause. Then Blocked asked, "How do you know she hasn't staged her own disappearance? She's been harping on that Krahl case in her paper for months. If she could make it look like someone was threatening her, it would be a great ploy to draw attention to her theory that Krahl's not the killer."

For a moment it took every ounce of restraint Cap could summon to keep from calling Sergeant Blocke a few names he might use only for a junkyard rat. His normally enthusiastic eyes became flat and hard and the muscles of his jaw tightened.

He measured his words in a steely voice, "Let me tell you something, Sergeant Blocke. Tia Burgess is not crazy. You think she's taken on a lost cause? Fine. She believes Ben Krahl is innocent. She wants nothing less than to dig out the truth— something the state's attorney apparently won't bother to do. Truth may not matter to the court anymore, but it matters to Tia. She wouldn't violate it by putting on some ridiculous disappearance act."

Sergeant Blocke's voice remained impassive. "We're having the Bronco dusted for fingerprints. We'll call you if we find anything."

"You find her!" Cap ordered.

He slammed down the receiver and walked to the window where he stood clenching and unclenching his fists.

Friday, July 5, 2003

Chapter 30 – The Storm

It seemed like long, leg-cramping hours after she began stomping at the rotted flooring, but Tia's efforts were finally rewarded. Something gave way under her tired foot and her broken sandal's heel pushed through into empty space.

Cooler air wafted from below through the small hole into the stifling attic room. She drew in the fresher air, gulping like a fish out of water, desperately grateful for the comparative coolness. Rivulets of sweat poured down her forehead and dampened her tired body. She reached for the second and last bottle of water, drinking it down in great gulps.

Momentarily refreshed, Tia began stomping with all her weight on the rotten and caving wood, then peeled back the faded linoleum with bleeding fingers. The wood underneath was riddled with termite holes and appeared spongy. She had broken completely through in one place. *Keep at it. Soon I'll have a hole big enough to slide through to—to what?*

What was underneath? Another room? A crawl space? Or would she drop some fifteen or twenty feet to a hard floor? She decided she had to take the risk. The power of a plan, even if it failed, was better than waiting helplessly for Mr. Evil-Voice to come back.

Leg muscles quivered from exertion. Eyes blinked back tears of tension. Tia had to rest, just a little while, and gather her strength.

She lay down on the dirty flooring and closed her eyes.

* * *

Somewhere on the west side of Woodsville, in the nondescript home of a one-legged Mexican who was currently gone on business, Mr. Evil-Voice leaned back and smoked his seventy-five dollar cigar. It was a luxury he allowed himself only in private when in Woodsville.

He prided himself on how well he blended in to the Woodsville underworld, and thought of himself as extremely clever. Even his arrests were planned to conceal his true identity. No one had the slightest clue how large his operations really were, including his so-called partner, a Texas border patrol officer who had been stashing away a very nice retirement fund for himself while looking the other way.

It was time to pay a visit to stubborn reporter girl. He had been thinking up a delicious plan for her that would eliminate the need for a suicide note. He was going to enjoy it. Maybe she would enjoy it too, for a short time.

A mixture of Ecstasy in her veins would make her willing for anything. She wouldn't know the drug was laced with his own lethal recipe. Even if she did know, she'd be compliant and alive long enough to serve his purposes.

When the cops found her body, they'd believe she had gotten hold of some bad stuff accidentally. He'd see to that. Just visit her Bronco and leave some used syringes behind. It wouldn't be hard.

The marks on her hands and wrists would look like bondage. He'd plant some porn magazines in the Bronco too, with pages ear-marked to the dominatrix stuff. It had worked on the woman he'd left in New Orleans. It would work on reporter girl in Woodsville, Wisconsin.

Or maybe he'd just knife her up good and dump her in the river. That had worked before too. There are lots of ways to get rid of an annoying problem, he thought, priding himself on how successful he had been in the past.

The key was to do your own dirty work. Then you don't have to worry about a hit man getting caught and turning state's evidence. He'd make that mistake only once. The hit man was doing fifty years hard time for another crime and was not likely to talk. Even if he did, no one would believe him, but that little oversight was not going to happen again.

Actually dirty work was not the term for it. He was beginning to think of it more as a craft. He found he enjoyed planning an unsolvable murder. He liked the challenge. Liked watching investigators wasting their time chasing down planted and diversionary clues. Liked knowing how cleverly he could outsmart them.

The first time he killed, it had left him panicky and shaken for several days. After that crime remained unsolved, he'd gained confidence. The second time he'd planned the murder so another suspect would get the blame. His plan had succeeded beautifully.

He was growing more confident in what he liked to think of as superior thinking skills. He had a real talent for killing. Maybe he would just take his time with reporter girl.

He inhaled once more, savoring the imported cigar, eager to begin but willing to restrain himself. Reporter girl wasn't going anywhere. He chuckled slowly, turning over in his mind the different methods he had chosen in the past, and thinking up new ones.

Planning the deed was half the fun, a way to revel in his own cleverness. He would finish the cigar first.

* * *

Once more Tia slept the deep sleep of nervous and physical exhaustion. Hours passed until she stirred, more from a muscle cramp than anything else. Again she awoke to a nightmare, blinking her eyes, aghast at her surroundings.

The naked bulb still burned. She was thankful for that. It would have been a worse horror to be locked in Stygian darkness.

She sat up, groaning from stiffness and rubbing her aching legs, then looked at her watch in horror. One o' clock, a.m. or p.m.? She had no way of knowing.

* * *

Twenty miles across the state line in Rockford, Illinois the last of the fireworks extravaganza had stitched blossoms on the canopy of night, flowers that burst into colorful bloom, then faded and slid down into the reflecting waters of the Rock River. Organizer Joe Marino breathed his final sigh of thankfulness for the pleasant weather, always a concern until the Fourth of July celebration was over.

Tired Woodsville residents had driven back to their neighboring city and settled the children in their beds.

Residential lights blinked out. The entire city slept quietly, blanketed by the calm July night. No one had any idea of the approaching storm, a tsunami wall of wind instead of water, freakish and unprecedented, already hurtling toward the city.

Mr. Evil-Voice decided to go out for a late dinner, something he rarely did, but on this evening he felt festive. Didn't he deserve a little celebration like everyone else in this land of the free?

He enjoyed a glass of imported Chianti and an excellent dish prepared with just the proper amount of seasonings rubbed on cubes of choice Texas Black Angus and served with a deliciously prepared stuffed portabella mushroom, sautéed in imported olive oil and topped with freshly grated parmesan and pine nuts. On the side were breaded artichoke hearts and a basket of finely baked breads. The food was almost as good as his favorite restaurant in Flower Mound, Texas.

For dessert he ordered fresh strawberries in a rich chocolate dipping sauce.

Evil-Voice tipped the chef modestly, wanting his evenings out to appear more like a luxury he had long saved for rather than a common event he could regularly afford if he wished. He often congratulated himself on being so very clever that no one would ever suspect he was not who he appeared to be.

At times he believed he was invincible. This night was one of those times. Why shouldn't he allow himself to have a little treat?

After driving to the lop-sided Mexican's home to stop for his tools, he decided to smoke one more cigar before getting down to the dessert of the evening, his "craft." Over the past few hours, he had been thinking that while playing a game with the cops was great fun, playing with his intended victims was something to be relished as well. He had always regretted not spending more time with that angel-faced blonde in Dallas. Such a waste. But then she had been . . . too willing. Too cooperative. The fun was in the resistance. The delicious fear!

He hoped the reporter would offer him at least some small challenge, just to keep things interesting. If she did, he might let her live a little longer.

* * *

In her attic prison, Tia worked feverishly to enlarge the hole in the rotten floor. She was making progress when she thought she heard the muffled sound of an approaching vehicle. She realized with heart-pounding fear that it was the only sound she had heard since her captivity. Maybe there had been cars passing by, but she had not heard any sound from outside until now.

Was it him? Her heart pounded a little faster, like a rabbit hiding helplessly in the brush as the hungry wolf snuffled closer and closer.

She listened. There it was. The unmistakable, screechy sound of the garage doors below her.

Sound was no longer trapped outside her attic prison, now that she had broken through the floor. Without waiting any longer, she struggled to squeeze her lower body through the ragged opening, stretching one leg down. She was greatly relieved to find a beam or joist of some kind with her toes.

It was a crawl space above a dropped ceiling over the second floor, perhaps slightly more than two-foot deep.

Okay, go for the crawl space and try to stay on a joist or a beam of some kind, she told herself. The sound of the garage door rattled the rickety walls from below once again, letting her know it was closing. The mad man would soon be here.

She strained her hips through and then her shoulders, holding her arms over her head as if she were squirming through an inner tube and under the water.

Only this wasn't water she slipped into. Tia had to twist her slender body unnaturally in order to get herself into a cramped crawling position. She wanted to put as much distance between herself and the escape portal as she could before her captor discovered it.

Unfortunately the crawl space was dark. Only a thin yellow stream of light managed to escape from above into the hole. It beamed down like a spotlight, revealing a disgusting array of beetles, dead wasps and assorted arachnids on the insulation below the ceiling joists. The rest of the crawl space was swallowed up by thick darkness.

Which way to go? She moved carefully along the beam, stifling a scream when a clingy spider's web spread across her face.

Footsteps sounded on the rickety stairs nearing the level of her head.

Tia bumped her head against a wall. This meant she had to move backwards if she was going to stay on the beam and hope to find where it intersected with another.

It was slow going. Her muscles ached and her eyes strained to see in the dusty and stifling space. At one point she slipped, her feet striking paper-thin insulation material directly beneath the beam. It occurred to her that whatever ceiling panels might lie under the insulation were probably as rotten as the flooring above her head. Scrambling to keep her balance she clung fiercely to the wooden structure, her breathing labored and her hands slick with sweat.

Almost directly above her head, she heard the sound of keys in the lock. Get moving, she told herself. But she froze, paralyzed with fear.

The door creaked open. She imagined Evil-Voice standing there in surprise. Then she heard a sound that made her flesh crawl. Laughter, a slow deep chuckle that seemed to come from some pit of vile mirth. It was the kind of laughter you might expect from a vampire about to sink his fangs into a helpless victim's throat.

A cloud of dust particles tickled Tia's nose. Not now. Don't sneeze now! She started to let go of the joists and pinch her nostrils together. Too late. The sneeze escaped. She couldn't control it.

The sound of his laughter, louder this time, spurred her to start moving again, anxiously. From around her came scrabbling, scurrying noises, then squeaking sounds.

Mice or rats!

Like most women, Tia abhorred rats, but at this point she'd rather face a whole nest of the vicious, red-eyed, naked-tailed beasts than the beast who was standing over her head, separated from her only by a rotted-out floor.

"You a clever girl, but don't think you gonna get away from me," Evil-Voice chuckled.

She would never fear rats again. The movie about some loser and his pet rat popped into her mind, making her wish she had a whole rat herd of rat-friends to command at that moment. She gleefully imagined the squealing herd erupting through the hole in the floor to devour the demon coming after her.

Footsteps, slow and deliberate, moved across the room above her to the hole. He was down on his knees. She heard him cursing the darkness. Then he spoke patiently, "I'm sorry to keep you waiting, my reporter girl. I'll be right back. You think I don't keep a flashlight in my car?"

More laughter. This time the footsteps moved rapidly out of the room and down the stairs. Tia moved rapidly too.

Chapter 31 - Wind

To the west of Woodsville, the unnatural storm rushed forward, a torrential tidal wall of wind power, uprooting trees and tossing garbage cans, mailboxes and picnic tables aside as if they were made of paper. The wind seemed to feed itself, gaining strength as it approached the city, and soon barn siding, roof panels and outbuildings went flying. Many observers later reported hearing a roar like a freight train and were convinced a tornado passed overhead, despite what the weather reporters said the next day.

Woodsville media would awaken to the devastation and soon be calling the July 5th, 2003 storm a "microburst" with wind speeds of up to 100 mph. Unlike a hurricane or a spinning tornado with centrifugal force, this wind blasted straight ahead like a giant, roaring locomotive on a straight, wide track of destruction. The gale struck Woodsville first around 2 a.m., then hurtled on toward Rockford, blasting that city with the same furious intensity.

Power lines were instantly downed over three-fourths of the community. A television station's tower toppled as if it had been made of toothpicks.

Before the storm hit Woodsville it gathered force enough to rip giant oaks and other trees from their roots like mere dandelions.

Tia had not yet heard the approaching roar. She could hear only the approach of the monster who was going to kill her if she didn't stop him.

She thought of how many times she had wanted to die over the last few years since she had lost Jeff and their child.

Then she thought of Cap's intensely blue eyes, his gentle voice, his passionate kiss. In that moment, she knew that she desperately wanted to live to kiss him again.

She had crawled along the beam as far as she could go and was squeezed against a corner in the gloom.

Maybe if he came in after her she would at least have a choice of two directions to flee from him. Perhaps she could manage to kick him off the beam and he'd fall through the insulation and the rotten stuff underneath it.

She didn't want to think he might have a gun and would have an easy time aiming a shot at her once he had her in his sight. How was she going to dodge a bullet?

Dear God help me get out of here, she prayed desperately, this time out loud. Was Jesus awake? This must be how Peter felt when the wind and waves threatened to swamp his wallowing fishing boat. The Lord was in the boat with him alright, but sound asleep.

Wake up, Lord! I'm sinking. Don't you care?

Then she saw the flashlight's beam moving through the crawl space, a wand of white light throwing the cramped area into an eerie pattern of moving shadows.

He was coming through the hole! She squeezed her eyes shut, unwilling to look at her tormentor, as if she could somehow keep him away by not acknowledging his presence. There was nowhere to hide.

The thumping of her heart might have been hopelessness knocking at the door of her heart, but she resisted it. A scripture sprang to mind. All things are possible to one who believes. She tried desperately to believe she would get out of this alive.

Evil-Voice had some difficulty squeezing his medium frame into the crawl space, but he was as determined as Tia had been, and he was in no hurry.

When he finally managed to heave himself through and was balanced on a joist, he shined the flashlight slowly around the area, across the beams and ancient insulation beneath them, over Tia, and back again to her pitifully cowering form.

"Ah. There you are," he rasped in delight, as if he had just discovered a tasty morsel.

"You gonna come here or make me come to you?"

She didn't answer him.

"You gonna wish you come here. I can make things easy for you or verrrrry hard. It's up to you." He drew out the word "very" with a great emphasis.

"Come and get me!" Tia spat out with a courage she did not feel. She turned her head toward him, trying to see if he had a gun, but the flashlight, beamed directly at her face, was blinding.

Evil-Voice had left the gun in the room above. He had other plans for Tia. The syringe in his pocket was loaded with a specially mixed hallucinogenic, a slowly fatal cocktail. All he had to do was get close enough to plunge it into her body.

Getting her out of the crawl space would be no problem. Just let the drugs act a few moments and she would become a cooperative zombie. She would do anything he suggested. She would even throw herself into the muddy Woody River if he asked her to.

Maybe he would.

Still, he didn't like the looks of the aged insulation material beneath him. The house had been specially equipped for holding hostages, not fortified for crawling on rotted ceiling joists. He knew much of the frame was eaten away by termites.

How long would these joists support him? He wasn't sure, and the uncertainty sharpened his enjoyment of the game. She was making things difficult enough to challenge his skills. This was going to be even more fun than he imagined.

Evil-Voice began moving toward her, laughing in a low, diabolical manner. She deemed him a madman, an evil Vincent Price character from some forgotten horror movie of her childhood.

If anyone in Woodsville had glanced out a window, he would have seen a display of impossible colors intermittently lighting the inside of towering and terrible storm clouds, the wind already pummeling the city. Mother Nature seemed determined to put the July fireworks display to shame with her own monumental display.

Suddenly roaring with impossible velocity, the furious wind slammed into the house with the force of an avalanche.

The termite-riddled building shuddered and groaned like a mortally wounded thing.

Hardly aware of the rage outside, Tia prepared to fight for her life, her muscles tense, her heart pounding.. With eyes now somewhat adjusted to the gloom, she could see a glint of psychotic glee in the eyes of her tormentor. He was no ordinary man. He was evil personified. It was clear that he would not let her live.

"You gonna wish you come to me. Maybe I let you die a little quicker, huh?" He threatened again, alternately purring and growling like a giant panther creeping toward her pitiful hiding place.

Nearing the corner space where she was trapped, he removed the hypodermic syringe from his shirt pocket. Tia could see the syringe glimmering like the fangs of a venomous reptile.

She looked frantically for some way of escape. And saw none.

* * *

Cap paced back and forth inside his bedroom. The unpredicted, freakish storm and his urgent sense of Tia in impending danger made him jumpy, unsettled and tired. But the idea of lying down was unthinkable. He waited, hoping desperately for the phone to ring.

It wasn't going to ring. Not at this time of night.

He knew that every detective in Woodsville was probably already sleeping soundly.

The night duty officers were snoozing at their desks or had pulled their patrol cars over to a sheltered spot for a little nap. The sleeping city rested, unaware of the approaching disaster. Veteran policemen knew there would be few calls for assistance tonight. Even the usual late-shift workers weren't out on the streets, their plants closed down for the patriotic weekend.

Though physically tired, Cap's growing sense of alarm would not allow him to sleep. What could he do? He glanced out the window, and saw the bellies of towering storm clouds, colored by flashes from inside, impossible hues of green, orange and amber.

It might have been beautiful under other circumstances. Tonight it was portentous of coming disaster and he was helpless to stop it. The storm was approaching rapidly.

Tia needed help. He could feel it in his gut, and he desperately wanted to help her. If it were not for the threat of this tempestuous night, he would already be out searching for her.

If anyone dared to harm her! His stomach muscles tautened at the thought. Heaven help the man who laid a hand on her!

The sight of those unnatural clouds made him think better of venturing out. He would wait until they moved on. Until then he paced the floor like a newly caged lion, anxiously probing its perimeters.

* * *

"I have a surprise for you, and you gonna like it," Evil-voice purred as he drew nearer. Tia slammed her foot backwards at his head, hoping to catch him in the throat.

The heel didn't connect. Instead she felt his hand grab her ankle and jerk her leg towards him, causing her to cling desperately to the beam, barely maintaining her balance. If she was having trouble keeping her balance, he must surely be having the same problem.

She kicked backwards again with strength fueled by adrenaline. This time she heard a grunt for her efforts. The flashlight he had been holding in his free hand smashed through the tar paper insulation and whatever substance lay beneath it. Farther below they both heard a metallic clattering sound.

At the same time, the faint light shining through the hole in the floor flickered and went out. Now they were plunged in total darkness. She heard her stalker mutter a curse.

Tia was vaguely aware of a keening outside. The house seemed to shiver on its very foundations, timbers creaking and groaning as the powerful blast continued shoving against it. Somewhere above parts of the roof ripped off and went airborne.

She felt his hand on her ankle again and heard the laugh. She tried to kick free but this time she couldn't shake his grip. With horror she thought of the syringe. Before she allowed him to stab her with some unknown drugs, she would take her chances and drop through the flimsy stuff beneath her.

Evil-Voice had secured a good grip on the calf of her leg with one incredibly strong hand. He held the venomous syringe with the other, raising it, preparing to plunge it deeply into her slender leg.

Was her life going to end like this? She struggled to kick him once more, determined to throw herself off the beam if she had to drag him with her.

Ripping, splintering sounds. Howling winds. Both exploded into the darkness of the crawl space. A spray of wind-driven rain burst through the wall, hammering her body with startling fury.

The joist tilted crazily. Tia scrambled for a handhold, vaguely aware of a huge tree limb ramming its way past her head with the force of a runaway train. The roaring blast swallowed up a descending scream, Evil-Voice on his way down to somewhere below her.

She felt herself plummeting also, a sickening, stomach flipping plunge.

Dropping through inky darkness, she found herself clinging desperately to a supple branch inside the house. From outside, the trunk of an enormous tree lay tilted against the shivering two-story house, a huge gaping wound ripped open in the dilapidated siding.

The intruding limb was supple and wet, and her desperate hands were losing their grip, but she felt the branch arcing downwards.

She dropped once more, her body landing with a thud on something solid. This time she lost consciousness.

The freakish windstorm spent its full fury in mere minutes.

Sudden silence was as deafening as the previous howling wind, the blast already moving on a steady path toward Rockford, leaving Woodsville littered with downed power lines, uprooted trees, torn limbs and debris.

The city looked like a war zone.

Tia opened her eyes, wet and sore, but exhilarated to be alive. She was lying on the second floor of the wrecked two-story. A large part of the tree had crashed its way through to the ground floor below her. Flickers of lightning continued to put on an after-show, giving Tia enough momentary light to see her way out of the storm ravaged structure.

She ran a mental inventory of her body. Everything seemed to be in working order. If she had a broken bone, she was unaware of it. Thank you God.

Get out of here now, her inner voice screamed.

Where was Evil-Voice? She didn't bother to look for him in the debris. Carefully picking her way over splintered siding, she found the stairs largely intact, scampered down and broke free through the torn wall into the coolness of the night.

She was standing in an older residential area of largely abandoned homes. It was not a part of Woodsville she had ever visited, but the sooner she could get out of it, the better.

This required wading over buckled pavement on grassy walks and sadly neglected streets through a soupy mixture, a flotsam of leaves, litter and debris. Dirty water poured off rain gutters and awnings and swirled in swollen gutters.

She had to pick her way carefully through the destruction, watchful for downed power lines. It was slow going.

The furious wind-driven rain had slowed to a gentle shower and felt wonderful to her tortured and dehydrated body. She lifted her face to the flow and breathed another prayer of thanks.

It took more than an hour to pick her way through unknown blocks to a business district. She was disappointed but not surprised to see that most traffic lights and streetlights were dark. How large an area the power outage covered she could only guess.

Somewhere a siren wailed, but from the looks of the streets, no police car or ambulance was going to get through, at least not to this area for awhile.

She made her shaky way along the sidewalk hoping to find a bridge and get back across the Woody River to the east side. Maybe she could find a gas station open with an operable phone.

That's when she noticed a glow from a nearby block. The outage had left one quadrant of Woodsville untouched. She swelled with gratefulness when she saw a 24-hour Mobil station ahead. Breathless and almost giddy with relief, she persuaded the storm-shocked night clerk to let her use his cell phone since telephone lines were down. Then she dialed Cap's cell phone number.

"Tia! Thank God, are you all right?" Cap exclaimed in a voice weak with relief. Every fiber of his being rejoiced to hear her voice. "Where are you?"

She managed to get a street address from the night clerk.

Cap instructed, "Stay right where you are, I'm coming to get you."

Like she had the energy or the means to go anywhere, Tia thought, her body trembling. The clerk offered her a bottle of water and a Hostess cupcake. She gratefully accepted the water.

Running out the door, Cap leaped inside his Jeep, glad he had four-wheel drive. He quickly discovered the north side of Woodsville was less damaged, free of the heaviest storm debris, so he detoured even farther north to White Pines Bridge and crossed over the Woody River. On the west side he plowed the Jeep through and over debris-littered streets until they became impassable, then leaped out and walked the rest of the way to the Mobil station on West Magnolia.

Tia had never been so glad to see anyone as she was to see Cap walking through the door. In a moment she was lost in his arms, trembling against his solid chest and heaving sobs of relief.

Overwhelmed with relief at finding her in one piece, Cap held her, fiercely protective, as if she might dissolve into molecules and be lost to him again. He was shocked at the bruised look in her eyes, huge and dark against the alabaster pale of her skin.

Tenderly he asked, "Tia are you hurt?" and added with some alarm in his voice. "If anyone has dared to lay a hand on you—"

"I'm okay. I'm—I'm—I'll tell you all about it, but let's get out here first."

It felt good to be wrapped in his strong arms. Safe. She wanted to stay there, her head against his chest, hearing the steady, rhythmic beating of his heart.

"When I couldn't find you I nearly went out of mind," he murmured gently, his lips against her rain-soaked hair. "I'll never let you out of my sight again, woman!" He realized he had spoken the words aloud, but at this point he didn't care. Anything he had ever wanted was a poor second to Tia. She was inside him like a fine wine.

He couldn't keep from covering her face with kisses. She wrapped her arms around his neck, stood on tiptoe and lightly brushed her lips against his.

A whip of desire arced through his body. Cap wanted to respond with a genuine kiss, but restrained himself. He accepted her kiss as an expression of gratitude.

"You're shivering. Here put my jacket on," he said, wrapping her inside his windbreaker.

They started out together. When she stumbled, Cap lifted her and carried her back to the Jeep, wanting to ask all kinds of questions, but also knowing she was too exhausted to re-live her ordeal at the moment. When he lifted her inside, she immediately closed her eyes.

Chapter 32 - Waking

The next time Tia opened her eyes, she was lying wrapped in a warm blanket on a comfortable sofa. She started to get up, but groaned from a sudden catch in her back and stiff muscles. Cap sat watching her from a chair. He grinned. He had stayed beside her during the hours she slept, afraid to leave. Besides, he liked having her completely in his care. She looked like a sleeping kitten, so charmingly vulnerable.

"Hello," he said. "I've been watching you rest, and you really are a Sleeping Beauty. How are you feeling?"

"I feel more like Waking Achy than Sleeping Beauty at the moment," she smiled back. "Thank you for coming to my rescue."

Then she noticed she was wearing some kind of a bathrobe, a man's bathrobe.

Reading her mind, Cap explained, "You had to get out of those wet clothes and that's all I had to offer you. Remember? You changed in the bathroom."

"Oh yes," she yawned. It was all coming back to her now. The whole nightmare. The attic. The terror of Evil-Voice. The storm. But she felt warm, rested and safe with Cap here beside her. Protected. What a welcome feeling.

He served her a cup of steaming coffee, and she told him the whole story.

*The July 5, 2003 microburst is historical fact.

* * *

It was several days before Woodsville dug out completely from the freakish storm's devastation and more than a week before Commonwealth Edison could restore power to the entire city a few blocks at a time.

Sergeant Blocke took Tia's statement and sent detectives to check the house, which she managed to direct them to only after she rode along with them. Cap also went with them, anxious to whisk her away so that she wouldn't have to see whatever they might found.

The body of Evil-Voice lay underneath the tree branches and a pile of debris, a splinter of which penetrated the temple of his head and protruded from his mouth.

Later, after all the fingerprints were run and cross-matched, authorities could only identify him as a small-time drug dealer from Texas, who had been in and out of the Woodsville County Jail and around the area for years.

They listened to Tia's story about his connection to the Jurowski homicide and his claims of belonging to some big operation.

They only listened. They had no evidence—nothing but her word.

Tia wept tears of frustration over her failure to find out more about Nancy's murderer from Evil-Voice. Then she dried her eyes and resolved, okay, it's back to square one.

She wrote a gripping account of her captive ordeal for the Weekly News.

She wrote a letter to Ben Krahl, apologizing that she had failed to get evidence from the man who had kidnapped her before he died in the storm. She told him to hang in there. She wasn't about to give up now.

Over the next few weeks, she wrapped her arms around Cap's waist while riding on the back of his Road King under a gorgeous August moon. They traveled over miles of terrain, stopping only to watch the diamonds of starlight shimmering off the water's surface and the tiny glow of lightning bugs winking through the trees.

On a warm September evening, she sat down to a candlelight dinner with Cap, served on his charming balcony overlooking a small, well-manicured lagoon near the Enchanted Woods golf course.

Cap thought she had never looked more radiant, dressed in a simple white sundress, the shoulder straps showing off suntanned shoulders, which spoke of their recent picnics together by the lake. Her satiny skin positively glowed in the golden rays of a spectacular sunset.

"I've been wondering what I was going to do about you since the first time you interrupted my breathing process," he said, taking her hand in his and watching her eyes intently, but keeping a smile on his lips.

She smiled back at him. "I didn't treat you very nicely."

"No you didn't, and I've been meaning to talk to you about that. I think I'll give you some time to make it up to me. It's probably going to take at least a couple of hundred years."

"And . . . what would I have to do during those years?" She asked, still smiling.

"Oh you'll have to accompany me on moonlight rides. Then we'll stop for midnight picnics underneath a canopy of stars. Of course there'd be lots of slave labor too—washing the car, my clothes and ironing my shirts."

Cap held his breath. Was he rushing things again? Her reply could be painful. An ear can pierce a human heart as fatally as a sword, he thought. But he had to risk hearing her response.

To his delight, Tia's smile broadened.

"I really like riding behind you on that Harley Road King. If it weren't for that I'd probably have to give this laundry thing a lot of thought," she teased. "But first I have a book to write."

"You can write all the books you like, but wouldn't it be easier if you had a husband to cook for you, say someone who knows how to make lasagna like this?"

Tia laughed. She loved lasagna. She loved Harleys. And she was falling in love with Cap Nemon. How could she resist? "That sounds suspiciously like a marriage proposal," she suggested.

"Then let me do this right." Cap left his chair, got down on one knee and looked up into her surprised eyes.

He was not smiling when he asked for her hand. This time he was completely serious.

A shadow of pain in her eyes caused his heart to pound.

"Cap, what if I can't have children?" she asked weakly, her lower lip trembling.

He didn't take his eyes off hers. Speaking gently and earnestly, he said, "Tia, we can't live our lives based on the what-ifs. What if the roof caves in tomorrow? What if green hair grows on my chin? Life doesn't come with any guarantees except the promises of God. I can't promise you everything you always wanted. But I can promise you this. You have my love, my heart and all that goes with it. I'm asking you for yours.

She didn't say yes.

Instead she leaned toward him with an achingly tender kiss that said more to him than words.

* * *

Only a few months earlier, Tia had never in her wildest dreams imagined that she would someday be thankful for the storms in her life. Storms are unpredictable and powerful. Nobody controls the wind. People can only control the way they respond to it.

Most people in Woodsville looked at the destruction, the disorder, and their inconveniences, and they cursed the July windstorm.

Tia looked up at the rainbow and thanked God. A storm had destroyed the happy life she once planned to live as her beloved Jeff's wife and as the mother of their children. Another storm had given her life back again. A new beginning. A new love.

Later that night, humming a tuneless melody she had picked up from Cap, she sat down at her word processor and wadded up the pages of the manuscript she had previously been working on. She was relieved, even happy to toss them.

At that moment, she was thinking of Nate Cash. He'd been so certain that Ben Krahl was innocent. She remembered what he said when she asked him, "What if the state's attorney doesn't act on your investigation? What if he just forgets about Ben and you and me and the whole thing altogether?"

Nate had answered with a twinkle in his sky blue eyes, "Then we go to Plan B. I'll have to write a book."

She lifted a glass to her lips. Those who live must represent those who did not live long enough to fulfill their plans. "Here's to you, Nate," she toasted.

Tia flicked the "on" switch of her computer and began to keyboard the words of the introductory chapter.

Like a vampire wrapped in the black velvet cloak of night, he waited, watching patiently. Because the house was set at an angle, he could see through open curtains on a side window of Nancy Jurowski's bungalow.

AFTERWORD

Meet the man on whose story this book is based. Shown in photo above is Ted Kuhl, # K-77710, Department of Corrections, P. O. Box 1900, Canton IL, convicted of the 1996 murder of a 29-year-old bank employee in Rockford, IL. Out of respect for the victim's family, her real name has not been used. She will be referred to as Nancy Jurowski in the following addendum.

At the time of this writing, Ted Kuhl, shown in above photo, has been in prison since 1997 for the murder of his girlfriend, shot down in the parking lot of Meadow Mart Mall in Loves Park, Illinois on December 7, 1996. Like the fictional character Ben Krahl, Ted was convicted without any forensic or scientific evidence. No motive was ever proved. No credible eyewitness ever testified. No murder weapon was ever found.

Ted's numerous post conviction appeals have been denied. He has exhausted his options, his finances and his hopes.

The man whose fictional counterpart is Rocky Miller has moved out town. He still refuses to speak with any investigators or reporters from the Rockford Labor News.

A convict on whom the character of Sycho Skare is loosely based, continues to write the author. He is serving 50 years for the drive-by-shooting death of Rockford woman, Paula Proper in

October of 1998. He has since denied knowing who killed Nancy
Jurowski

Lynn Jordan, the character loosely based on Skare's co-
defendant for the homicide, has lost her appeals. She also is
serving a 50-year sentence for the 1998 drive-by shooting of
Rockford woman, Paula Proper.

The late Joe Lamb (fictionalized as private investigator Nate
Cash) has a daughter, Joyce Lamb, a successful author of award-
winning mystery suspense novels and her assistance with this book
is greatly appreciated.

While the author obviously has had some of the same
investigative experiences and witness interviews as the fictional
reporter, Tia Burgess, the resemblance ends there. Tia Burgess,
Cap Nemon and Mr. Phillips are entirely fictional and not intended
to represent any person alive or dead.

It is the author's great hope that this book will somehow spur
new interest in Ted Kuhl's case. Or better yet the truth will finally
emerge which will prove Ted's innocence beyond a shadow of
doubt—clearly visible and no longer just a shadow in the rain.

For those who are interested, a letter on behalf of prisoner,
Ted Kuhl, written to the governor of Illinois, U.S. congressmen
and the Illinois Attorney General would be greatly appreciated by
his family and friends who have exhausted all avenues to prove his
innocence.

Readers will find a fascinating read in the following copy of
forensic scientist Arthur Chancellor's report, a highly professional
analysis of the Ted Kuhl case based on police reports, witness
statements and court records.

Investigative Consultant

Arthur Chancellor, forensic scientist V – Mississippi Crime Laboratory, Batesville, MS, (since May 2001)
Previous Positions
Operations officer, Ft. Campbell District Office, US Army Criminal Investigation Command, May 1999-May 2001 (retired from US Army Criminal Investigation Command as Chief Warrant Officer Four in May of 1001
Commander – Special Agent in Charge 31st MP Det (CID) Ft. Campbell, KY (Sept. 96 – May 99)
Commander – Special Agent in Charge 90th MP Det (CID) Ft. Sill, OK (Jan. 95 – Sept. 96)
Team Chief – Crimes Against Persons, 44th MP Det (CID) Ft. Lewis, WA (May 93 – Jan, 95)
Team Chief – Crimes Against Persons, 44th MP Det (CID) Ft. Lewis WA (Nov. 91 – May 93)
Special Agent, Level One Drug Suppression Team, Heidelberg, Germany (July 88 – Nov. 91)
Team Chief – Drug Suppression Team – Ft. Campbell District Office, KY (Aug. 86 – Oct. 87)
Other assignments as CID Special Agent, Military Police Investigator (Jan. 74 – Nov. – Aug. 86)
FORMAL CIVILIAN EDUCATION
Masters in Criminal Justice Administration, Okla.
City University, Okla. City, 1996
Bachelor of Arts – Criminal Justice – St. Martins College, Lacy, WA 1994
Associate Arts – Law Enforcement Technology – Austin Peay State University, Clarksville, TN 1984
FBI National Academy, Quantico, VA session 185, 1996
Military Police Basic Course – Advanced Individual Training (AIT) Ft. Gordon, GA 1974
Military Police Investigator Course, Ft. McClellan, AL 1979
Primary Leadership Development Course, Ft. Sherman, Panama 1980

CID Basic Course, Ft. McClellan, AL 1981
CID Advanced NCO Course, Ft. McClellan, AL
US Army Air Assault Course, Ft. Campbell, KY 1985

Warrant Officer Candidate Course (WOCC) Aberdeen Proving Grounds, MD 1986
CID Warrant Officer Basic Technical Course, Ft. McClellan, AL 1986
Defense Language Institute Presidio Monterey, CA 1987-88
CID Warrant Officer Advance Course, Ft. McClellan, AL
Warrant Officer Senior Staff Course, Ft. Rucker, AL 1999

SPECIALIZED INVESTIGATIVE TRAINING
Productive Interrogation Course, Tyson's Corner, VA 1981
Bloodstain Pattern Interpretation, Corning, NY 1984
Basic Forensic Pathology Course (Armed Forces Institute of Pathology, 1984
Hostage Negotiations (FBI) Ft. Campbell, KY 1984
Homicide and Sex Crimes Course, (FBI) Schwinefurt, Germany (1989)
Special Agent Laboratory Training, USA CIL, Atlanta, GA 1993
Hostage Negotiations, US Army Military Police School, Ft. McClellan, Al 1994
Child Abuse Prevention and Investigative Training, Ft. McClellan, AL 1994
Advanced Homicide Investigation, New Orleans, LA 2000
Bloodstain and Crime Reconstruction Course, Ft. Campbell, KY 2000
EXPERT WITNESS QUALIFICATIONS
US Army – Narcotics Investigation (84)
US Army – Narcotics Investigation, drug crime scenes (93)
Greenville, Mississippi – Crime scene analysis (03)
Bolivar County, MS – Crime scene analysis (03)

TEACHING/INSTRUCTOR POSITIONS
Schleswig-Holstein State Police Academy, Eutin, Germany (1981-91) Lecture – American Police Drug Investigative Techniques (Lectures conducted in the German Language
US Army Drug Investigators Course, Heidelberg, Germany (1988-91) Lectured on undercover operations, drug recognitions, working with informants
St. Martins College, Lacy, WA (1994) Guest Lectured on Basic Homicide Investigation
Austin Peay State University, Clarksville, TN (1997 to present)
Course - LEN 2010 Drug Identification and effects
Course – LEN 2020 Criminal Identification (on-line course)
Course – Understanding Terrorism (on-line course)

Harriett Ford

Mississippi State Police Academy, Pearl, MS (2001 to present)
Course – Death Investigation
Course – Advanced Crime Scene
Course – Adult Rape and Sexual Assault
Mississippi State Police Academy, Morehead, MS (2001 to present)
Course – Intro to Criminalistics and Crime Lab
Institute of Police Training and Management, Orlando, Fl (2001 to present)
Course – Adult Rape and Sexual Assault, Connecticut State Police Academy, Orlando, FL (2001, 02, 03)
Course – Acquaintance and Drug Facilitated Rape Course
Connecticut State Police Academy, Pensacola, FL and Yorktown, VA (2003)
Course – Advanced Adult Rape and Sexual Assault, Connecticut State Police Academy (2003)
Renegade Law Enforcement Training, Tallahassee, FL (2002 to present)
Course – Crime Scene Investigation form the Detective's Perspective, Irving, TX, 2002
University of Mississippi, Oxford, MS (2002 to present)
Course – PS 374 Criminalistics

Publications
Three Dimensional Reconstruction of a bullet path: Validation by Computer Radiography, Journal of Forensic Science, Volume 40, NO 2, March 1995. Co-authored with William R. Oliver, Mitchell Soltys, Jim Symon, Aziz Boxwala, and William Gormley
Certifications
Police Supervisors Certificate, Washington State Police Academy, Olympia, WA (1994)
Police Middle Management Certificate, Washington State Police Academy, Olympia, WA (1994)
Instructor Certificate, Mississippi State Police Academy, Pearl, MS (2002)
Special Awards or Recognition
Selected as 1st Infantry Division NCO of Quarter (1978)
Kentucky State Police Commissioner's Award (1987)
International Narcotics Enforcement Officers Association award for Narcotic Enforcement efforts (1990)
Selected as US Army CID Warrant Officer of the Year, (1996)
Appointed as a Kentucky Colonel, 2001

244

Military Decorations
Legion of Merritt
Meritorious Service Medal (four oak leaf clusters)
US Army Commendation Medal
US Army Achievement Medal (silver oak leaf cluster)
Enlisted Good Conduct Medal (four knots)
NCO Professional Development Ribbon
Humanitarian Service Medal
National Defense Service (star device)
Army Service Ribbon
Air Assault Badge
Professional Affiliations
International Association of Chiefs of Police (1995 to present)
American Academy of Forensic Science (1996 to present)
International Association for Identification (2000 to present)

Arthur Chancellor's Analysis

Findings and Professional Opinion:

A complete and concise review of the police reports, witness and suspect statements, photographs, and other documentation presented for analysis have resulted in the following professional opinion:

There is insufficient forensic, physical, testimonial and/or circumstantial evidence presented to conclusively establish that Ted Kuhl was responsible for the 1996 shooting death of Nancy Jurowski (whose real name does not appear in this report out of respect for her family members).

The evidence presented in the police investigation fails to establish any logical motive or rationale for Ted to murder Nancy.

There are strong indications that the alleged confession and/or admissions made by Ted to police were obtained through improper police interrogation techniques (according to my training in Productive Interrogation).

There was no evidence that police made any effort to corroborate or validate Ted's last statement to them. In fact, other witness statements to investigators were in direct contradiction to his so-called "admission" statement, prepared by police. These contradictions were not reconciled.

There are strong indications that major witnesses, Ricky Mueller and Christa Peterson, were substantially pressured through coercive police interrogation tactics and possible governmental misconduct.

The use in court of an eyewitness, Mueller, who has substantially changed his account of events 16 times and then fails a polygraph examination is counter to accepted police and investigative practices.

The basic facts surrounding the homicide, time of day, location, method and events immediately preceding are inconsistent with either a spontaneous "heat of passion" type event OR a premeditated murder committed by Ted.

Although the police insist that there were only two shots fired that night, there is both physical evidence and eye witness testimony to indicate there may have been up to four shots fired.

There are at least *three witnesses*, other than Christa Peterson (Nancy's longtime friend) and Ricky Mueller, who observed an unidentified person near Nancy's vehicle prior to the shooting. This person fits the physical and clothing description initially provided by Rick to 911 and investigators.

Failure to establish prior ownership or possession of a weapon by either Ted or Nancy and failure to locate the weapon after the shooting is more consistent with the homicide being committed by the unidentified suspect, and not Ted.

There were no police reports made available for review that indicate any efforts to locate other potential suspects, although private investigators presented documents which indicated *several* potential suspects were actually in the area that night.

A homicide does not happen in a vacuum. There are always events leading up to the crime, events that take place during the actual homicide and events following. Those events are used to determine, identify inconsistencies and consistencies in the circumstantial, physical and testimonial evidence collected in the investigation.

The events leading to Nancy's death can be described as normal, pleasant socializing with friends. There were a number of events during the day with would indicate no animosity or conflict between Ted and Nancy—the tour of the scuba shop, buying a Christmas tree, taking the tree to her house, Ted's visit to Nancy's mother to deliver a gift, and their agreement to meet for dinner and drinks at the Backyard Grill.

By all witness accounts, the four main participants (Ted, Nancy, Christa and Rick) showed no conflict or arguments between them or anyone else. No conflicts that could have cause a violent outburst or rising tempter between Ted and Nancy was evident. A lack of this type of "conflict" prior to the shooting makes "the heat of passion" or spontaneous act inconsistent with the facts as presented in the case file.

Personality types of both Ted and Nancy, as provided by friends and witnesses, were inconsistent with the "heat of passion" or violent outbursts by either person. Ted has no criminal history and no history of any acts of violence, according to family members, friends and neighbors who have known him since childhood.

Such violent acts as spontaneous crimes of passion resulting in injury or death, without substantial provocation or threats, are normally found in persons with a history or background of violence, quick tempers or other irrational behaviors. There is no indication that Ted or Nancy had such a history.

Nancy's death was consistent with being a premeditated and very planned incident. Meaning specifically, the perpetrator clearly intended to harm and kill her. What is not clear based on the police investigative documents is who the perpetrator actually was, and whether Nancy was the actual intended target.

Part of any homicide investigation is the identification of suspects. Three factors are used: Motive, Opportunity, and Means."

In simplistic terms, we are looking for a suspect with a reason or motive to kill, who has the chance to commit the crime and who has the ability or the weapon. Each of these focuses is discussed in detail below.

The Motive:

The motive is basically the actual underlying cause or reasons behind the death of the victim. While it is not a legal necessity to prove in order to convict, motive is extremely important when it comes time to identifying a suspect.

Simply put, people do not wake up in the morning and decide to commit murder. There is always a reason (motive) behind the perpetrator's actions. Some of the more common motives include monetary gain, revenge, jealousy, love, sex and marriage, and/or some other personal conflict.

(Note: there are some crimes in which the actual underlying motive is only understood by the killer and may never be clarified until they are captured. Such better known examples would include the well-publicized Son of Sam slayings, the Tate-Labianca murders by the Charles Manson family and the Zodiac killer murders.)

By all accounts, Nancy and Ted Kuhl still enjoyed a close personal relationship. Although they did not live together any longer, it was apparent they still saw each other socially, and on occasion, intimately.

The only conflict discussed in any of the documents provided for review about their personal relationship was Nancy's desire to have children and Ted's insistence against it. This was apparently the cause of their breakup, but again it was by all accounts, rather amiable and they were still seeing each other frequently.

The second area of potential conflict discussed was Nancy's request to Ted to have her name taken off the mortgage on the house they had purchased while living together. There was no indication in any of the statements that this conflict was more than a verbal request by Nancy.

The money Nancy had loaned Ted for the down payment of his house had already been repaid months earlier. Thus, there did not appear to be any friction over money aspects of the house.

There was mention by witnesses of Nancy's concern that Ted and Christa might possibly be seeing each other, but there was no indication that this had caused a long-term conflict or that this would have sparked a violent response from either Nancy or Ted.

Further, statements from both Christa and Ted deny any such relationship prior to or after Nancy's death. He had purchased the plane ticket for Nancy to accompany Christa on a trip to California. Christa also purchased her dress for Nancy's funeral— not Ted.

Minor personal conflicts between Ted and Nancy were not violent or long lasting. Such personal problems or conflicts that evolve into motives for a homicide have traditionally come to the attention of family and friends over a period of time before an explosive disagreement.

If this were the case, it would be consistent and expected that family and friends would be able to identify specific times and events in the recent past when heated arguments, accusations, or even physical assaults occurred (as in the case of Howard Purcell, tried and convicted in Rockford's staircase homicide He had stalked and attacked his estranged wife with a stun gun before finally shoving her down the stairs).

It would be consistent that these more violent conflicts, if they existed and were increasing or becoming more intense, would be common knowledge among friends of Ted and Nancy. Because there was no mention of any such personal conflicts, this should be eliminated as a motivating factor.

professional opinion:

"Based on the documents available, there does not appear to be a clearly identifiable, rational or logical motive behind Ted committing Nancy's murder. "Furthermore there does not appear to be any tangible or intangible benefit derived by Ted from Nancy's death that could even be remotely construed as a motive.

"As explained previously, nothing happens in a vacuum. Normal, law-abiding people just do not wake up one morning and suddenly decide to kill someone. Particularly someone with whom they have enjoyed a close personal or intimate relationship, and without a single sufficient provocation or reason."

Opportunity:
Based on the case facts, Ted would clearly have had an opportunity to shoot Nancy in the parking lot, since he (along with others) was in the immediate area prior to her injury. However, because of the continuing type of personal relationship between them, it is somewhat incredulous to believe Ted would choose such a public place to commit a murder.

It is obvious that he could have easily lured her to another more private place and made sure there were no other witnesses available to interrupt or observe, which would make far more sense if he had indeed planned the crime.

Professional opinion:
Choosing the location of the homicide in a public area, with the chance of discovery and observation so great, with no escape plan following the homicide, is somewhat hard to believe. Especially when other opportunities existed that would have made it considerably easier to escape detection.

Means:
The means or ability to commit the murder is centered on the weapon used to inflict the fatal injury. This was the most difficult to evaluate because the actual weapon used was never found. Further, no evidence was ever presented to show that Ted or Nancy ever possessed the weapon prior to the shooting.

Failure to establish prior ownership or possession of a weapon by Ted or Nancy, or even to locate the weapon after the event is more consistent with an unidentified person being involved in this homicide.

Based on the facts in the police investigation, I don't see any elements of premeditation on Ted's part. The problem with premeditation in this case involves the following facts and circumstances which were NOT ADDRESSED by police investigative reports.

1. There was no physical or testimonial evidence presented which would place the murder weapon in Ted's personal possession prior to the shooting.

Obtaining a gun beforehand, and keeping it until use could be evidence of premeditation. That is not apparent in the material available for review.

Instead, the gun suddenly appears, is used to kill, and then disappears never to be found.

2. For this to be a premeditated event, the weapon would have to be in Ted's possession at the time of his entry into the restaurant. Based on all witness accounts, after their departure from the restaurant, Ted, Nancy and Christa all walked together into the parking lot. There was no indication that Ted deviated to any other place in order to obtain the gun.

3. Concealment of the gun prior to use becomes the next issue.

Where could Ted have hidden the weapon that would not be observable? The clothing he wore that night does not appear to be the type in which it would be easy to conceal a weapon.

Therefore, the most likely hiding place would be in Ted's leather jacket. Since the police were not able to determine the exact barrel size of the pistol used, there is no way to accurately describe if the jacket's design would accept the bulk or size of the pistol.

Also, because the jacket was removed when they entered the restaurant, the pistol remaining inside the pocket would have stood a good chance of accidental discovery, such as someone bumping or jostling it.

Although it might also be possible to secret the weapon inside his trouser waistband, the chances of discovery would be considerable. This risk of discovery seems an inconsistent action for someone contemplating a murder in just a short time later. There is no indication that this was ever a consideration in the police investigation.

4. There is no logical explanation as to what happened to the weapon following the shooting. Although this was addressed several times during Ted's multiple versions of what happened, it was never established what Ted was supposed to have done with the gun.

This is important because after the shooting, Ted's actions were observed by dozens of independent witnesses and yet no one observed any suspicious actions consistent with depositing a weapon or other object in any location.

5. The weapon did not obviously remain in Ted's possession afterwards, because of the encounter with the police officer who clapped Ted into handcuffs, patted him down and placed him into the patrol vehicle.

6. There is no motive or underlying reason for this murder.

7. There was no evidence presented to place the gun in Nancy's possession before the incident.

Statement Analysis:

In this particular investigation there were a series of multiple statements taken by police from three significant persons: Ricky Mueller, Christa Peterson and Ted Kuhl.

Witness Statements:

In my review, each witness is evaluated individually.

Rick Mueller was an important witness. A close friend of Ted's, he was part of the group with Nancy, Ted and Christa at the Backyard Grill preceding Nancy's murder.

Additionally, Rick was actually in the parking lot at the time of Nancy's murder and was one of the first persons to make a 9-1-1 call notifying police. He later become one of the chief prosecution witnesses and essentially was an "eyewitness" to the actual shooting of Nancy.

However, it is important to note that over the course of several interviews with police, Rick began changing his eyewitness accounts. Initially claiming to have observed an unknown person "walking from left to right" and shooting Nancy. Claiming that at the time of the shooting, Ted was already turned away from Nancy walking towards his own truck parked next to Rick's vehicle.

Later, after numerous police interviews, he changed his story again, claiming to have observed that it was actually Ted who shot Nancy.

It was in his last statement, given on Dec. 17, 1996 when Rick admitted to having purposely lied and provided false information to the police in previous statements. According to Rick, he lied because he was "afraid of Ted," and feared that something might happen to himself or to his family.

Based on this fear, he claimed he provided false information to the police, basically to "protect" Ted, and thus to keep him from going after Rick and his family.

The importance of this statement is the fact that Rick's effort to initially provide "false information" to the police was apparently done without any prompting or request from anyone else.

Instead he says he took it upon himself to lie to the police and protect Ted, who he knew to be a murderer. The chronology and synopsis of each police contact and the varying statements furnished by Rick are important to document at this time.

Rick's initial contact with police took place within seconds of the shooting. He was already at his vehicle and immediately after the shooting, he got into his vehicle and drove out of the parking lot. While driving, He used his cellular phone to make the first 9-1-1 call reporting the incident.

It is important to note this call was made literally seconds after the incident, basically allowing no time for him to devise a plan to deceive the police.

In the 9-1-1 transcripts, Rick clearly states that someone has been shot in the parking lot and over the course of several minutes, provides the dispatcher with a basic description of the person he saw fire a gun at Nancy.

Professional opinion: So great is the significance of spontaneous or excited utterances made by people under stress that they are accepted as exceptions to the hearsay rule and are often admitted into evidence.

The feeling that under pressure in a stressful situation, with little time for the speaker to plan or think of a "lie," such statements are viewed as being truthful.

In a very real sense, Mueller's initial 9-1-1 call can and should be viewed as "spontaneous utterance."

Additionally, the written transcript of the 9-1-1 call also verifies the second contact with police. This is when the initial responding patrol officer announces over the radio the description of the suspect as provided by Rick.

During the second meeting with police, Rick provides the same description of the shooter as a male, wearing a leather jacket, baseball cap and tan or light colored pants. This same basic physical description was later provided by two other witnesses of a male seen in the area immediately prior to Nancy's murder.

Rick's third contact with police was at the same time as the initial responding officer to the scene. It is listed as the third contact because of the overt nature of Rick's efforts to identify a potential suspect observed in the area.

Rick was providing the description of the suspect in the parking lot, when he pointed out a suspicious vehicle parked nearby.

This observation caused the police department to respond and make a traffic stop on the vehicle. The driver was stopped and the patrol office made a "field interview," releasing the driver apparently based solely on his denial of any involvement.

Rick's fourth contact with police was at the police station, Dec. 7, 1996. Rick stated he had departed the Backyard Grill shortly before Ted, Nancy and Christ and was already at his vehicle when the other three entered the parking lot and began walking toward Nancy's car.

At the same time, he saw an unknown person approaching from left to right toward Nancy's car. Rick reported hearing a scream and observed the flash of a gun.

This places Ted walking away from Nancy toward Rick, while the second unknown person is at Nancy's vehicle delivering the fatal wound.

The importance of this statement is Rick's observation of a second person standing next to Nancy, firing a pistol. Especially since Christa and one additional witness have reported the exact same observations.

Improper Police Influence

Ted's vehicle was parked in one of the spaces within the same row as Rick's. This would put Ted's foot travel consistent with walking towards his car and away from Nancy at the time the fatal shot was fired.

Rick's fifth contact with police took place on Dec. 7, 1996, on page 21 of "Lead 3" police report of Tim Oberg. Following Rick's initial interview, he returned some 30 minutes later with additional information about the shooting. No police report was found to indicate what new information was provided.

His sixth contact on Dec. 12, 1996, was an oral interview at the police station, documented by police officers in an investigative report. He indicated there was something on his mind by "physical indicators" (according to the report).

The seventh contact came On Dec. 15, 1996, when Rick notified police that Ted was coming by his house and they intended to go trap shooting. Based on this information, police set up a surveillance of Rick's residence until after Ted departed.

The eighth contact with police was that same date, when Rick went to the police station and repeated his initial statement, describing an unknown person walk from left to right, raise his arm up and fire a weapon. The difference was Rick's claim that the person he observed was Ted.

***(It is important to note that this statement was given the day AFTER Rick failed his lie detector test in Chicago. He was very nervous at this time and indicated he feared police suspected him.)

Rick says that while he was waiting at the convenience store for police to arrive he called the Backyard Bar manager "Rich." It is important to note that some of the first questions he asked Rich dealt with what happened in the parking lot. He wanted to know if they caught the shooter, or "saw the person that did it."

Hanging up with Rich, he said he then called his wife to say he would not be home. Surely he would have told his wife what had just happened. Then he claims to have called Tom Hogland to tell him what was "going on," and asked him to come to the store because he was afraid.

Later when he was enroute to Loves Park Police Department, Rick said he called Tom yet again, this time speaking with Rick's wife (who answered the phone) and telling her about the event.

During these four phone calls to: Rich, Rick's wife, Tom Hogland and Hogland's wife, Rick is presented with four opportunities to tell someone that he knew who was actually Nancy's murderer. Yet he fails to do so. Even though he was already away from the scene and far from the person he claimed he now feared.

From a behavioral perspective, the phone call with the greatest importance is the one to Tom Hogland. This is based on Rick's own statement that he was scared. This implies a special relationship of trust and security during a time of perceived danger.

Yet the first person he calls for help, Tom Hogland, is not provided the information Rick has about the "feared" person (supposedly Ted) or that Ted just committed a murder.

Additionally, he was supposedly afraid for his wife and family, yet in the initial phone call to her, he does not warn her of any danger posed to them by Ted.

During his ninth contact with police, Dec. 17, he finally retracts elements of his earlier statement, says he did not tell the truth, and now reports that he never saw a second person at the scene that night.

Instead he claims the figure was Ted. Rick indicated he never actually saw Nancy or even who or what exactly Ted was shooting at. The basic sequence of events he now says is this: Ted approaches Nancy from left to right, raising his arm and firing a weapon. Then he turns toward Rick's vehicle. Suddenly, based on what Rick claims he just saw, he is afraid of his best friend who is now approaching his own vehicle.

However, reading the words used to describe what happened that night, we see a major conflict with Rick's new statement.

This conflict can be seen as the first evidence of improper influence by police personnel. The improper influence is the changing of his statement to reflect the police theory of the crime rather than actual observations by a witness.

Rick is very clear that he never actually saw exactly what Ted was shooting at and further that he never actually saw Nancy in the area at the time the gun was being fired.

Yet, based on his LIMITED observation of Ted firing a gun toward an unknown object, (he wouldn't have known Nancy was dead if this statement were true) now he is caused such anguish that he fears for his safety and flees the scene to avoid Ted. This is inconsistent with his own statement. Why should he fear Ted if he did not even know Ted was firing at a person?

Interestingly, WITHOUT OBSERVING ANY VIOLENT ACT, he fears for his safety from Ted, his "best friend" and someone he has known for over ten years.

This fear is felt when there is no indication that Ted made any threatening gestures or statements towards Rick. Literally within seconds of being so afraid of his friend that he needs to escape, he sets about protecting this same friend by giving false information to police.

Professional Opinion:

This dichotomy of Rick's conflicting statements was apparently never recognized or reconciled by police. Failure to even address these conflicts is seen in cases where police willingly agree or accept those facts that fit their theory of the crime, yet disregard any fact that does not.

Rick Mueller's tenth contact with police was on Dec. 18. He was taken to Reid and Associates for a voluntary polygraph examination as a verification of the statement he provided to police the day before. The results of the polygraph indicate he showed deception on the following relevant questions:

1. Was Ted Kuhl the individual you saw with his right arm outstretched in the parking lot of the Backyard Bar and Grill at the time you saw a flash and heard a shot? (Yes.)

2. On Dec. 7, did you see Ted Kuhl fire a gun? (Yes.)

3. Before you walked into the Backyard Bar and Grill on the night of Dec. 6, 1996, did you know Nancy Jurowski was going to be killed? (Yes.)

4. Did you dispose of the gun that was used to kill Nancy? (No.)

(The polygraph indicated he was not truthful on any of the above answers.)

Mueller's eleventh contact with police was during the "pretext call" made by Rick to Ted and recorded by police. Rick apparently believed he could obtain incriminating statements by Ted during this call. However, although Rick directly accused Ted of shooting Nancy, there were no incriminating statements made by Ted at all. In fact, Ted was steadfast in his denial of any involvement in Nancy's death. (Ted even stated, "Come on buddy. I was there. Then where's the gun? If that's what you really believe then tell the police.")

A review of the transcripts of the recorded call reveal the extent of police pressure being applied to Rick to come up with additional information and obviously implicate Ted as the perpetrator. This pressure included efforts to directly accuse Rick of being somehow involved in the Nancy's death.

Mueller makes the following statements in the taped transcript:

1. "Tom called me today and asked me if I am sane. I'm not sane no more. I have been upset ever since this has happened. I have had everyone in the world interviewing me and talking to me."

2. "They are torturing me over this, and I need my sanity back."

3. "I am thinking. I have been thinking for the last week. I have been going crazy. I can't eat. I can't sleep. I have lost enough work."

4. "I have been pressured and everything has been brought to me, and I know what I saw."

5. "Well they're making me feel like a real big suspect and I had nothing to do with it, and I need to know what I have to do to save you and me."

6. "I am the only witness, and I got everyone breathing down my neck, and wanting to know what I saw and I know what I saw."

Continuing with the event analysis, the aspect of Rick's behavior at the scene and immediately following must be addressed.

Rick, in his Dec. 17, 1996 statement, asserts that he gave false information to the police because of his sudden fear of Ted following the shooting. Yet, his behavior following Nancy's death, is inconsistent with the behavior of someone who is deathly afraid of another person.

This inconsistent behavior is best demonstrated in the following situations as provided by witness statements:

1. The first time Mueller and Ted came into contact with each other following the homicide was at the Loves Park Police Department when they were waiting to be interviewed. Police reported that when they came into contact with each other, Rick with tears in his eyes gave Ted a consoling hug and Ted responded with a "pat on the back." (No fear expressed toward Ted.)

2. Immediately upon their release by police, Rick, Christa and Ted all went to Ted's residence to talk and console each other. (No fear.)

3. Witnesses place Rick standing side by side with Ted at the funeral home during visitation. (Again no apparent fear.)

Following the funeral, Rick drove Ted back to his house. (He's alone in a vehicle with a man he says is trying to kill him.)

(*Beau and Carol Brannon, mutual friends, testified that Rick invited Ted to go skeet shooting with him the next day after the murder—an unreasonable request if Rick was truly afraid that Ted was trying to take his life.)

The importance of these behaviors is to contrast Rick's actual actions with later statements made to police about his rationale for making a false statement. His claim of experiencing immediate fear for his own and for his family's safety, is simply not born out by his immediate and subsequent action toward Ted, supposedly causing his fear.

The interview of Mrs. Mueller on Dec. 19, is of great importance when evaluating Rick's behavior following the murder. According to Mrs. Mueller, Rick never said anything to her (about fearing Ted Kuhl) until after he had returned from taking the polygraph examination on Dec. 18. This was three weeks after the event and the day before his wife was interviewed that Mueller finally decided to tell her what he had told the police (that Kuhl was the gunman, and if he were truly afraid for their safety, logic dictates he would have warned his wife immediately.)

The twelfth and apparently the last contact with authorities prior to the actual trial took place when Rick testified at the Grand Jury on February, 1997. (At that point in time, Rick's position was that he had seen Ted fire the weapon, but that he did not actually see what Ted was shooting at.)

Professional opinion.

It is widely known and accepted that there are often problems with obtaining information from witnesses, particularly those who were eyewitnesses to violent acts. This is especially prevalent in cases wherein the victim was a close or personal friend of the witness. Because of these problems, it often becomes necessary to conduct numerous interviews of witnesses until the full and complete story is obtained.

There is a fine line, however, between interviewing to obtain necessary information and improperly influencing a witness to "change his story" so it reflects police theories of the crime, or matches other statements or physical evidence collected during the investigation. There are certain witnesses that can be influenced to change their story.

An example of this can be seen in instances wherein an innocent man confesses to a crime that he really did not actually commit. Professional literature on police interviews and interrogations indicates that this is a very real possibility with some witnesses and suspects. This is why there is a legal rule stating that a man cannot be convicted of a crime based on his confession alone.

Instead, there are legal requirements placed on the government to provide corroborating evidence of the confession in order to use it against the suspect in court.

These same criteria should be applied by the detective in cases of "eyewitness testimony." Specifically, there should be independent corroborating evidence to validate a witness testimony. The problem with Rick's statement is the fact that it was not corroborated by ANY other independent evidence.

The other problem with Rick's statement is that he is conveniently able to avoid stating he saw Ted shoot Nancy. Instead, he says he saw Ted shooting "something." The chief question in this instance is if Rick was able to identify Ted, why was he not able to see what he was shooting at? Nancy was the obvious target. Yet there was no indication she was on the ground or out of sight when she was shot. This very suspicious inconsistency was not addressed.

Reviewing this file, I see where the police could have validated or corroborated Rick's statement, but made no attempt.

1. Event reenactment: Return to the parking lot scene and recreate the event as close as possible. Specifically, go there during the same time of year, same time of night, using the same lighting conditions. Place vehicles in the parking lot where they were located that night to determine Rick's position in the lot, and if it was possible for him to even identify Ted as the person who actually fired the shot at Nancy.

Statement reconciliation: Rick has failed a polygraph examination over the "new information," yet there is no effort to determine why he has failed, by reconciling his new statement with previous statements. Obviously there is something in his later statements that is causing him trouble, otherwise he would have passed the polygraph. Reconciliation should have taken place to determine why he was having problems passing the polygraph. Then additional testing would be appropriate to ensure that he was telling the truth about whatever statement he provided.

Professional opinion:

Relying on a witness who has made repeated conflicting statements and then failed a polygraph examination, without further effort to determine WHY the witness failed, is counter to accepted police investigative practices.

In this case, the polygraph was correctly used as an investigative tool to determine the veracity of Rick's new statement. However, the results were apparently ignored when they failed to coincide with police theory of the crime. This casts serious doubts on the credibility and objectivity of the entire police investigation.

Additionally, if the police declined to use, or were not influenced by the results of Rick's polygraph, then the question should be asked, why was the test used in the first place? It is assumed if the results were favorable to their theory of the crime, it would certainly have been used to whatever extent allowed by state law.

Christa's And Rick's Stories First Matched

According to Christa's original statement to police on Dec. 7, 1996, Christa, Ted and Nancy all left the Backyard Grill together, walking into the parking lot to Nancy's vehicle, parked the furthest away.

Christa reported that she said her goodbyes when they arrived at Nancy's vehicle, then turned and walked to her own car. She was scraping off the windows when she heard a scream and saw an unidentified person by Nancy's vehicle. Seeing the threatening gesture by the person, she dropped to the ground and attempted to get underneath her car.

As she dropped, she heard shots being fired. Christa reported that she could not see exactly what was going on at Nancy's vehicle, but detected Ted running away from the scene with the unknown person shooting at him. The shooter then fled to the south. Ted arrived at her position within seconds and fleeing gunfire they ran back into the restaurant together.

Christa also stated that she believed there were at least four shots in the parking lot. Her statement is clear to this point . . . "I heard some shots and saw this guy shoot at Ted and Ted was dodging the bullets."

Again with this statement, we clearly have a witness who places not only the unknown person in the parking lot, but now is also actually shooting at the only other person in the immediate area, Ted.

It is important to note the fact that Christa's initial statement actually MATCHES RICK'S FIRST STATEMENTS TO POLICE.

The main difference is Christa's inability to provide a detailed description of the shooter, because of her position and actions subsequent to the shots being fired.

Christa was next interviewed by police on Dec. 12 and basically repeated her earlier statements without any major deviations. There were minor changes in the description of the unknown shooter, but substantially, it was the same information.

The next interview with police was Dec. 19. It is important to place this interview into the chronology of events that had taken place within the previous few days.

It was on the 17th of Dec. that Rick radically changed his statement to implicate Ted in the death of Nancy. It was on the 18th of Dec. that Rick failed his polygraph, and it was on the 19th of Dec. (same day of Christa's interview) that Rick placed the "overhear" call to Ted and Ted suggested going to the police department to allow Rick to accuse him of a criminal act in front of the police.

It is apparent that Christa's interview was obviously designed to take place simultaneously with Ted's interview.

The investigative report detailing Christa's interview was more in line with a police interrogation of a suspect, rather than an interview of a significant police tactic when dealing with a witness suspected of not being forthcoming in her statements. It is clear from the actions of the police as described in their written report, that they are relying on information provided by Rick (Dec. 17) as the basis of what they referred to as "inconsistencies" in Christa's statement and other information.

It is important to note that during the initial stages of this interrogation, Christa provided the same basic details of the event as she had provided in her previous interviews.

However, the tone of the interview drastically changed when Christa was directly confronted by police with an accusation that she was involved in a "conspiracy to cover up Nancy's murder."

Additionally, the police attempted to challenge other aspects of her statement, even down to the actual position of her vehicle. She refused to say her car was facing north when they accused her of lying.

The interrogators admittedly accused Christa of lying to the police about other details of her statement. This change in attitude toward Christa can be seen as the first attempt to directly influence her statement through inferences of her own personal involvement in Nancy's death.

The police report also details Christa's verbal and physical reaction to these accusations as follows:

". . . She (Christa Peterson) was adamant about the accusation. Peterson was very upset and was given time to calm down. She was permitted to smoke a cigarette that she had with her. She was given several scenarios about the homicide, but she refused to say they were accurate if she did not see what was described in these scenarios.

Peterson was not adding any information not already included in her statement and said she does not recall anything else from the night in question. Her story remained consistent.

The suggestion was offered that her car was parked facing the opposite direction, which would have placed her facing Nancy's car, and she would have seen the shooting. Peterson was told there were pictures to support this, and she again refused to alter her story.

Peterson was told that if the pictures proved she was not being honest, she had probably lied about other areas of the investigation. She said the car was parked facing south, not north as was suggested.

This information from Peterson is accurate.

She did not give police any information that was inconsistent with her original statement."

It is important to note the police indicated to Christa that she was being re-interviewed based on "inconsistencies" between statements. A review of the witness statements reveals far greater CONSISTENCIES made by Christa and Rick than ANY inconsistencies. These include the following:

1. Both Mueller and Peterson recounted similar events that took place inside the restaurant prior to the event.

2. Both Mueller and Peterson describe the same series of events as they left the restaurant.

3. Both Mueller and Peterson clearly place an unknown person standing adjacent to Nancy at the time of the event.

4. Both Mueller and Peterson heard a scream from Nancy.

5. Both clearly place Ted some distance away from Nancy at the time the shots were fired.

6. Both reported the shooter held the weapon in the right hand.

7. Both reported multiple shots being fired.

8. Both detailed Ted's attempt to escape the area following the incident.

At this time it is important to reiterate that there was an additional witness inside the Backyard Bar and Grill who also reported: an unknown person adjacent to Nancy prior the shooting and detected four shots (consistent with Christa's and Ted's report of up to four shots being fired.)

Two Witnesses, Same Stories
Rick Had More Motive Than Ted

On Jan. 8, 1997, the police offered and Christa accepted an opportunity to take a polygraph examination. During the pre-test portion, she provided the same basic information as she had to police during each of her earlier interviews.

After the polygraph test, the examiner stated Christa was being truthful in her statements to police regarding the events of Dec. 7, 1996. The examiner did indicate trouble in certain portions of the examination dealing with her observations of Ted's activity.

The examiner determined she may have had trouble contrasting her own reflections with information received from the police—she was told that Ted had in fact confessed to shooting Nancy. (He had not.)

Although she had not seen who shot Nancy, believing that Ted had actually confessed may have caused a reaction at that point of the exam.

The next interview with police was on Jan. 13, 1997. Apparently this interview was at Christa's request. She asked if Ted was about to be arrested and expressed concern for her own safety.

Interestingly, she expressed concerns that Ted was being considered a suspect, primarily because there did not seem to be any motive for the murder. She wanted to know why he killed Nancy and why he was not yet arrested since she believed he had confessed.

Detectives denied any specific knowledge as to a pending arrest and began the interview. As part of this process, detectives again went over her statement.

However, like she had done each proceeding interview, Christa repeated the same basic details she had observed that night.

As with her other interviews, police began to "press" Christa for more details concerning Ted's actions, implying that she was not telling the truth or was withholding information.

This is documented in several parts of the report by statements such as, "Christa became defensive."

The detectives also covered aspects of the possible motive behind the murder. Detectives reported Christa's "concern" about Ted's lack of motive.

Professional opinion: The interviewing officers reported both a physical reaction and an attitude change when Christa was essentially challenged on the truthfulness of her statements. A defensive, or even aggressive response at the suggestion that she was lying or withholding information, is an expected response from a truthful person who has been accused of lying.

The last official contact available for review is Christa's grand jury testimony. A review of transcripts helps to document POSSIBLE GOVERNMENTAL MISCONDUCT, in that while they were waiting to testify, Christa and Rick were placed in the same waiting room where Rick openly discussed his proposed testimony with her, specifically saying that he was going to testify t he actually saw Ted shoot Nancy (another change in his story).

This new information, coupled with prior knowledge of Ted's so-called "confession" (which the police had told Christa during her interviews was a confession to murder) may have induced or attempted to induce Christa to change her testimony or to be uncertain as to what exactly she had observed that evening.

Whether this was the government's intention or unintended result, the fact remains that Christa was subjected to influence and pressure to alter her account of the events.

Based on a review of the transcripts, Christa appears to have been treated more as a hostile witness rather than an eyewitness to the event.

Ted Kuhl

On Dec. 7, 1996, the first written statement made by Ted was completed at the police station. The most significant thing about this statement is the absolute lack of detail about the incident itself, and what happened immediately after Nancy's death.

This is in striking contrast between the interviews conducted at the same time with Rick and Christa, which were completed, in much greater detail.

There was no police report accompanying the statement to determine if there was any reason behind the limited amount of information obtained from Ted.

Significant in the statement, Ted does report he believes that there were multiple shots fired: "Two for sure, four possibly, but couldn't swear to it."

Review note:

Ted apparently prepared a sketch during his interrogation, as did the other two main witnesses, but it was not among the documents provided for this analysis.

Ted's second contact with police was on Dec. 19, 1996, when Rick placed the "overhear call," (recorded by investigators as he spoke with Ted).

Rick's state of mind and other aspects of his participation were previously discussed.

However, the importance of this call is the fact that Ted not only does not make any admissions, he refuses to meet with his accuser alone and instead insists Rick make his accusations to the police.

After the phone call (instead of running to hide somewhere as a guilty person confronted with crime), Ted immediately calls the police and reports the call, asking to meet with detectives at the police department to confront Rick. This was a huge risk if he were actually guilty.

Then Ted traveled to the police department, expecting to confront Rick and his allegations.

He was asked instead to go to another location for another interview. It is clear from the text of the written police report that officers fully intended to interrogate Ted when he came to the police station.

Professional opinion:

State law dictates that in the course of an investigation, a suspect must be informed of his legal rights.

It does vary from state to state and being unfamiliar with Illinois law, it is difficult to determine if the interrogators violated Ted's rights to self-incrimination when he was interviewed without benefit of a rights advisement.

Normally, a rights advisement is indicated when the investigation has centered on one suspect and the purpose of the interview is to solicit incriminating statements from the interviewee.

It is clear that by the Dec. 19th interview, police believed Ted was the offender and had begun to focus on him to the exclusion of all other possible offenders.

The purpose of this interview/interrogation was clearly to elicit incriminating statements. Eventually at some point several hours into the interrogation, Ted was advised of his rights.

The question with the rights advisement becomes, why was it completed hours after the first incriminating statements were made?

Theoretically, the rights advisement should have been initiated once incriminating statements were obtained and additional such statements were being sought.

In some jurisdictions, when incriminating statements are obtained from an interviewee, without benefit of a rights advisement, a "cleansing statement" is required prior to continuing the interview.

A cleansing statement essentially is a clear advisement by police, basically stating that even though incriminating statements were made without benefit of rights advisement, the interviewee has no obligation to continue with the interview.

A legal expert needs to evaluate whether Ted's rights were violated at this time.

Ted's Interview Analyzed:

During the Dec. 19 interview, Ted made several statements detailing different versions of events that took place on Dec. 7, 1996. It is interesting to note that the police initiated these variations based on their statements that Ted's versions of events were in conflict with physical evidence and other witness accounts.

Ted said he was present when Nancy was shot and killed, however his version was not consistent with what they believed happened and therefore Ted was challenged.

Based on that challenge, Ted changed his story again. He was again challenged. And again, until police were satisfied that his story matched other statements to confirm their theory of the crime.

Professional opinion: It is common police practice that multiple versions of the same event provided by a witness should be viewed as deception.

Only someone with something to hide has difficulty recalling exactly what happened during the incident under investigation, theoretically.

However, multiple versions are not unusual, especially when the incident involves the death of a loved one. In these situations, there are also many different issues that may affect the witness, including:

1.) Denial. In the sense the interviewee does not want to believe or accept that the incident actually took place, the victim was actually hurt or killed.

2.) Guilt. Not necessarily guilt from direct participation in the event, but rather feelings of guilt because they were not able to prevent the incident from taking place or to protect the victim from harm.

3.) Use of alcohol or drugs prior to the incident by the witness. Alcohol especially interferes with memory, perception and sequencing of events. Ted had been drinking that afternoon and night.

4.) The interviewer's attitude toward the interviewee. Aggressive and insistent interviewers may inadvertently or intentionally influence witnesses to provide statements that conform to the interviewer's (police) theory of events, rather than what the witness actually remembers. This point was also covered when detailing Mueller's statement to the police. Along this same line would be the interview technique used to obtain the admissions and confessions. The best example of this and the one I believe was used for this interview is the "good-cop, bad-cop" routine.

5.) The length of the interview. There is a time in every interrogation, when the interviewer runs the risk that the interviewee has been worn down to the point they will sign a statement against self interest in order to escape the interrogation process. I believe Ted reached this point during 14 hours of questioning following a full work day.

The most important aspect of the police interrogation and subsequent admissions is the fact that neither Ted's oral admissions nor final written statement make any sense when compared to any other evidence documented in this case. (That is one reason Ted gave for signing the police hypothetical statement, saying he was convinced they would soon realized it could not possibly be accurate.)

Further, throughout the remainder of the investigation, there does not appear to be any effort made to corroborate any of the statements made by Ted.

There is a legal maxim that roughly states, "A man cannot be convicted based on his confession alone."

Yet in this case, it appears the only real evidence police have is what they were able to obtain through questionable interrogation techniques.

That evidence basically consists of Ted's and Rick's inconsistent statements without verification.

What Was Left Undone?

There were several observations and/or forensic examinations that should have been completed as a matter of routine in these types of cases. They are as follows:

1. There was no gunshot residue (GSR) sample taken from Ted's hands (or it was not mentioned in the reports). Such an examination would have been used to determine whether he had recently fired a gun, and would be considered an important part of the preliminary investigation. His clothing tested free of residue.

Ted's hands were not examined for bloodstains. If he was in close proximity to Nancy as he held the weapon to her head (as alleged by Rick, who also later claimed Ted was 50 feet from her when he fired the gun) the high velocity bloodstains could have been observable on his hands. These stains would have resulted in what is known as "back spatter," caused by blood and tissue expelled from the body at the point of entry. This is a very common forensic finding in these types of cases, but never mentioned in the reports.

Professional Opinion:

Witness statements were provided for review. It is interesting to note that in at least three statements taken from independent witnesses, there was "consistent" evidence to facts and circumstances as reported by Ted, Christa and even the initial statements by Rick.

The most important revelations from these witnesses are the presence of a male (matching the overall clothing description as initially provided by Rick) walking in the parking lot prior to the shooting.

Based on their statements, the actions of this unknown person, making a claim that he was waiting for someone in the bar, can only be viewed as suspicious and certainly a person to be looked at.

There were no reports provided to indicate what steps the police took in locating this person.

No Forensic Evidence:

As part of the event analysis, a review was also conducted of the various reports from the Crime Lab covering the forensic examination of the physical evidence recovered. From the material provided, there was no physical or forensic evidence that could link Ted to the shooting of Nancy.

The bullet fragment recovered from Nancy and from the amusement center should be compared on the Integrated Ballistics Identification System through the state crime lab to determine if the weapon used in this homicide was ever used in another violent crime. If it were used after this incident, then it would be very strong evidence that another person was the actual killer.

The police believe the multiple gunshots reported by Ted, Christa and other witnesses were a result of echoes within the parking lot. However, there was nothing to indicate any efforts were made to verify this fact. A re-enactment should be considered to determine if echoes are in fact produced by gunshots in the area.

Shooting reconstruction examination

The Illinois State Police completed a shooting reconstruction in an attempt to determine the relative position of the shooter based on the final impact point in the ceiling of the arcade. Based on their analysis it was not possible to accurately determine the position of the shooter within the parking lot.

A possible bullet projectile was discovered in a light pole in the parking lot where Nancy was shot. (It is still visible there today.) Its presence lends credence to Christa, Ted and other witnesses who reported more than two shots being fired during the incident. There was no indication that police ever made any efforts to link this impact point to the homicide. Instead it was arbitrarily eliminated from involvement in the incident by the police without explanation.

Professional opinion/conclusion

Based on the material submitted for my review, there does not appear to be sufficient evidence or information to conclusively prove and/or establish exactly who shot Nancy Jurowski The only evidence available that implicates Ted consists of Rick's and Ted's statements, both of which are of very questionable value due to the manner in which they were obtained.

There does not appear to be any effort made to corroborate either Rick or Ted's statements and they are basically accepted at face value once they match the police theory of events.

I find the most difficulty in understanding the police theory of events leading to the homicide. I find no logical motive. I do not see any evidence of where the weapon came from or where it went afterwards. Therefore I see no means to commit the crime. And finally, I see the time and location of the homicide as being very inopportune.

I am struck by the dichotomy presented by police of Ted "the intelligent murderer" who is able to obtain a weapon, conceal it until it is needed, hide it and later obviously dispose of in (in 12 seconds) so that it was never found again. But at the same time, Ted picks a public place with other witnesses present, when he could easily have lured Nancy to another location and killed her without any witnesses. Choosing the parking lot, he is left without escape route or chance to dispose of the weapon.

Lastly, that he was able to formulate such a plan without involving anyone else, that he was able to hide his motive for wanting to kill from even his closest family and friends, but then willingly present himself for interrogation for such an extended time without benefit of counsel is not consistent.

In my opinion, this investigation suffered form what is known as "tunnel vision," wherein police develop a theory of the crime and no effort is made to look at any other possibility. Evidence that matches that theory is accepted. Evidence that tends to point in another direction is ignored.

I do believe this was a premeditated homicide. I do not believe Ted was the murderer. There are just too many facts to eliminate him from involvement in the case. It is clear from witness statements that a second unknown person was present who most likely killed Nancy.

This was verified through Rick's initial statements, Christa's statement and one witness inside the restaurant. Two other witnesses further observed this person several times preceding the homicide as he walked through the area claiming he was "waiting for someone inside."

Premeditation Scenario:

Waiting until Ted and Nancy parted company, appearing out of the darkness, immediate delivery of a fatal injury with the pistol, doing so by ambush, leaving the victim no chance to defend herself, without any conversation or personal confrontation with her, then shooting other rounds at the potential witnesses before fleeing the scene, having a planned escape route and being able to leave the scene unobserved—these are marks of premeditation. It is all consistent when the "unknown" male suspect is substituted as the murderer. It is totally inconsistent whenever Ted is considered a suspect.

The analysis and professional opinions reached in this case are based solely on materials made available for review in conjunction with sound investigative principals.

"The receipt of additional materials and information not previously provided may result in altered findings and opinions."
Arthur Chancellor, Investigative Consultant

STATEMENTS REGARDING THE TED KUHL CASE

Rockford, Illinois — State's Attorney Paul Logli's statement regarding the Ted Kuhl conviction:
"It is beyond the authority of this prosecutor or any prosecutor to simply agree to a retrial of a case without a substantial, conclusive basis for such decision. This is especially true when the effect of that decision would be to overrule a jury that heard all the evidence in the case and determined unanimously that the defendant (Ted Kuhl) was proven guilty beyond reasonable doubt. There is no evidence to factually prove that Kuhl is innocent of the crime, or that someone else besides him is factually guilty of the crime. This office has no choice but to rely on the decision of a jury, trial court and appellate court of this state, all of which found the evidence sufficient to convict Ted Kuhl beyond a reasonable doubt in the murder of Nancy Jurowski"

Albert and Roseanne Kunze, Ted's former employers:
"There is no evidence to factually prove Kuhl guilty. The jury did *not* hear all the facts. We were appalled that the state's attorney and Judge Michael Morrison both admitted full knowledge of the star witness, Rick Mueller's 16 untruths. It's a fact that these 16 changes in his story were withheld from the jury, and yet the judge stated that the outcome would have been the same. With virtually no factual evidence at all, it appears the jury rendered the guilty verdict based on reasonable *suspicion* rather than reasonable doubt."— Albert and Roseanne Kunze (Ted's former employers)

Stanley Cohen, award winning journalist and author of the book, "The Wrong Men":
"Those who do the arithmetic attest that eyewitness error accounts for more than half the wrongful convictions in the United States."

Private Investigator and former investigative reporter Joe Lamb:

"After months of reviewing case documents and interviewing available witnesses, it is my belief that Ted Kuhl is not guilty of this crime and that both he and Nancy are victims of a tragic injustice. We have identified people associated with three violent street gangs who were present the night of the murder and whose presence was overlooked in the investigation. We believe one of them killed Nancy."

Former Illinois Governor George Ryan:

"I will have no more to do with this machinery of death." — spoken as Ryan commuted the sentences of 167 prisoners in January of 2003, calling the system "terribly flawed," after 13 death row inmates were exonerated by DNA evidence. That number continued to grow to 111 nationwide during 2003. Ryan made national news in 2000 after placing a moratorium on the death penalty in Illinois.

Ted Kuhl:

As much as I love and miss my freedom, I love and miss Nancy even more. I want the man who killed her to be found. I believe she deserves the truth to come out.

Source Information

The Rockford Labor News featured the following series of articles on the Ted Kuhl case written by Harriett Ford:

In Cold Blood Dec. 13, 1996

Why? Impatience Testy in Loves Park Murder Case February 7, 1997

Murder, Lies and the wrong man in prison? April 7, 2000 (Part II follows in April 14 issue).

Wrong Man Locked Up? Killer on the Loose? April 14, 2000

Victim's Family: Case Closed, Conviction Was No Mistake (Mother Debunks the 'Wrong Man' Theory" April 28, 2000

Who Did Nancy Fear? May 12, 2000

Ted Kuhl's Lack of Emotion Damning? May 19, 2000

Jealousy or Premeditation Theories Make Little Sense May 26, 2000

Who Had A Gun? Where Did It Go? June 2, 2000

Was There Time to Hide A Gun? June 9, 2000

Who Was Stranger Prowling the Lot? June 16, 2000

Krista Peterson: "I Never Had An Affair With Ted" June 23, 2000

False Confessions! Why Do They Happen? June 30, 2000

How Many Pieces of Puzzle Missing? July 7, 2000

Imprisoned Ted Kuhl: "Much as I Miss My Freedom, I Love and Miss Nancy More" July 14, 2000

"Witness At Scene: I Was There; Ted Did Not Kill Nancy" Friday, July 21, 2000

Figure This One Out: No Motive, No Gun, Not Witness: So Why Is Kuhl in Prison? July 4-5, 2002

Will Someone Have The Guts To Say Mistakes Were Made? August 1-2, 2002

Investigator Convinced: Wrong Man Doing Time And Killer Remains Free (Detailed Report Given Officials) August 8-9, 2002

Stench Ripens: 40 Years, Blind Justice or Just Plain Blind? New Facts Point to Bungling (Where's Judicial Concern?) August, 15-16, 2002

Interest High In Kuhl Case August 22-23, 2002
In Kuhl Murder Case: New Facts August 29-30, 2002
In Ted Kuhl Case: Many Confident Logli Will Do What's Right
September 5-6, 2002
What Will Logli Do? Kuhl's Court Motion Set September 12-13,
2002
Kuhl's Son Seeks Fairness: An Open Letter To Paul Logli "You
Have The Power That Few Possess" September 19-20, 2000
At Kuhl Murder Trial: What The Jurors Never Heard   September
26-27, 2002
What If the Jury Had Heard All Known Facts In Case? October 3-
4, 2002
Ted Kuhl Series Continues: SA Wants Court To Keep Lid On,
Prosecutor Asking Judge Grubb to Overlook New Defense Facts
October 10-11, 2002
Next Kuhl Court Date Thurs., Oct. 24 October 17-18, 2002
Shameful Situations: Faith in Judicial System Is Badly Shaken In
Cases Such As Kuhl's Conviction November 7-8, 2002
Beleaguered Lady Witness Wonders, Doesn't Truth Even Matter?
Disappointment in Justice System November 21-22, 2002
When The Wait Is Unbearable November, 28-29, 2002
Jury Contamination: Something Else To Ignore In Kuhl Murder
Sentence? December 5-6, 2002
Logli's Silence Surprising in Botched Case December 12-13, 2002
Why, Why, Why? Innocent But Still They Confess December 19-
20, 2002
Getting Away With Murder December 27, 2002
The Injustice of Legal Mistakes: Wrongs Made Right Come
Terribly Late January 2-3, 2003
Really Now! Is Our Court System That Badly Broken? January 23-
23, 2003
Night of Murder: Open letter Add to Fires of Contention That
Conviction Was a Shameful Injustice January 30-31, 2003
On Murder Night: Too Dark to Tell February 13-14, 2003
Joe's Unfinished Work Should Not be in Vain (More
determination to Exonerate Kuhl) February 20-21, 2003

Could You Pass The Test? False Confessions March 6-7, 2003
With Information Now at Hand: Veteran Detective Convinced A
New Trial Would Free Kuhl March 13-14, 2003
Injustice In Botched Kuhl Case: Does No One Really Care? Too
Many Questions Never Even Asked March 27-28, 2003
In New Trial Quest: One Last Chance for Kuhl in July May 8-9,
2003
The Kuhl Imprisonment: It Couldn't Happen But It Really Did
(Mystery Remains in Motiveless Murder and a Conviction Defying
All Logic) June 26-27, 2003
Attorney Peter Nolte: Nothing Has Gone Right In Kuhl Case July
10-11, 2003
Before His Death: Joe Lamb Asked Why the Hush In Ted Kuhl's
Case? His questions deserve Answers July 24-25, 2003
Points to Ignored Suspect: Loves Park Caller Stirs Kuhl Case
August 21-22, 2003

ADDITIONAL SOURCES:

Liebman, James, et al. A Broken System: Error Rates in Capital
Cases, 1973-1995. 2000. The Justice Project.
http://justice.policy.net/report.
A Broken System, Part II: Why There Is So Much Error in Capital
Cases, and What Can Be Done About It. 2002. The Justice Project.
http://justice.policy.net/jreport.
Will, George F. "Innocent On Death Row." The Washington Post.
April 6, 2000. P. A23.
Turrow, Scott. Ultimate Punishment: A Lawyer's Reflections on
Dealing with the Death Penalty. New York: Farrar, Straus &
Giroux, 2003.
Turrow, Scott. Dead Men Walking Free. TIME, October 28, 2002.
Turrow, Scott. Reversible Errors. New York: Farrar, Strauss &
Giroux.

Loftus, Elizabeth psychologist, University of California, reference study on false memories implanted

Saul Kassin, William College psychology professor specializing in the psychology of confessions.

Cohen, Stanley, "The Wrong Men," Barnes & Noble, New York, 2003

Kurland, Michael. How to Try a Murder, handbook for armchair lawyers. McMillan, New York, New York, 1997

Author's Biography

Harriett Ford is a veteran reporter/columnist for the Rockford
Labor News in Rockford, Illinois. She made the top 111 out of
11,000 candidates for Ann Landers' position when the famed
advice columnist left the Chicago Sun Times and moved to the
Tribune in the late 1980s. Ford has written the popular Sara and
Sadie's Sense and Nonsense, an advice and humor column
appearing weekly in the Labor News since 1990.
She currently resides in Missouri where she is working on a
second book. Ford is a member of the Ozarks Romance Authors
organization, and the Ozark Writer's League.
Her husband of 41 years, John, is the love of her life, along with
two daughters and four grandchildren.

Printed in the United States
74365LV00003B/16-33